MONSTER IN ME

MONSTER IN ME

CRYPTID ASSASSIN™ BOOK EIGHT

MICHAEL ANDERLE

DISRUPTIVE IMAGINATION®

Copyright © 2020 Michael Anderle
Cover Art by Jake @ J Caleb Design
http://jcalebdesign.com / jcalebdesign@gmail.com
Cover copyright © LMBPN Publishing
A Michael Anderle Production

LMBPN Publishing
PMB 196, 2540 South Maryland Pkwy
Las Vegas, NV 89109

First US edition, July, 2020
eBook ISBN: 978-1-64971-087-1
Print ISBN: 978-1-64971-088-8

THE MONSTER IN ME TEAM

Thanks to our Beta Readers

Jeff Eaton, John Ashmore, and Kelly O'Donnell

Thanks to the JIT Readers

Dorothy Lloyd
John Ashmore
Diane L. Smith
Jeff Goode
Deb Mader
Peter Manis
Jeff Eaton

If we've missed anyone, please let us know!

Editor
Skyhunter Editing Team

CHAPTER ONE

T his is exactly why I hate being so close to the ocean. All that money spent on getting my hair perfect is simply wasted. I should have known better, dammit. Everything in her genetics screamed curling hair, and humidity in the air tended to add considerably more body, which rendered all the products she used so rigorously utterly useless in keeping it straight.

At least this time, she would only be a half-hour at the most. Her plane was only scheduled to stop to refuel. Thanks to the tightening customs regulations in the European Union, she wasn't even supposed to leave the aircraft. Thankfully, in private airstrips like this, they were a little more understanding of the necessity for someone cramped in the tight confines of a plane to take a brief walk and have a quick nicotine fix.

"Thank you, Andrei," she muttered and as she raised the pale brown cylinder she'd put her bodyguard through the trouble of lighting between her lips.

"Of course, Miss Chavez."

She took a deep drag, held her breath for a few seconds, and let her breath out slowly. The acrid smell of the cigarette filled the air around her. She didn't usually indulge in her dirty little habit but there were times that it was needed. Fortunately, she had taken to leaving her pack of imported Sobranies and her lighter with the bodyguards her board of directors insisted she travel with.

Before she'd smoked even half, the gates of the airstrip were pulled open to admit a long black limo and a gust of wind that cut in from the Mediterranean. It made her shiver, although she wasn't sure which circumstance was the cause. The vehicle was quickly followed by a second limo, which drew in before the gate was shut once again.

Chavez flicked her long black hair back behind her and stood motionless, waited for the vehicles to approach, and winced reflexively.

"I can almost feel the humidity adding more body to my hair," she muttered, dropped the cigarette, and crushed it under her shoe.

Two men exited the vehicles after their security made sure the area was safe. One of them was older—almost ancient, she thought—with what was left of his white hair pulled back to frame his bony head. She could almost see the veins through his translucent skin, but he walked like someone who was well used to moving under his own power despite using an ornate cane with a sapphire-encrusted ivory handle for support.

The second man was different. He was well-built with no need for padding in the shoulders of his gray suit. His dirty-blond hair was already receding despite him only being halfway through his thirties, but he made no effort to hide it. He carried himself with the kind of attitude that was drawn from an ability to not care what other people thought of his appearance.

"*Caballeros*," she greeted them after she'd shaken their hands firmly. "I appreciate you meeting me on such short notice, but as you are well aware, I cannot remain here for too long."

"We appreciate you having this meeting away from curious and unwelcome eyes and ears, Miss Chavez," the younger man stated in a heavy Serbian accent.

"Please, call me Sofia," she answered smoothly.

"And you may call me Matija," he responded.

"Magnus," the older man introduced himself in what sounded like a Danish accent. "It is a good thing that we are now on a first-name basis with each other, given the business we are to embark on. Trust is of paramount importance at this stage."

"Agreed." Her hand slid to the pocket she used to carry her cigarettes in and she restrained a grimace when she remembered they were no longer there. Maintaining this kind of business face could be as stressful as anything she had ever done in her life, but her family required it of her. And they had taught her well.

"Our base of operations has already been set," Matija continued, took a phone proffered by his bodyguard, and handed it to her. She immediately passed it to Magnus. "It is a small island off the coast of Algeria and already has all the infrastructure we need installed. The location originally used as an airbase for the Allies during the Second World War and was repurposed in 1982 as a nuclear missile silo by the United States government, although no nuclear weapons were ever transported to the island in question."

"I suppose it would have been a little too much to ask for it to be already running on nuclear power," Sofia grumbled.

"The solar and wind power stations will be more than sufficient," he assured her. "That is what the island has been used for over the past twenty years, but the bases fell into disrepair and the Algerian president was more than happy to turn them over to us for bananas as long as we promise to sell the electricity produced to them at a good price. Besides, he suddenly needs a quick influx of cash given that he has very unhappy rebels on his hands."

"Will those rebels be a problem?" Magnus asked.

"They are funded by the US government and are more interested in the larger population centers and the oil reserves," Matija explained. "They have no interest in the solar and wind farms. We should be safe in our endeavors as long as we continue to pump electricity into the city."

"It's a good cover," she noted. "And the extra profit provided should be enough to dissuade them from encouraging any other parties who might show interest in purchasing it."

"Agreed." Matija drew papers from a briefcase. "I've already had the necessary personnel moved into the facility, and they've worked on repurposing it. The location should be ready for operations in the next few days. I'll let you know when and that will conclude my investment in this project."

Sofia nodded. "I'm on my way to the American base to see to our investments in the area. While there, I'll purchase the Pita plant we need—I have already identified the likely source and am sure they can be persuaded to supply at least one to start with—and I'll import the biomass that will be required with the last shipment of soil. The experts I'll bring in have told me that having everything on an isolated location like an island would help with conducting controlled experimentation without the unforeseen variables that affected the original experiment."

"Affected?" Magnus grunted and tapped his cane on the ground for emphasis. "That is one way to describe the unmitigated fuck-up we now see spreading through the Sahara."

"On the bright side, that fuck-up is what allows us to have access to the non-terrestrial substance that was denied us in the last round of bidding." She tapped her thigh lightly. If they finished this meeting quickly, she would have time for one more smoke before taking off again. "With that in mind, we should have complete control of the biological product that is exposed to the liquid extracted. The lessons learned in the Sahara experiment will serve us well in that regard. Providing the goop, as it is called, the specialists, and the biological material required for testing as well as the fertile soil meant to cultivate what we produce will conclude my investment in this project."

Sofia and Matija both turned their eyes on the older man as he tapped the ground lightly with his cane.

Finally, the old man spoke. "The security personnel are already en route to a way station, after which they will be transported to the island in question. Consultants have already discussed the possibility of outside governments interfering with our project, and they suggested a terror tactic."

She narrowed her eyes. "Please don't tell me we'll have to fund terrorists. Not again."

"Nothing like that. Our purchase of alien biomass is illegal, and the creation of more of our own is even more so. With that said, every country on earth wants what the Zoo produces, but none would like to have it produced on their soil, if you will. The threat of that would mean having strict sanctions imposed, as no other country would want to trade with one that could be transporting alien...spores or something across their borders. Such tactics should keep our investment in this project safe until we are willing to liquidate said investment."

It wouldn't be the end of the man's involvement. Sofia had worked with Magnus for a while now and knew that he wouldn't simply stop at seeing a return. He would milk this for every cent it was worth and turn it in for the insurance money when he'd bled it dry.

But pointing that out to him wouldn't end well. She'd seen what happened to the partners who challenged him. There was a reason why he was still at the head of an empire when his children's children were having kids of their own.

The old man's attention turned to her directly, and she had to resist the urge to pull away from the intense gaze. "What happened to Levinson's concern over the project? Has his curiosity been sufficiently satisfied or will he need to be otherwise handled?"

Sofia sniffed. "No. When he asked, I had proof that what I was working on was a cannabis project, meant to genetically design higher-grade marijuana plants for sale. That stopped him cold, although he had a weird look on his face. I think he might have assumed I was stupid for the attempt since the market has already been flooded with genetically designed weed products. Or maybe he simply thought I was getting high on my supply."

Magnus scowled. "He could still be a problem in the future."

"I doubt it, but if he is, I will handle it. It's too early for us to drop bodies, especially the kind that will be investigated under a microscope by federal agencies, local police departments, and about a dozen different insurance companies around the world. They ruin my dinner party schedule."

He was clearly not convinced, but he knew as well as she did that they couldn't afford to have curious eyes focused on how they spent their time outside of attending official functions.

"Very well, then," he said and tapped his cane decisively on the tarmac. "I believe this concludes our meeting. It is best for us to not be seen together if at all possible. You may contact me in a more secure manner later once everything is set up on the island."

Another tap of the cane—which she should be used to by now but which irritated the shit out of her—showed the end of the conversation as Magnus turned and moved to his limo. The door was already open and waiting for him and he climbed inside without a second's hesitation.

"Until we meet again." Matija offered a small bow to her before he turned away, and in less than a minute, both vehicles had left the airstrip.

Sofia turned to the men waiting for her. Andrei already had her pack of cigarettes and the lighter out and lit one for her, and she took a deep drag before she exhaled slowly.

"Fuck, I don't know why I ever tried to quit," she whispered, closed her eyes, and enjoyed the sea breeze for the first time since she'd landed. "When can we get the hell out of here?"

"Refueling should be another five minutes, ma'am."

"Thanks."

This was only a way station before what was bound to be the more difficult part of her trip. The fact was much more difficult to process. She would need to have a nice long vacation somewhere cold when she was finished with this, not somewhere warm and sunny. No, somewhere cold and with snow, preferably in Switzerland.

She finished the second cigarette and felt the buzz in her body from the nicotine starting to calm her.

"I think we should board now, Miss Chavez."

She nodded, flicked the cigarette away this time, and watched it bounce across the tarmac. Andrei fell in behind her as she turned on her heel and hurried to where the plane's steps were still in place for her to board once more.

There was no point in lingering for some customs official to decide to ground her and make sure she wasn't carrying something illegal. She wasn't, but the delay would simply not be acceptable.

"You do see why this is a concern, right? I don't need to explain it to you."

Niki could hear Jennie sigh over the phone despite the whining of airplane engines behind her.

"Of course I do, Niki, but you don't need to worry about Desk. She's more than capable of taking care of herself."

"Someone tried to hack into her servers. Someone from inside the DOD. They attempted to get their hands on her code."

Her sister laughed. "And were rewarded with about fifteen terabytes of midget bondage porn for their efforts."

"Do I even want to know—"

"She keeps it in reserve in case someone tries something with her. Plus, it's almost impossible to delete, so the chances are the person is hopefully saddled with a host of not safe for work content they can't explain until they go ahead and reformat their computer."

"Honestly, that sounds like something Vickie would do."

"Who the hell do you think taught Vickie everything she knows?" the woman responded with a laugh that sounded smug rather than apologetic.

The agent tugged absently at her hair and nodded. "Okay, fair point. Still, it worries me that someone thinks they can get away with trying to steal some of her code. And why the hell would they want to do that?"

"Because the DOD has paid out of their noses to get their hands on decent AI software lately, and someone probably thought they could get a promotion or something if they simply took advantage of the fact that they're housing one of the most advanced AIs in the world in one of their servers. Not only that, they'd have been sorely disappointed. Both Desk and I have agreed that she shouldn't be limited to a single server and have taken steps to secure critical code in various other locations, some of which even I am not aware of. I have to say—and sadly, I cannot receive the accolades I deserve—I have created an AI that exceeds even my expectations."

"A little full of ourselves, aren't we?"

"Can you honestly tell me Desk isn't the best AI you've ever worked with?"

"Well, sure, but given that I haven't worked with too many AI's in the past, that bar isn't set very high."

"Well, take it from my considerable technical expertise that Desk is among the best in the world. It took me years to develop her. Besides, do you think I would have anything but the best looking out for my baby sister?"

"Wha—you're my baby sister!"

"Yeah, keep telling yourself that."

Jansen walked slowly to where she stood and looked a little uncomfortable that he'd overheard her conversation with Jennie. She smirked when she reminded herself that he at least put on a good show of looking uncomfortable. It was very unlikely that the man was anything other than perfectly comfortable with overhearing what other people were saying, given his former role as an intelligence asset.

Niki covered the mic on her phone. "Yeah?"

"Our ride's here. Speare has reservations for us in the Aria. I guess as a job well-done gesture?"

"Maybe." She grimaced. "Or maybe he realized there is a benefit to putting your people in a hotel that doubles as a casino that makes most of its money from people gambling. Either that or maybe he got a special group rate. Do they offer any benefits for DOD operatives?"

The man shrugged. "Hell if I know. But we should get going. Maxwell won't wait for long. He got a hefty bonus and he's aching to spend it on some prime rib."

She laughed. "All right, let's get moving. Why didn't you get a bonus, though?"

"It's a timeline situation. We started working for the DOD at different times, so the years of service anniversary falls on different dates for us. Idiotic bureaucracy is what it is."

"Right. Start the car. I'll be right there."

Jansen nodded and jogged to where Maxwell had already started the vehicle.

Niki pulled her hand away from the microphone. "Okay, sis, I need to get going."

"Yeah, it's adorable that you think putting your hand over a phone's mic still keeps the person on the other side from hearing. I'll talk to you later?"

"Not if I kill you first," she muttered before she hung up. It wasn't a good idea to be the one to get between Maxwell and his prized prime rib. Besides, Taylor would put the three of them through their paces over the next couple of days to familiarize them with running and working in the suits he'd sourced for them. Any opportunity for relaxation and enjoyment they could get their hands on before the taskmaster got his hands on them was worth it.

The drive into Vegas had its unique brand of breathtaking qualities. Despite the sheer amount of greed and backstabbing she knew was happening, there weren't many sights in the world quite like entering the Strip. People who were some of the most talented at catching the human eye and not letting go had put work into making every building there a masterpiece.

The Aria certainly fit that description. A valet already waited to open the doors for them and took the keys to the SUV from Maxwell's hands as they stepped inside.

"These digs are a little more..." Jansen let his voice trail off as they headed to the front desk.

"Opulent." Niki finished his sentence for him. "The word is opulent. Vegas is the capital of the over-the-top luxurious hotel stays, and not many people would complain about that when their rooms are comped by the DOD."

The man nodded and stopped at the front desk, where the receptionist smiled in greeting. "Hi, we have reservations under the names Maxwell, Jansen, and Banks."

"Of course. One moment while I check those."

The woman behind the desk typed the names on her computer and smiled, but with a hint of confusion. "I'm sorry. I have a reservation for Trond Jansen and Tim Maxwell, but I don't see any reservations under the name of Banks. Hold on one moment. I'll talk to my manager."

She pressed a button next to the phone and in seconds, a man with balding hair and a cheap suit hurried from an inner office. "Hi there. Ms. Niki Banks, correct? You'll have to follow me. There was a small change in your reservation."

Niki narrowed her eyes. "I'm sorry...is there a problem?"

"Problem? Heavens no! It's only that your reservation

was upgraded at the last minute. If you'll join me in the Sky Lounge, we'll get you checked in lickety-split."

Jansen mouthed the two last words as she gestured for them to check in.

"I don't suppose you could tell me who upgraded my reservation?" she asked as the concierge ushered her to the lounge.

"Of course, ma'am. Naturally, we tend to not share such details, but the gentleman who arranged it said he wanted to surprise you. He mentioned something about you two being involved and that this was a way to show—and I quote—that he means business."

"I'll go ahead and assume that this was done through McFadden's Mechs?"

He paused. "No, but the man who made the arrangements said his name was McFadden. Taylor McFadden. He stressed that this was not a business arrangement but rather quite personal."

She smirked and held her bag a little closer. "Sleep in a beautiful suite tonight, for who knows what tomorrow will bring?"

The concierge kept the smile firmly on his face, but there was a hint of a twist in his eyebrows. "I beg your pardon?"

"Nothing. Never mind. Look, I've been on a plane all day, so I don't suppose we could simply fast-track the whole check-in process?"

"Naturally. That is the function of the Sky Lounge. Right this way, ma'am."

He proved true to his word and the process was even quicker since there was already another credit card waiting on the file for her reservation. In under a minute, she was whisked up in a private elevator to one of the largest hotel rooms she had ever seen.

"Holy shit," Niki muttered as she gaped at her surroundings. "It's bigger than my house."

The concierge had nothing to say to that. All she could do was stare through the massive windows that overlooked the Strip.

"If you need anything—anything at all, at any time of the day or night—call me on the hotel line." He bowed stiffly at the hip before he turned away and returned to the elevator.

Opulent was the only word she could think of to describe the suite. Everything was bigger and more impressive than it needed to be. The small coffee table next to the window was already laden with gift baskets filled with chocolates and other treats, as well as an ice bucket with a bottle of Dom Perignon chilling inside.

A selection of other drinks stood near a placard with the extensive room service menu available.

Niki doubted that she would peruse the menu yet, but the bottle seemed to look at her invitingly.

She put her suitcase next to the bed and stripped out of her clothes. In a few minutes, she slipped into one of the complimentary bathrobes while the tub filled with hot water. It had been a while since she let herself soak in a bath, and she wanted to do it right.

The bathtub was set into the floor and a few small steps enabled her to slip under the warm, bubbly water. A couple of different surfaces provided space for her to put her full glass down as she settled into the somehow cushioned surface.

The gentle water jets had already begun to press into the sore muscles of her back and shoulders and made her groan audibly as she slid a little lower into the water. With a sigh of contentment, she closed her eyes and simply enjoyed the luxury Taylor had provided for her.

As her arms spread wide, they bumped into something and her eyes jerked open. Another gift basket that she'd missed was set beside the tub. She picked up the sheet of paper left on top and smirked when she read the note Taylor left for her.

For all your sore muscles, past, present, and future, it read, with a small winking emoji. He'd asked them to provide it with the note too. The guy had some fucking balls to him.

"Maybe that's what attracts me to him," she muttered to the bubbles. "I like me a ballsy man."

CHAPTER TWO

The Mojave Desert was a little too cold for comfort at night, and the chill lasted into the early morning.

Still, he'd always liked the cold over the heat. The fact that he had moved to Nevada of all places showed how great he was at thinking these decisions through.

But the idea of working for the next few years and selling McFadden's Mechs to the highest bidder didn't sound like something he would do in the end.

Then again, Taylor thought as he pressed the accelerator down in the four-by-four, maybe he wouldn't still be alive then.

"What's the matter?" Vickie asked and nudged his arm from the shotgun seat.

"Is it weird that I haven't written a will?" He didn't much like the question and he scowled as he leaned back in his seat.

"Why...why would you have written a will?"

"Because I don't exactly live a safe life. In the end, if something does manage to kill me, I don't have any next of kin to claim everything. If I don't have a will, it'll end up in a court or a bank or something and everything I've done will go to nothing and no one."

"Well, if you were ever to write a will..." She tapped the armrest lightly with her nails. "Who would all your shit go to?"

"You guys. McFadden's Mechs is yours as much as mine, and that would need to continue."

She turned to face him. "Well, that's obvious enough, but I'm talking about your personal shit. Like, I assume you have a decent amount saved for a rainy day—all you former military guys do—and if you don't have any next of kin for that to go to, it'll end up in the hands of whatever bank you have it in. So I'm asking you, as a friend, where do you want all your personal assets to go?"

Taylor gave her a sharp glance. "What you're asking is how much I'll leave to you."

The hacker shrugged. "Well, I didn't want to know that outright, but sure, let's go there." She turned and faced him fully, her eyes wide and a cheeky grin playing across her lips. "If you die, what will I get?"

He couldn't help but laugh. "Have you always been this greedy or is it a more recent development?"

"More recent. You know how they say that getting a substantial sum of money doesn't change a person's personality but only amplifies it?" She fixed him with a teasing look and after a few seconds, leaned closer and nudged him in the arm with her fist again. "You know I'm kidding, right? And I don't want you to even think about not being around for the long haul."

"Yeah, I know." He smiled and shifted to nudge her

shoulder with his fist in response. "But yeah, you're probably as close to next of kin as I'll have. You and maybe—hopefully—Niki. And I feel like I might owe Jennie something for everything. Bobby will probably be the executor, so he'll get a good amount too. But aside from that...yeah, this is a little depressing to even think about. But it's the kind of shit you have to consider just in case."

"Fuck that. I will live forever and you will too, Tay-Tay. We're this close to the technology granting people eternal life." She held her forefinger and thumb up less than a centimeter apart.

"Yeah, there's a small problem with the technology that's supposed to help us live forever."

"What's that?"

"It happened to grow a big fucking jungle in the middle of the Sahara. I'm sure it won't be a problem for you, right? Since we'll live forever."

"Well, yeah, semantics. They should find a way around the murderous monsters any day now."

Taylor nodded. "Yeah. I'm it."

They pulled off the main street and proceeded down a handful of dirt roads into the desert, where the tough terrain turned rocky and hilly. After about ten minutes, they drove into an open area well hidden from the highway.

The rugged, inhospitable area was more or less what Taylor had been looking for, and the seclusion was not a bad idea either. He couldn't help but admire the wilderness around them. It had remained almost completely untouched by humanity for the past few years since the train yards and the warehouses had been abandoned.

"All right, folks!" Taylor called. Tanya, Niki, Elisa, Vickie, Maxwell, and Jansen had already dismounted and began to equip themselves with the suits he had brought or those Bobby had loaded in his truck. "This location is mostly abandoned and about fifteen klicks from the Vegas city limit. It used to be a way station into the west of the country where numerous trains passed through, but things have changed. The world moved on and left us with a primo area to get to know our suits. Get dressed up because the dancing will be fun."

"Fun for who?" Maxwell asked, already mostly finished with strapping his suit on.

"For me."

"I wish we could have ended up in the nuclear testing sites," Vickie muttered. "But the military is still all like 'but the radioactivity will kill you' or 'how did you get this number' about it."

Taylor grinned. "Well, I guess it's up to us to use our imaginations and make this as fun a place to train as they would have been."

"And by our imaginations, you mean…"

"Mine, yes."

They all suited up and the training in their little improvised obstacle course in the warehouse had helped them become a little more familiar with moving in the suits. Still, they were a long way from the natural motions he needed to see from them.

Vickie jumped from one foot to the other and tried to show off a little, but all he could see was the fact that she had too much lag between her movement and the suit's.

She was adjusting to the slower reactions, which was okay for training, but it would get her killed in the field.

She jogged to where he stood. "So, what will we do today?"

"Adjust your suit's reaction sensitivity for one thing."

"But I'm still getting used to it on this setting!"

He nodded. "That's the problem. That quarter of a second of a delay will get you killed. The closer to your reactions the suit is, the quicker you'll pull the trigger. I don't need to tell you that the person who pulls the trigger first is usually the one who walks away, right?"

"Unless you miss, which is what higher sensitivity would do for me."

"Unless you train for it." Taylor winked and nudged her arm. "You got this."

The hacker scowled. "Ugh, fine, I'll do it, but don't you laugh at me if I trip over my feet again."

"Pinkie promise. Hold that thought. Why...how did you... If Elisa is here, who's covering our phones? I thought you found someone, but I only now realized that no one arrived and there are no new people on our security system."

She looked at him with a carefully blank expression. "I...I did find a temp. There's a shortlist of people we trust so I called in one of those."

"All those people are here. Except for Jennie. You don't have Jennie on the phones at the shop, do you?"

Vickie looked aside and refused to meet his eye. "I... Desk. Desk is there—in a way—taking all the calls and making recordings for us to listen to later if we want to. Elisa said she wanted to get a little work done in her suit and would I be a good manager if I didn't let her go to the training she wanted to attend?"

"Huh." He grunted. "That's surprisingly mature of you. I don't know what to make of that."

"I'm simply that awesome?"

"Awesome enough to adjust those sensitivity settings to a more combat-friendly level?"

She mumbled something he couldn't hear but he assumed was a curse on him, his family, and his cow and he moved to where Niki seemed to struggle a little with the suit she wore.

"You look uncomfortable," Taylor noted.

"Hi there, Captain Obvious," she snapped.

"That's Major Obvious. I was promoted. But that's neither here nor there. Why the hell are you uncomfortable? I thought you were the one who had a little training? I need to have you as the teacher's pet who helps everyone else get with the program."

"Fuck no." She moved the suit around her hips. "These new suits are…well, suffice it to say that I'm a little outside of my comfort zone."

"Well, that's what the training is for. Once you've expanded your comfort zone, the suit will feel like it's a second skin and merely an extension of your body. And that will give you, like…fifteen different kinds of edges."

"You do realize that the metaphor falls apart there? Knives aren't supposed to have more than two edges."

"Ninja throwing stars?"

"Is that what you think of me?" She cocked an eyebrow. "As a shuriken?"

"You are whatever you need to be in the field of battle.

The thing that keeps you alive when you fight ever-evolving monsters is the ability to evolve yourself. Now, get your ass moving. In fact, everyone get your collective asses moving. We have training to do!"

They were already responding. Taylor could already feel the naked heat of the sun beating down on him. He was tempted to join them in the training, but he would see far more of their technique and capabilities if he watched them from afar. Bobby would push them from the front lines.

Besides, it would let them bond over being annoyed with him.

"Come on, guys!" he shouted over the comms where he was now seated in front of the computer that Vickie had set up for him to monitor all the suits' functions. "The day's a-wasting and you're all standing around! Do you want to know how to kill fuckers with those suits or not?"

He grinned when he imagined all the scowls in his direction, but it was difficult to feel bad. His workout was scheduled for later in the day, and with Bobby upping his game, Taylor needed to be ready to explain a few bumps and bruises. Hopefully, being at the front lines would tire the fucker out somewhat.

Niki leaned on her knees and dragged in a slow breath. The memories of Taylor's gift of a luxurious hotel room with a nice bubble bath were long gone. All she could think about was how goddammed hot the sun got in the Mojave. There was no sunburn thanks to the suit, but she wouldn't complain if the rest of her life was spent in the comfort of an air-conditioned office.

"No, that's not true," she whispered and moved the suit slowly to give her aching muscles a little time to recover.

"What's not?" Bobby asked and removed his helment. The man didn't look fresh—at least not from the redness of his cheeks—but he didn't look as tired as he should have.

"I'm...talking to myself. Hold on, Bungees, is Taylor pushing us harder than he needs to for some reason, or is this more or less how you guys were trained?"

He shook his head. "It's definitely not the way we were trained."

"So he's putting us through our paces for no reason?"

"I didn't say that. We were trained as regular military. It was then something of a shock when we went into the Zoo, one that all of us had to get used to or die trying. I think he's trying to develop a training regimen that prepares people to head into the jungle. Believe me when I tell you that I've been as tired as you feel right now. I'd rather it was in a safe training environment than out in the middle of a fight for your life against a horde of critters out for your blood. Conditioning is important out there, or do you think that Taylor is some kind of freak who's like that naturally? That he didn't have to work for it?"

Niki shrugged. "I imagine his physicality might have something to do with it."

"It doesn't play as big a role as you might think."

Bobby stopped talking immediately when Taylor strode to where they stood.

"You guys have some skills," the tall redhead admitted as he packed the rest of his equipment. "I'm fairly sure I threw everything I had at you and you walked away under your own power. That's fucking impressive. All of you."

Vickie looked a little more exhausted than the others and he picked her hand up and lifted it to bump her closed fist against his.

"I'd flip you off if I had the power and energy to do it," she complained.

He pulled her closed fist toward him and tugged the middle finger out until it was upright and directed at him. "There we go."

Even she couldn't hold the laughter back. "You're the best, Tay-Tay."

"I know." He squeezed her shoulder gently. "Eat tons of protein to rebuild all those muscles and you'll be back at it in no time, I promise."

"Thanks."

He turned to where Niki and Bobby stood, and the agent could almost feel that the two of them needed to talk about something on their own.

"I'll see you later?" she asked, not sure what she was hoping for but it popped out before she could stop herself.

"Yeah, I'll send you a message," he answered and patted her on the shoulder. "You guys are good to head back to the hotel on your own, right? In the SUV?"

"Sure, but Maxwell will have to drive. He's the one who's more or less alive at this point."

"Don't think I missed that."

Taylor dragged his gaze away from Niki's SUV to where Bobby studied him carefully.

"Missed what?"

"You might be decent enough with sleight of hand, but at your size, there are some things you can't do without it being noticed. Slipping a note into Niki's pocket is one of them."

He drew a deep breath of the cooling desert air. "Yeah, I guess. Leonard and even a certain consultant manning our phone lines at the moment—"

"Desk."

"Right. Even she thought it was a good idea for me to make my move with Niki—which, unfortunately, includes not fucking up by keeping her in the dark about the fight that's coming up."

Bungees folded his arms in front of his massive chest and tilted his head to the side. "So let me get this straight. You'll wine her, dine her, get on her good side...and then tell her that you're setting up a fight."

"Pretty much."

"A fight with two mob tough guys."

"You are correct, sir."

"With no suit or protection."

"Yep. That's about the plan in a nutshell."

Bobby stared at him for a few seconds before he broke into laughter. "I hate to say it, but you will never get laid, dude."

Taylor opened his mouth to reply but ended up with a simple nod. "You're probably right about that, but at least I'm being up-front and honest about it. She's said that it's important for people to be honest with her."

"Well, the sex—if you ever get any—will probably be over the top."

"I don't want her feelings to get hurt, you know? I can live with blue balls. Hell, we all had to live with them when we were still in the military. But I can almost guarantee that having a .45 emptied into said balls is a whole lot fucking worse."

"You make a fair point." Bungees couldn't help but laugh at the comparison. "You know it takes crazy to know crazy, right?"

He shook his head. "I have no idea what you're talking about."

"Sure. Are we working out tonight or what?"

"Yeah, if you're not too tired from today's training. I think I need more focus on my footwork since it'll give my ribs a chance to recover from that hook you caught me with."

Bobby shook his hand firmly. "Sounds good. I'll see you after I drop everyone else off."

Niki sank into the bath with a drawn-out sigh. It didn't escape her that this was the second in as many days and she had begun to feel like a cliché, but she couldn't help the fact that it would help to circulate more blood to her sore muscles. The Epsom salts the Aria had provided her with were also known for their anti-inflammatory properties.

A selection of choice chocolates rested on one of the surfaces next to her as well as a couple of sports drinks to help replenish all the liquids she'd lost out in the desert. At that moment, she felt like she could simply lie and soak for days.

Things probably wouldn't work out that way, but she felt less annoyed with Taylor about the harsh training he'd put them through. The guy did know how to get on her good side as well as he knew how to get on her bad side.

She picked up the remote and turned on the tv in front of her. A handful of drama shows and police procedurals were unappealing so she changed the channel repeatedly until she came onto a show called *Say Yes to the Dress*. She was too old and gave too few fucks for her to feel anything like shame over enjoying her favorite shows, guilty pleasure or not. While she wasn't particularly proud of it, the shame factor had gone a long time before.

Besides, it had sentimental value. She used to watch it with her mom when they spent time together. Despite all the difficulties she had gone through with her family, watching a group of women try dresses on in Manhattan with her mother and Jennie was a memory she held close to heart.

Of course, it meant that the show had been going for fucking ever, but that wasn't the point.

"Sorry, honey," Niki muttered with a cube of Belgian chocolate in her mouth. "But the bride isn't supposed to show that much cleavage on her wedding day. It's so tacky."

The showrunners agreed, and the dress was exchanged for something a little less revealing, although not by much.

"Okay, that's more skin than I'm comfortable showing." She popped another piece of chocolate into her mouth. "But hell, if I had a body like that, I would probably flaunt that shit too."

It felt a little too judgmental, but it wasn't like the girls would hear her. Plus, they were being paid a fuck-ton of money to try on dresses to be judged by their peers around the world. It was her job to enjoy it by judging the quality of the dresses.

"It's not like I'll ever spend that much money on a dress I'll wear for one day. The dudes get to either rent or keep their tuxes for a hundred other occasions, but the bridal gown is the most expensive and is then put away some-where for the rest of my life. Fuck that."

She was talking to herself and the realization made her chuckle. The commentary was simply part of the experi-ence, whether there were people to watch it with her or not.

The show continued until her skin began to prune. If she stayed any longer, she would spend the night in the water that was still warm after almost an hour. She pulled herself out with a low, guttural groan as her muscles protested being moved after spending so much time prone. She decided she'd simply watch the show to its conclusion when she got into bed—and maybe after some room service.

Niki wrapped herself in a robe and picked her shirt up from where she left it. She had a bad habit of tossing her clothes into a pile on the nearest surface or the floor, and Jennie had tried all their lives to get her out of it. The old habit remained, however, and she brushed some of the dust off that had collected on the article of clothing in the desert.

Something slipped out of the pocket and she immedi-ately reached to try to catch it before it landed on the floor.

She regretted the impulse almost instantly as every muscle up and down her back screamed in protest.

"Oh...fuck me." She gasped and stretched gingerly to pick the envelope up from where it had fallen. "I'll kill him —slowly and painfully. Put ice picks into his arms to pin him down and beat his ass to death."

The envelope was small, the kind used to hold a gift card or something. Taylor had slipped it into her pocket at some point, but she had no idea when.

She withdrew it and frowned at the contents for a few seconds before they made sense around her bathtub and exhaustion stupor.

Will you join me at the MGM Grand L'Atelier de Joël Robuchon this Friday night? She recognized Taylor's handwriting. It wasn't terrible or sloppy but it was still plainly written by him. There wasn't anything pretty and no frills were added. *If your answer is yes, a car will arrive to drive you there at 8 PM.*

"How the fuck..." she muttered and shook her head. The dumbass had forgotten to tell her how she could accept the invitation. Did he expect her to talk to him about it beforehand or would the car simply arrive at eight regardless of her answer?"

He had probably put considerable thought into this but it was very clearly not his forte.

"Fine," she answered and placed the card on the bedside table. "I'll kill you Saturday and eat with you Friday night. There's no sense in letting a good meal go to waste."

CHAPTER THREE

"Mr. Marino, the conference call you wanted to set up is waiting for you."

Rod looked up from his computer screen. His current task was to check the reports for the evening before, mostly so his pit bosses could say he had looked at their take for the evening. They were in something of a dry spell so there was nothing of real interest. Three weeks remained until the next big fight and it would be a while until a holiday would justify having a poker tournament that would draw the casual gamblers in.

They were still making money but not enough to catch and hold his attention.

He tapped the place where he had to sign and scribbled something beside his finger before he flung it into the out tray. Other people were paid to pick up whether someone was trying to cheat him, after all.

"Sure...ummm..."

Dammit, which secretary was this? The last one had

been sent to work for someone else after she had forgotten about a couple of his golf appointments. They had sent a replacement in but he couldn't remember her name for the life of him.

"Stephanie, Mr. Marino. Should I connect you to the call?"

"Yes, thank you, Stephanie."

Marino needed to work on having someone long enough that he didn't have to learn a new name every other fucking week.

His screen connected to the conference call that was cast quickly to his tv instead. This gave him a full view of the group of men he had tried to connect with over the past week or so. They were all as busy as hell, and he wouldn't hold it against them for not having the time to be at his beck and call. That said, he expected them to at least honor an agreement they had made to meet when they said they would.

All seven of them were present. *La Cosa Nostra* wasn't known for its civility, even among its ranks, but the kind of respect each of the men commanded was something he aspired to.

"Good afternoon, Don Marino," an older man with a second chin and a bald spot on his head muttered and straightened in front of his screen.

"Good afternoon, gentlemen, and thank you so much for taking the time to speak to me. I know we're all busy men and I don't want to take up too much of your time."

"We appreciate that." The second man was younger and looked like he had once been a model many years before.

"And while you need not clear any of your casino business with the rest of the family, the favor you have shown in keeping us in the loop of those fights you do host is a favor that will not be forgotten."

"I do have questions regarding the conditions of this fight since it will likely not be sanctioned by the Nevada Gaming Commission," another added.

"You don't need to worry about the NGC," Rod assured them. "The relevant authorities have been notified and paid to turn a blind eye to what happens in my casino on the night in question. You don't have to worry about that."

"That was not what I meant. We know you are capable of keeping the local authorities under control. My point is that if the rules are not the kind that would be found in a sanctioned fight, they need to be laid out before any of us would be willing to put any money down on it."

"Oh, right." He pulled up the rules that had been drafted for the fight beforehand. "It'll be a fight between two of my men and an outsider who I've worked with over the past few months. You should already have the details, but it will be a bare-knuckle fight with as few rules as possible. A cage match, if you will."

"If two of your men are involved, how can we know this is an even match? No one wants to watch a stream of an outsider pummeled into unconsciousness by your men. There is little interest or money in such demonstrations."

"The man they will go up against is former army and straight out of the Zoo besides," Rod explained. "His complete military history is part of the info package I sent you all—although most of it has been classified, which says enough on its own. You'll find this man is no walkover, and…well, suffice it to say that I will invest considerable capital in this and I expect there to be adequate return."

"Even so," the oldest of the group, a lean man with a hooked nose and almost no hair, retorted with a thick Italian accent. "We will need more information on all three fighters before we commit our resources to transmit the fight online. You understand, yes?"

"Of course." He made a note of the suggestion on a nearby pad. "You already have the details on my two fighters, but if you need more information on the newcomer, I will provide it."

The rest of them looked more or less satisfied with his response, and he drew back from the screen. "If there are no more questions?"

"We will contact you when we have more information, Don Marino," the fossil of a don replied and tapped the screen a few times before one of his assistants hurried forward to end the call for him.

The others dropped out and Marino took a moment to rub his temples which throbbed for some reason. Talking with the dons located across the country always gave him a headache.

"Stephanie?" he asked over the intercom.

"Yes, Mr. Marino?"

"I'll need a list of the people I have available for a side project. Nothing too dangerous or too exhausting, merely gathering information from people who probably won't be overly welcoming."

"Will do, sir."

The woman worked quickly enough and was the kind of calming presence in his office that he needed. He hoped it lasted and she became a regular around him. Maybe then he would be able to focus on his work instead of trying to remember the secretary-du-jour's name.

CHAPTER FOUR

The MGM Grand was only a couple of blocks away from the Aria, and Niki wasn't so debilitated by the training that she couldn't walk that far. Still, it was nice of Taylor to want her to have the best treatment from door to door and so made sure there were always people helping her and making her feel like a lady as much as possible.

Besides, from what she could see on her maps app, it didn't look like the walk was that pleasant, even by Vegas standards. There was no way she would waste the outfit Desk had helped her select while jostled by the crowd of random tourists who made their way home after a long day of sightseeing in the unbearable heat.

And making the walk in heels was not what she would ever consider, no matter how great they made her ass look. The shoes weren't something she wore often enough to justify heading out for a half-mile walk simply for the hell of it.

The limo was already waiting for her when she reached the door and the driver opened the door as soon as she stepped outside. That was the kind of thoughtfulness she doubted Taylor had in mind. It wasn't in the man to treat anyone like a delicate princess, so this had to come from the car service. They probably asked the receptionist to give them a heads-up when the person they were waiting for came down.

"Shall we?" the man asked with a passable attempt at a posh British accent.

"We shall indeed," Niki replied and stepped into the car, careful not to let the dress gape and reveal anything compromising in the process.

The drive was predictably short, and the driver was quicker than she expected. He was already opening the door for her before she had finished shoving one of the bagged snacks into her purse. The man showed no sign of being surprised or even that he had seen her doing it, but it was impossible that he hadn't.

Still, if he didn't make a fuss, maybe it wasn't that big a deal.

Niki stepped out of the limo and she immediately saw Taylor standing at the door, waiting for her. Him wearing something overly fancy wouldn't feel right and he knew it so instead, he'd chosen something classy and relaxed instead. The gray suit jacket and slacks complemented his powerful frame, and the white shirt matched his paler skin. She couldn't help but let her gaze drift over the two buttons he'd left undone to reveal his collarbone and a sliver of skin beneath.

She straightened her dress before she finally spoke to him. "Well, well, well. Don't you clean up nice? You're rocking the professional-casual look there, aren't you? Did you have this outfit laying around somewhere for a special occasion, or did you have to go shopping for it?"

He laughed and for the first time, she realized he felt a little nervous over the date. The vulnerable look about him was oddly endearing and certainly more attractive than the Neanderthal-esque confidence he usually wore like a suit of armor.

"I plead the fifth," he responded after a moment. "Shall we? I hear this restaurant has the best gourmet French Tapas served in a modern space with counter service in Las Vegas."

"Did you read that in the Google reviews?"

"Maybe."

"Well then." Niki extended her hand and Taylor took it and tucked it in the crook of his elbow as he led her inside.

She liked the more cultured look he had worked on, and from the attention the rest of the women in the restaurant gave him, so did they. It wasn't anything too obvious or overt. Most of those present were on dates or attending business dinners with husbands or boyfriends, but the subtle glances were all she needed to see. And the fact that they repeated the hasty study every few seconds when they thought no one was looking made it worse.

"What do you think of these stilettoes?" she asked as the *Maître D'* prepared a table for them.

He tilted his head back to study her and nodded. "They make your ass look great, I won't lie."

She smirked. "Well, yeah, that's why I chose them. But I mean the heels."

"Is this a trick question? They work on making your ass look great?"

"I mean are they thin enough to stab a bitch with? I'm asking for a friend."

"Oh, okay. Well…uh, sure. You'd have to put a little extra oomph to get them through but yeah, you could stab a bitch with them, especially if you go for the eyes. I wouldn't recommend them for kicking, though. Why, do you plan to use them to stab someone?"

Niki shrugged as the *Maître D'* indicated that their table was ready. "Maybe. They're a pain to wear anyway."

"I'd hold off on that until after dinner at least. Not only do I not want to get kicked out, but I do want to see you in them for a little while longer."

She laughed. "You're looking scrumptious yourself if you don't mind me saying so."

Taylor grinned and held her chair out for her to sit. "Sorry. I'm a little nervous and I guess that comes with me sounding like a creep."

"A little. But all things considered, I'm nervous too. We might as well get in a couple of mentions about how good we both look. It's better than inane and useless small talk."

"Amen to that."

Another waiter appeared and poured them a glass of French white wine each. He advised them that their first course would be out shortly before he retreated to the kitchen.

"So, I have to ask," Niki started and took a moment to sip her drink before she continued. "Well, I guess this counts as small talk, but it also means we need to get to know each other a little more. So is your family as crazy as you are or are you a black sheep?"

He almost snorted his wine. "Well, that's a little rich

coming from a family that incorporates you, Jennie, Vickie, and two versions of Desk."

"It simply means I know crazy when I see it."

"Ah. Good point." He took a moment to dab his lips with the napkin before he responded. "No, I don't think they are as crazy as I am, although it has been a while since I've seen them."

"But you returned from the Zoo...well, relatively recently."

"It's a long story, but I was...uh, okay. Let's say cut off from the rest of my family. It wasn't pleasant and I joined the military immediately after that."

Niki leaned a little closer. "What happened?"

"My dad and I had words about certain things he's done in the past and has no regrets over. My mom took his side. Things got heated, and he pushed me. I broke his jaw and was kicked out of the house and told in no uncertain terms that I wasn't welcome there. I found the nearest signup office in the area and I never went back. My mom sent me a couple of letters while I was stationed in the Zoo but I never opened them. I think I left them behind when I came to the US, but I'm not sure."

She nodded. "Well, I guess that answers my question."

"How so?"

"Well, for them to cut ties with someone like you, they'd have to be crazy, right?"

Taylor smirked as the waiter approached with two plates, placed them on the table, and retreated quickly. "You know, that sounded suspiciously like a compliment."

"It was meant as one." She smiled her most dazzling smile as she nudged the food on her plate with a fork.

"Changing the subject somewhat, I hope there are more courses to this. When you order Maine lobster, you expect there to be more...you know, lobster to it."

She couldn't help a smile when she realized that compared to Taylor's massive frame, the food seemed much smaller—and comedically so.

He nudged the plate and nodded. "There are four courses and a dessert, so I think we're set for that. Unless all the portions are this small, in which case I might need to stop at a burger joint on my way home. Seriously, how the hell do they get away with charging so much for so little food?"

Niki shrugged and took a mouthful, and her eyebrows raised almost of their own volition. "Okay, it might be that they charge for the quality instead of the quantity."

A slight scowl was his only response before he took a mouthful. "They damn fucking better. I ordered steak for the fourth course and it had better not be this small."

She couldn't help a small laugh as she had already finished the tiny portion and dabbed her mouth before the waiter came to clear their plates. "Do you mind if I ask you another personal question?"

Taylor looked like he had expected this part of the evening but hadn't looked forward to it. He wore a similar expression when he was steeling himself for a fight against a horde of Zoo monsters. "Of course. What do you want to know? Although I assume Desk has already looked into my life thoroughly and shared all that information with you."

"Fair, but there's information that even Desk isn't privy to."

"Don't tell her that."

"Right...but... Okay, I don't know how to ask this right, but here goes. You've explained to me in the past why you slept around so much. I don't think I would ever understand that myself, but you did apply some logic to it, which is more than most guys are willing to do." She wiped her hands on her napkin when she realized they were suddenly sweaty. "I guess my question is why are you so willing to stop now?"

This wouldn't be easy.

Rod stared at the list of contacts Stephanie had compiled for him. Most were the pit bosses he used in the casino and he wasn't sure they were the kind of people who would get the job done properly. And while he didn't want to have to spell it out to anyone, the chances were that they would end up on Taylor's shit list as well.

Of course, he was looking to make money on the last two idiots who had interacted with the man but he didn't need it to happen more than once. If people were going to get killed, they should not be members of his crew.

He leaned back in his seat and scratched his cheek for a few long seconds before the solution struck him. It wasn't the best idea he'd ever had but he was on something of a timeline.

Galvanized by this new possibility, he pressed the button on his landline to connect to the outer office. "Stephanie, would you mind coming in here for a second?"

"Of course, Mr. Marino."

Moments later, she stepped inside. There wasn't much

difference between her and the other secretaries he'd had in the past. Her long, blonde hair was held in a rigid pony-tail, and her dark-green eyes were covered by a pair of full-framed glasses. She was a little taller than most, though, and her heels added only a couple of inches to a lean, deli-cate frame that was perfectly and professionally comple-mented by the gray skirt suit she wore.

"I have a job for you," he explained and motioned for her to take a seat. It was late but the woman made no indi-cation that she wanted to leave soon and simply sat across the desk from him. "There are three men who I will do business with, and I'd like you to meet them and take down some relevant details about them."

"Details, sir?"

"Background, height, weight, arm reach, that kind of thing."

"It sounds like a tale of the tape for a fight."

"Something like that."

"But for three men."

"That is correct."

She had a notepad and made notes quickly. "Is there anything I should know about these men beforehand? Should I expect any trouble or resistance to these questions?"

"Well, not the first two on the list. They are employees of mine, and if you tell them I sent you, they'll be willing to provide you with anything you need. The third might be a little more problematic, which is why I'll send you—someone he won't...well, expect to cause any trouble. The last two guys I sent to talk with him left some bad blood, and I hope you'll be a little more diplomatic."

The woman added a few more notes. "I should then collect all the details relevant to fighting that they would be willing to give me, yes? As for this third man...Taylor McFadden, how diplomatic should I be?"

"Okay, don't offer it up, but I'm sure he'll require it. But negotiate first and get as much as you can out of it."

She didn't even blink. "I'll let you know what I've learned on Monday, is that acceptable?"

Marino's eyebrows raised. "I...yes, very acceptable. Let me know if McFadden gives you any trouble."

"Of course. Will there be anything else, sir?"

He shook his head. "You can head home for the night. I'll do the same in a little while myself."

CHAPTER FIVE

Taylor didn't answer immediately. Instead, he toyed with his wine glass and even waited until the waiter arrived with the next course. The pepper-crusted beef tenderloin looked and smelled divine, and Niki felt bad for making him choose between answering her and digging in.

"You can go ahead and eat if you want," she said finally as he took a sip from his wine. "It's not an easy question so I don't expect there to be any easy answers to it."

He looked at her and smirked. "No, no, it's fine. You're perfectly entitled to ask it. Honestly, I expected you to ask it a while ago before you agreed to go out on a date with me. I've already told you that the long and the short of it is that the Zoo is a love the one you're with type of place. You be with whoever you can since tomorrow, you might be going through some monster's digestive tract."

She tilted her head with a small frown and he hurried to apologize.

"Sorry, that wasn't the most appetizing metaphor. But the fact of the matter is that you take comfort in the arms of almost any willing human partner you can find. The first few times it was merely about the sex for me, but after that, it became a little more. It's about knowing that the people you have a beer with today might be gone tomorrow, so you crave a human connection, however small and fleeting."

Niki nodded slowly. "That was a surprisingly eloquent answer. I'm impressed."

"It was something a therapist told me. It didn't make much sense to me at the time, but over the past few months, I guess I've warmed to it. Maybe the hack knew what she was talking about."

Her expression thoughtful, she cut her pepper-crusted beef tenderloin that had remained untouched. "Was there ever anyone a little more special than simply getting your…only the human connection aspect to it?"

He scratched his chin and she knew she wasn't imagining the way he avoided her gaze. She also knew he was trying to be honest—maybe a little too honest—and he wasn't sure of the consequences of answering every question the way he was.

Still, he had to know she wasn't the kind of girl who would ask something she didn't want the answer to. And even if that wasn't quite true, she wouldn't create a scene or make him regret telling her everything she wanted to know. That wasn't the way to reward his good behavior.

"Well…there was someone," he admitted finally. He took a mouthful of the filet mignon and chewed slowly as if to give himself time to think about what he would say. "I met her during my first couple of months in the Zoo. Of course, on my first run in there, I was one of the only survivors and things had spiraled a little. She was a sergeant and almost stereotypically hard-assed. We were both stuck there while our tours lasted and made a couple of runs together and overall, it was fun. More than that, we trusted each other and both had the...addiction to the adrenaline high that came from heading into the Zoo."

He paused for a few seconds as he focused on his steak.

Niki wasn't great at simply waiting for the end of a story. "What happened to her?"

"We went into the jungle one day and she didn't make it out," he answered simply and took a sip of his wine. "I managed to get her dog tags out, though. We had a small get-together at the bar that night, everyone raised a glass, and that was kind of it. I guess I told myself never again after that. When you get used to the life, you start to feel like a junkie. You hate heading back in but after a while, you start to miss it. And that makes it feel worse, until eventually, you...slip and then, that's the end."

Taylor still didn't meet her gaze and she almost didn't want him to. The guy had put up such a huge wall between himself and the rest of the world, and this rare peek into what he was protecting was more than fascinating. She didn't want to do anything that would make him retract into that shell of his.

After a short silence, he shrugged. "And then you get Stateside and it's not the same. That kind of mentality has no place in the civilized world, and you need time to adapt to it. Even then, even looking down the barrel of what might be your last chance to live in the world again, you still feel that...something. Like you've adapted to live in an alien world and you're no longer fit to be among humans."

She placed her hand on his arm and squeezed gently. He seemed to not notice it for a couple of seconds before his gaze locked on her fingers. In silence, he stared at her hand while she simply waited, and he finally shook his head and looked at her.

"Huh, I...said that all aloud, didn't I?"

Niki smiled. "You did but I didn't mind. You're in your head so much that it's nice to see you willing to talk and shit."

He smirked and nodded, then glanced at her hand before he covered it with his.

"Is that what you're afraid of, though?" she asked as the waiter came to take their plates. "Slipping back into old habits? Old mentalities?"

Again, he took a moment to think. "Well, the jobs you provided helped to avoid the rebound and eased me back into civilized society. I guess you could say I got onto a recovery plan before I ever had to worry about it. I didn't want to go back, and the easy battles you brought me into were more than enough to keep the adrenaline junkie in me sated."

"So dropping a helicopter on yourself...that was easy?"

"An easy decision to make, if nothing else. It was the recovery that was long and difficult. A recovery I wouldn't have had to make if I died on that mission, which would have been an acceptable result if you'll remember."

She waited until the waiter had placed their dessert plates in front of them—chocolate sable and coffee Chantilly cream topped with a helping of coffee ice cream.

"I do remember. I guess that was the first time I saw you as more than simply a useful Cro-Magnon tool to be thrown at the monsters whenever they cropped up and made a mess of things. You were an ass, though."

"So are you saying that was the first time you checked my ass out?"

Niki didn't want to answer that, but the man had been surprisingly frank all night and it didn't feel right to not return the favor. "No. Not by a long shot."

He grinned and took a bite of one of the cookies. As with the rest, the portions were way too small and the dessert was finished almost before she had a chance to properly enjoy it. The waiter was on the ball, cleared the plates immediately, and nodded when Taylor gestured for him to bring the check.

"Well, in fairness, that appreciation went both ways," he noted as the young man returned with the leather folder containing the check. "I was merely too much of a gentleman to let you see it, is all."

"If you think you were in any way subtle about it, you are woefully mistaken." She made a move to intercept the bill before he could to see exactly how much the whole four-course-plus-dessert meal had cost them. He was quicker and snatched it out of the young waiter's hands before she could stretch far enough.

"Don't even think about it," he warned, peeked inside quickly, and slipped his credit card in before he handed it back. "I happen to know that being on a government employee salary is no fucking picnic. I was in the army for a while, so I know a thing or two. Like that it's much worse than being a government contractor."

Niki grinned as the waiter returned with the card. Taylor was already on his feet and circled to where she began to stand. She still had a little trouble with her heels as they moved to the entrance, where the limo was already waiting.

"You know, Taylor, a girl might hypothetically be very flattered by what you did," she noted as they reached the door and she waited for him to pull it open for her.

"Really? Well, was this...hypothetical girl flattered?"

She tilted her head and allowed herself a smile as she ran her fingers down his arm. "You could say this hypothetical girl was very flattered. Hypothetically."

They stepped out to where the limo waited and he cut in front of the driver to open the car door for her. The man in uniform didn't look very happy about it but remained silent.

But she wasn't ready to leave yet. It was clear that Taylor didn't expect to get straight to it on their first official date and she was happy about it herself, but it felt a little off to simply leave him the way he was.

With a hint of hesitation, she leaned closer. Even with her heels on, she managed to stretch the extra few inches she needed to place a light kiss on his lips. He didn't seem surprised—or, at least, he didn't pull away from her as she ran her fingers down the hard planes of his chest that were barely contained by the casual suit he wore.

A few seconds ticked past and Niki finally drew back and paused to straighten the delicate fabric of her red dress. She cleared her throat as, exactly as it had with the meal, everything in her wanted so much more.

He sucked in a deep breath and his tense shoulders relaxed as she raised her hand to wipe a hint of lipstick that had smudged onto his lips.

"You know, it usually takes a whole fucking lot—almost an act of God—to get me to open up like this, Taylor, and you've pried at those walls with a crowbar," she whispered breathlessly, unable to resist trailing her hand down his neck and chest. "But don't...don't screw around with it, okay?"

"Will do." His voice was thicker and raspy like it came from the throat as he nodded and stroked her hair tenderly. "Thomas will take you to the hotel now."

He seemed as uncomfortable with the situation as she did, but as they both made to part ways, the hint of a pause showed that neither of them wanted this to end yet. Maybe it was the right thing to do, but something animalistic in her wanted to drag him into the limo with her.

Instead, she slid into the vehicle and he closed the door behind her. Niki exhaled a breath she hadn't realized she'd been holding. Like she was unconsciously aware that she wouldn't be able to hold herself back from him if she had to breathe his scent for any longer.

The sound of conversation from the front of the car brought her attention to the here and the now. Taylor had circled and slipped the driver something before he retreated and let them drive off.

"So what did he have to say...Thomas, was it?"

"Thomas, yes, ma'am. Mr. McFadden gave me cash and his credit card info. He told me to take you anywhere you'd like to go for the rest of the evening and make sure you're safe. Oh, and if anything were to happen, to give him a call so he could come running."

"Holy shit." She couldn't help a soft chuckle as she settled into her seat. "Well, I have champagne and a couple of glasses here, Thomas, and it would be a shame to waste them. Let's drive the Strip and see that water fountain I've heard so much about. A nice relaxing time is about what the doctor ordered at this juncture."

"Of course, ma'am."

It buzzed persistently. Again.

Vickie had tried to set her phone to silent in the past but, like magic, that was when everything went to shit and she always woke to fifty calls, hundreds of texts, and people in desperate need of her help. It was like the universe told her to stay connected at all times. Or else.

And yet people assumed she wasn't busy doing something else—like, say, sleeping—and thought they could call her at any time of the night or day to tell her they needed her help.

"Sure, I'm that fucking good but hell, how will they survive if I'm not around to pull their asses out of the fire?" She straightened in her bed and put her glasses on. No way would she take the time to put her contacts in.

It was Niki and there were three missed calls from the same damn number.

"I swear to God if that dumbass redhead hurt my cousin in any way, I'll make sure the whole fucking world sees that video of him in his high school play," she grumbled, pressed redial on the last call, and leaned against the headboard as the tone dialed.

It only rang a couple of times before the woman picked up.

"What's up, my cousin!"

The extended last syllable grew higher and higher until she needed to pull the phone away from her ear.

"Hey...hey there Niki... is everything okay?"

"Everything is fucking awesome is what it is." Niki slurred her words a fair amount, which reminded Vickie of other times when she'd seen her cousin get drunk. "I had a great fucking time with Taylor. The food was great, but there wasn't much of it—it's like these French places always assume the people eating there are on a diet or something. I don't know what to do about them. But then Taylor sent me off with the limo driver and the minibar was stocked, let me tell you. Was...was stocked."

The hacker shook her head and took a moment to make sure that it was Niki who called. "Who are you and what have you done with my cousin? Because I'll have you know that I have a very particular set of...I have friends who have a very particular set of skills they've acquired over a very long career."

"Psshh, of course it's me. Don't be silly."

"Well, this Niki sounds suspiciously like she's having a good time and is completely swept up by a guy and I happen to know that her having a good time is simply not fucking possible."

"Well your...happen to know is wrong. Besides, Taylor has a very crunchy exterior and a very tasty body under it. And hey, I like me some crunchy."

Vickie winced. "Ew. I don't want the mental image of the two of you getting hot and heavy with each other."

She heard the woman laughing on the other end of the line. "We didn't have sex, silly. Not yet anyway."

"Again, ew."

"I haven't thought that through yet but I've fallen for him, Vicks. I've fallen hard and I don't want to get up."

"First of all, that's a very tasteless joke."

"I know."

"Second of all...come on, man." The hacker rubbed her temples. She wasn't used to having to be the grown-up, especially not with Niki.

"I'm so screwed. Well, not screwed screwed, but...you know what I mean."

"I won't make any promises for someone else to keep, but you have to know that Tay-Tay is trying his best."

Her cousin snickered. "Is that what you call him? Oh, I'm so calling him Tay-Tay from now on."

He wouldn't like that. "Okay, fine, whatever, but...yeah, this might be as close to being in a rom-com that you'll ever be, and if you honestly want to hear my advice on this... Well, he's throwing himself all-in. I'm not saying you should do the same—especially since I know your all-in behavior—but that's his level of commitment. As far as I know, anyway."

"I know..." Niki said something else but she moved away from the mic on her phone, which made it difficult to hear, although Vickie could hear liquid sloshing inside a bottle before she returned. "This is cool. I like it. And I don't want to fuck it up, and I don't know...how."

She grimaced and shook her head. "Woah. If you called me to ask for a relationship map, you're shit out of luck, coz, because I'm as lost in that particular minefield as you are. But you can always give me a call if you feel a little down or out of sorts and shit."

"Thanks, coz. I'm—shit, it's two in the morning. I'm so sorry. I wasn't even thinking... Fuck, do you have school tomorrow?"

"Eh, it's Saturday, so no. And even if it were, I can always fudge my attendance records if they get pissy about me getting into class late. Don't worry about it. Drop me a line if you ever need to talk. I can't say that I'll ever have any good advice to give you, but I've been told I'm one hell of a listener."

"Will do, coz. Peace...out!"

The line cut off as the woman uttered a very loud and uncharacteristic whoop and Vickie could only shake her head.

"Fucking idiots," she muttered, put her phone on the charging port, and pulled her glasses off. "But hey, Tay-Tay pulled off the first date. Good on him."

He had to admit, the desert was far more private than being in the American Base. It held fewer prying eyes and ears, and there was nowhere to hide unless someone happened to be made out of sand. Satellites could pick up images, but sound would be impossible. The woman had chosen a location that would not allow anyone to listen in on what they would talk about.

Still, Sal Jacobs couldn't bring himself to feel comfortable. Being asked to meet with secretive people who flashed large sums of money around, liked their privacy, and didn't want anything that was said in their meeting to be repeated elsewhere had ticked every single box of the untrustworthiness bingo.

"You look tense," Madigan muttered and patted him on the shoulder. "Don't worry. If they try anything, I'm here to protect you."

He couldn't help a small smile and he straightened his spine as the woman approached him. She was tall and her dark hair was tied in a tight bun as she studied something on a tablet one of her bodyguards brought to her. The two men with her and the handful near the vehicle were probably some of the hardest, toughest killers money could buy, but he would put his money on Madigan every day of the week and twice on Sundays.

The woman finally finished what had held her attention on the tablet and approached them, a small, professional smile on her face. "Dr. Jacobs, I must say your reputation precedes you. Your abilities and that of your team are almost legendary in these parts. But I've found it wise to not put much stock into reputation. It is, for the most part, gossip and people talking. I do not trust it until it is proven as fact."

"Well, given that I have no idea who the fuck you are, we should say that I have heard absolutely no gossip about you." Sal folded his arms. "And if you're trying to say you don't think my team and I are capable of living up to that reputation, I have to ask why you're willing to do business with us in the first place."

"Because of your reputation," she answered with a small, sly smile. "Once you can prove to me and my group that your reputation is fact, things between us are solid."

"And how do we go about proving that? We won't run tests for you to prove our abilities."

"Of course not. The proof would be in the pudding, as you Americans say. The going rate for a Pita plant these days is considerably lower than it was a few months ago, yes? But still a small fortune—five million dollars, American, according to my people. I would be willing to pay fifteen million for such a plant collected fresh from the Zoo. Your reputation tells me you are capable of this, yes?"

He exchanged a quick look with Madigan before he nodded. "Sure. We'll need to see some of that upfront."

"The going rate is five million, so we pay five million up-front. The other ten will be paid on delivery. Those are my terms."

One of the bodyguards came forward with a hefty briefcase and opened it to reveal a weighty stack of one-hundred-dollar bills.

Sal retrieved his phone immediately and dialed into the line his technical support kept open at all times. "Anja? Are you there?"

"Always," the young Russian woman answered.

"Can you run a scan on a cash deposit for me?"

"Sure. Turn your phone camera on and hold it over the cash in question."

He did as he was told and didn't bother to look the bodyguard in the eye. Although he wasn't a small man—a little over six feet and a hundred and eighty pounds—the guards were all taller and larger than he was. It wasn't good for his ego to start making that comparison.

"Okay, it looks clean," the hacker said after a few seconds. "The software checked the bills and they're all legit, with no trackers, dye packs, or anything else that might be a problem. The count is up to five million dollars. Are we going on a shopping spree?"

"I wish. I'll call you back." He hung up and studied the woman carefully before he looked at Madigan. His partner looked as uncomfortable with the arrangement as he felt, but she nodded slowly.

"Your terms are acceptable," Sal noted, took the briefcase from the guard's hands, and snapped it shut. "We'll let you know when we have a plant for you."

The woman smiled. "Excellent. I look forward to your call."

She snapped her fingers but the men were already mounting up and preparing to move out. One of them held the door of the Hammerhead open for her and in under a minute, they accelerated away from the area, leaving a rising cloud of sand kicked up on their way to the American base.

"Do you think if I ever snapped my fingers like that, I could get the Heavy Metal team to jump into action like those goons did?" Sal asked.

Madigan shook her head. "I doubt it. Back to business—how do you feel about them?"

He scowled, his gaze fixed on the moving vehicle as he lugged the briefcase of cash to where she had parked their Hammerhead. "They might as well have spelled out 'we're going to kill you when you finish the job' with pom-poms."

She studied them for a few moments but shrugged and folded her arms in front of her chest. "Well, yes, but it's not like it's the first time someone's tried that with you."

"You're right, it's not, but it's only exciting the first time around. After that, it's simply fucking annoying."

"The money's good. Better than any of the jobs that we've taken lately."

"Well yeah, it would have to be to make it attractive."

"So instead of simply waiting for them to backstab us, we backstab them. You know, proactively."

Sal pushed the briefcase into the back and made a mental note to find a way to deposit that amount of money in a single transaction since there was no point in having that much cash liquidity. Too many people were desperate enough to be tempted by that kind of reward. "We'll need to track them to where they take the plant for a retrieval."

"I'll say South Africa." Madigan climbed into the driver's seat and turned the vehicle on. "Or maybe somewhere in South America."

He settled into the seat beside her. "Nah, my money's on the US."

"They had accents. Hers sounded South American but her goons all sounded like they grew up speaking Afrikaans."

"Sure, but you only get that arrogant and throw money around like that when you work for an American company. Probably somewhere on the west coast, if I had to be more specific."

She eased the vehicle away from the dunes and toward the road. "Okay, that's a fair point. So what do you think, should we give Agent Banks a call? Let her know there's someone in her jurisdiction trying to get their hands on something illegal and incredibly dangerous?"

"Probably. Especially if they're trying to breed their own Pita plants—or, God forbid, start their own Zoo."

Madigan scowled. "On American soil? I fucking hate it when they try that."

"I could be wrong."

"You could, but when was the last time that happened?"

Sal paused to think about it as she chuckled and raised an eyebrow at his concentration. "I don't know. Last winter, I think."

CHAPTER SIX

The Mojave was hard on the eyes even at the best of times. When the sun beat down, it was difficult to look at unless Niki wore sunglasses.

And it seemed even they wouldn't be enough to help today. It was early and technically still in the acceptable time of day to be out and about. Despite this, her head pounded and her mouth tasted like she had gargled the same dusty sand she stood on, and she couldn't help but feel like she was about to die a very slow and agonizing death.

"Today will fucking suck," she muttered, leaned against the hood of her SUV, and considered climbing inside and cranking the AC to the maximum until the rest of their group arrived. Taylor was running late and so was most of his team, which left her, Jansen, and Maxwell to wait for them in the middle of the fucking desert.

The two men didn't look like they minded. They discussed something that had happened to them at the casino tables the night before, but she had zoned them out when their voices hurt her head too much. They knew she was hungover and were probably talking extra loudly to make her miserable.

Mission accomplished.

She tried to turn quickly when someone tapped her on the shoulder, but her body responded sluggishly and she winced. Vickie stood behind her, carrying a paper tray with two disposable cups of coffee.

Niki hadn't even heard the girl's car pull up. Although it was a Tesla and therefore quieter than most cars, she should still have been aware of her arrival.

"You look like shit, cousin," the hacker commented and handed her one of the coffee cups.

"Yeah well, I feel like shit, so at least it's accurate." The black, bitter coffee did help somewhat, but not as much as she'd hoped it would. "Champagne always gives me the worst hangovers. I have no idea why. Honestly, I don't remember it getting this bad with scotch."

"It's common. You don't feel it as much with the champagne so you end up drinking much more. It's not rocket science."

The agent nodded and took another sip of her coffee. "I guess that makes sense."

Her eyes were immediately drawn to the massive black truck called Liz when it pulled in beside her SUV and raised a cloud of dust as it came to a halt. Bobby's truck drew in directly behind and Jansen and Maxwell stopped their bantering and readied themselves for another day at the office.

Taylor climbed out of the truck and looked a little sprier than she felt, but she narrowed her eyes when she saw that he looked like shit as well. He wasn't hungover—if he ever got hungover anymore—but his right eye was darker than the left and there was a bandage on over his right eyebrow. His left cheek was also a little discolored and swollen.

Niki took another sip of the coffee to make sure that she wasn't seeing things. "Is it only me, or does it look like Taylor's been in a fight?"

"It does look like he's been in a fight," Vickie commented. "And if he looks like that, I'd hate to see what the other guy looks like."

He waved at them and jogged over, but the hacker beat a hasty retreat.

"Hey," he said by way of a greeting. "I need to talk to you about something if you're not...um, busy."

It was nice of him to give her an out if she wanted one, but she shook her head. "I'm merely a little hungover. Which is about a rung of improvement over what it looks like you've been through. Did you have a head-butting contest with a car?"

"More or less," he admitted. "But that's not what I wanted to talk to you about. Well...it is, but there's context involved that I think you should know about. People have told me I should keep you in the loop even though we aren't...uh, even though there are no rings involved in our relationship yet."

She narrowed her eyes. "Okay..."

"First things first, Bungees did this to me."

Her eyebrows raised in astonishment. "I...okay. Can I ask why or is this one of those 'you do not talk about fight club' moments?"

"No, nothing like that. Well, again, I suppose it could be, but no."

"I have to say, you're not making much sense here, Tay-Tay."

He flinched visibly at hearing her say the nickname—like she'd slapped him with it—but pushed forward immediately. "It's a long story. It started when two assholes came along and threatened Bobby and Elisa while they were at the shop and I wasn't. They wanted to find me since they were working for Marino and he wanted to have a word with me, and the whole thing escalated. Nothing happened, thanks to Bungees, but when I did that job for him, I said one of the conditions was to have a decidedly unfriendly chat with the two assholes in question. He agreed and once the job was done, he had a few conditions of his own. He wanted it to be a cage match, streamed online, with bets available for the select few. You know, Vegas shit."

Niki nodded slowly. That was a fair amount to process in less than a minute and she was still getting through her first coffee of the day. She took another sip and a few necessary moments to consider what he had told her.

"I take it the two assholes accepted the fight offer?"

Taylor nodded. "From the way Marino described it, they were anxious to get into the cage with me too. These mafia fuckers always want to show off how tough they are, and the way they saw it, the first guy to take me on and win would have those bragging rights. All things considered, with the shit I've put their family through, I guess there's a very cushy job with a ton of benefits and perks for the guy who has that on his record."

She grimaced but it made sense. Guys like Marino had ways to make a profit off anything and everything they touched. "Okay."

"You're...taking this far better than I thought you would. I expected there to be at least a couple of threats regarding the inevitable fate of roasting my testicles over an open fire while they're still attached to me or something."

"No, not at all, although if you want threats, I do have a couple of choice ones. I even have one that involves using ghost pepper to spice your balls while I roast them over burning coals."

He shuddered at the thought. "I think I'll pass. But are you okay with this? Really?"

Niki couldn't think of anything else to do but shrug. "I'm more interested in the fact that you considered my feelings to the point where you thought to tell me about this despite the lack of my noose around your neck."

"More like a ring around either our fingers."

"I know what you think."

"That's not...entirely true." He took a sip from his coffee and looked around the desert. "But I think a lasso might be a little more appropriate. Around you instead of me, though."

A very unattractive snort emerged before she could stop herself and she barely managed to not spill her coffee. "Okay, I'll be more careful with my flirting from this point forward."

"Why?"

"To keep my mind from being dragged off a cliff and into a gutter by that lasso of yours."

He smirked. "Well, okay, but I hope it doesn't last too long. I look forward to joining you in a dive off that cliff."

She took another deep swig of her coffee until she drained the dregs and put the empty cup onto the hood of the SUV. "You know I'll be there with you, right?"

"Be where?"

"At the fight. I'll stand right beside you."

Taylor gaped at her and let her take his coffee without even a slight protest. "Okay. Why, though? Not many people would want to be close enough to the cage to hear fists connecting."

Niki tilted her head and leaned closer to grasp him by the collar of his shirt. This time, she dragged him to her height and pressed her lips to his mouth, and her tongue danced with his. He tasted of sweat and coffee, and she loved it although she wasn't sure why. There was something hard about the taste like the rest of his body was.

She pulled back, not caring that the rest of the crew were watching. Or maybe they weren't. It didn't matter.

"Because, Taylor McFadden, I might as well have branded your taut ass with my name. It's mine, and that means I'll be there, close enough to be in the potential splash zone. And you can bet your ass that I'll shoot any fucker who tries to cheat his way to a win in that cage. And if you die, I will take necromancer lessons so I can raise your spectral ass to bitch at you for the rest of my miserable life. And speaking of asses, I don't pay you to stare at mine all day, so why don't you fucking help me get into my suit?"

"Honestly, the ass-watching is more of a perk of the business." He smiled in the way only he could as she walked to where Bobby was still unloading the crates from his truck.

"Do you think we should do live ammo training?" the mechanic asked as his boss stepped up to help him.

"Tomorrow," Taylor asserted.

They weren't the kind of men she liked hanging out with. It wasn't even that her parents had told her to avoid guys like them for her entire life up to the moment when she moved out of their house. She'd followed their advice until she ran out of money on her way to Los Angeles and ended up in Vegas.

Stephanie stopped giving a shit about what her parents thought of her life choices at the point when she had to pay her way through college and they didn't bother to attend when she graduated *summa cum laude*.

Who the fuck didn't go to their daughter's graduation?

She adjusted the blonde wig she chose to wear and her glasses while the two men continued their attack on the punching bags that had been set up in front of them. The whole area had been created by a professional, and both men had trainers who shouted instructions in their ears.

Vegas was the place to find trainers like that. This was where all the fighters came when they wanted to make it big, and the same went for trainers.

These guys weren't the types who would fight in the UFC or one of the hundred boxing organizations in the world. They were brawlers, men who had grown up fighting—and not simply play-fighting. These men had fought from a young age for their survival.

And some dumbass by the name of Taylor McFadden had challenged them both.

"Have you met Taylor McFadden?" she asked as one of them took a break to sip his water. "What do you know about him?"

"He's a punk." The man spat, wiped the water that spilled from his lips, and returned to the punching bag. His powerful arms and shoulders rippled with every strike.

The second man was a little larger but he seemed more subdued. "I never met the guy, but I've seen him. He's big and he knows how to throw down from the sound of it. And he has…what you call, *sfere di ottone.*"

She needed a few seconds to remember the Italian she'd learned during her semester abroad. "Brass balls?"

"Something like this, yes? He killed men. Very powerful men in the *famiglia*, and what did Don Marino do? Hire him. It's not a man you fuck with lightly."

Stephanie took note of the man's words. "Why…why are you fucking with him, then?"

"Can you imagine what can be gained by the man who takes that reputation of his away?"

She gaped and shook her head as the man returned to his training. They were doing this because they wanted the glory of it. The fact that they would fight him two on one didn't even register. It was both unbelievable and interesting to see.

"Good talk," she whispered, snapped her notebook shut, and turned toward the door.

"I need to have a word with this McFadden fucker."

CHAPTER SEVEN

The phone line was busy yet again.

It wasn't surprising at this time on a Saturday but still, there was no reason why there was no forwarding number available. The business they operated, in her reasoning, catered to people who had emergencies that couldn't wait for business hours.

Stephanie pressed the end call button on her phone and dialed it again. Marino wanted the details on McFadden before Monday and she wouldn't leave her boss empty-handed. She knew what he was. It wasn't like he tried to keep it a secret. Everyone in fucking town knew. And the more she found out about Taylor McFadden, the more she realized there was more to the man than met the eye.

Someone had stolen millions of dollars of Mr. Marino's money—Don Marino, she reminded herself—from an armored car and nothing had come of it. The heist had been perpetrated by men in full combat armor suits and McFadden happened to own a mechanic shop that fixed suits of combat armor.

"Holy shit," she whispered. "He did the heist. On Marino's orders or his own?"

"Excuse me?"

Someone had picked up. Fuck.

"Uh…hi, who am I speaking to?"

A pause followed on the other side of the line. "How can I help you?"

The woman's voice seemed weird but not for any reason Stephanie could put a finger on. It sounded normal in every way except…maybe the accent?

"My name is Stephanie Cordray and I would like to speak to Taylor McFadden, please."

"What might this be with regard to, Miss Cordray?"

Again, the voice unsettled her somewhat. "Well, to be perfectly candid, it is regarding an athletic endeavor he will undertake in the next couple of weeks."

The pause that followed was longer than the first. "Are you one of his exes? Because I happen to know that Taylor is looking into a very serious relationship and is not on the market for any more…flings."

The guy's assistant knew about his personal life. Talk about involved.

"No, nothing like that. He'll be in a cage match sponsored by Mr. Marino, and I would like to talk to him about that on Mr. Marino's behalf. Do you think he would have the time for that?"

"I don't think he's available today, but depending on what data you require, I should be able to help you. I think you'll find there isn't much about Taylor McFadden that I don't know about."

Stephanie narrowed her eyes. "Is that so?"

"I think you'll find there isn't much in the world that I don't know about. Stephanie Cordray, age twenty-seven and a half, born in Denver, Colorado, to Joseph and Yasmin Cordray. He's a welder, she's a schoolteacher. Oh, recently divorced—that's sad to see."

She knew what was happening. The assistant was trying to get under her skin. "How?"

"If you think there's anything about your boss and the people who work for him that I don't know about, you're way too naïve to work for someone like Rod Marino. That man, thus far, has been too much of a threat to the people I care about for me to not be personally plugged into every aspect of his life."

A little startled, she nodded and when she remembered the woman couldn't see her, she added, "Fair enough."

"With that said, what exactly does Rod Marino want to know about Taylor McFadden that he doesn't already?"

Caught by surprise, she tried to work out how the conversation had suddenly shifted from veiled threats to compliance. After a few seconds, she finally looked at the notes she had been taking. "Um…oh, right. Do you know if Taylor has ever been in a fight before? I mean the professional kind of fight that there would be a highlight reel of?"

"Well, given that McFadden joined the military a few weeks after his eighteenth birthday and didn't leave until less than a year ago, I can confidently say his fight history has mostly been off-camera and not with humans. At least, not professionally."

Stephanie wrote it down. "So, no professional fighting history."

"Not with humans."

It took her a few seconds to realize what the woman was talking about. The man's record indicated that he'd spent much of his time in North Africa and these days, that meant he spent his time running into the Zoo. She vaguely recalled mention of some ZooTube site that posted videos and had become a fledgling Zoo-centered industry that rapidly gained popularity. In five years or so, they would make movies, tv series, write biographies, and have interviews with and about the crazy fucks who went into that place.

Maybe having two guys fighting him wasn't such a bad idea. Crazy went a long way when there weren't any rules in the fight.

"Was there anything else you wanted to know?"

Stephanie moved her pencil down the list of questions she wanted to ask. The next five wouldn't matter if he had no fighting history. "Do you know what kind of fighting style he uses? What his training is?"

"What, are you scouting for the competition?"

"The people making bets want to know more about him than simply how he keeps his beard looking so nice. Do you know what kind of training he's been through?"

"The Army has a very particular kind of training and it isn't one that goes by any name. Or, rather, it goes by so many names that it's tough to simply put it down on a tale of the tape. But if you want to, you can call it the MAC, also known as Modern Army Combatives."

"Yeah, well, that's what they teach the grunts in boot camp. Much more goes into what they teach the guys after that."

"If you don't know already, I don't know what to tell

you. They teach men like Taylor to kill, which is similar to the training they use for the thugs Taylor will fight. It should make it interesting."

She sighed. This would go much smoother if she could have this conversation face-to-face with McFadden.

"Okay, let's go over the basics then. Do you have his height, weight, and arm reach?"

"Height is six feet, six and a half inches. His weight fluctuates depending on how much water weight he carries. He's just gotten out of the hospital and physical therapy too, but his average should be between two hundred and fifty-five and two hundred and sixty pounds. Arm reach is a little over eighty-six inches. Do you want me to convert any of that into metric?"

The details matched what Marino had on the man, more or less, although it did look like he had put on almost ten pounds since the physical he had taken when he left the army. Whether that was water weight, fat, or muscle remained to be seen.

"No, thanks. I can convert it all easily enough for those that need it."

"Do you need to know anything else?"

"Not unless you can get Taylor to talk to me in person."

"I'll try but I won't make any promises. Besides, you owe me a favor now."

Everyone had their hands out these days. Stephanie didn't know what she could promise to this woman but if she could, she would make good on it. Having contacts outside of Marino's business interests was always a good thing.

"How can I help you?"

"Let me know the details you'll be sending to the other bettors too. The chances are that I'd like to put money down on the fight and I'd need to make an informed decision."

"Are you sure you're not merely spying for your man Taylor?"

"Well, look at the pot calling the kettle black. That aside, though, I have money to make on the fight too."

She sighed. "Fine. How do I contact you when I have all the information?"

"Call this number again and if you get someone other than me, ask for Desk."

"Desk?"

"It's a nickname. You don't think I'll give you my real name, do you?"

"I guess not." She heaved another sigh and resigned herself to the fact that the woman wouldn't be more forthcoming. "I'll talk to you later, Desk."

Something still felt off about the voice, but she chose not to spend too much time thinking about it. She had all the information she would need on McFadden, although a little more wouldn't go amiss if she could get it.

"It'll be one hell of an interesting fight, whatever happens." She knew she wasn't talking to anyone except herself but at this point, most people thought she was another of Marino's bimbo secretaries and she preferred them to keep thinking that. She was safer this way.

Stephanie pulled her blonde wig off and let her natural, black hair fall free for a couple of seconds before she drew in a long, deep breath.

"Fucking mobsters, military fighters, and greedy hackers. Maybe I should go back to Denver."

She had to give it to the fucking Serbian, he did know how to choose a location.

Of course, the view probably wasn't what Matija had in mind when he purchased the facility. In fact, she doubted the man had set foot there or ever would, but Sofia felt it was important to see what was happening on-site with her own eyes.

The island was a few miles off the coast of Algeria, and with that kind of exposure to the elements and the sheer power of the ocean, it was no wonder no one had tried to settle there until the Second World War. The waves had pounded against the rock until it was little more than a pillar protruding from the ocean with a nice little green area on the top.

It looked small from afar but it was much larger once her helicopter landed.

A handful of technicians and specialists were already waiting for her when she was escorted away from the spinning rotors of the helicopter.

"Miss Chavez, we are honored that you would choose to visit us at this time," one of the leading specialists shouted over the sound of the helicopter powering down in the background. He sounded vaguely South African like her bodyguards, but she had a difficult time placing accents in English.

"Thank you, Dr. Minnaar. I've wanted to see this for some time now." She looked around the top of the island and her gaze settled on the single, fortified building at the center. It was barely five thousand square meters if she were to hazard a guess, and it rose to three stories. "I have to say, it was far more impressive in the files you sent my office but at least the solar panels are up and running again."

"Ah, yes…well, the building is what was left when the Americans decided to abandon this base, and it was meant to look unimpressive. You will understand when I say it is only a cover—a tip of the iceberg if you will. The structure will house our personnel and is also where we will operate the solar panels and the wave power plant at the bottom. We keep what energy we need and send the rest to the mainland. In addition, it is where the desalination plant will be operated once it is finished and operational."

"Desalination?"

"Yes, we need clean water and enough rises from the waves for us to filter and use both for survival and for the projects you would like to undertake. The soil has already begun to arrive, and we have started the greenhouse three levels down. It is the largest area of the complex with the most open space, once built to house intercontinental ballistic missiles. I think it interesting that life will take the place of what was once intended to house weapons of extinction."

The man had a point. There was something irony-like in that concept.

"Pardon me—and I do not wish to speak out of turn—but when will the object of our projects be delivered?" he continued. "Even with basic tools and simplified processes,

I can tell you that my team and I are most anxious to begin our work here. In the right hands—which is to say yours—the very world will be subject to change."

"I know," Sofia answered and her voice quieted as the engines in the background wound down enough for them to have a conversation at a normal volume. "And the Pita plant will be delivered shortly if all goes well with the contractors we hired for the job. Like you, they are the best available. Now, what say you we get the tour out of the way so I can tell my board of directors how fantastically well the work is going here?"

"Of course, Miss Chavez. If you will follow me?"

CHAPTER EIGHT

"Oh, God, I'm such a fucking cliché."

There was no one else around to hear her and the only people who would know how much of a cliché she was would be the housekeeping staff who constantly had to replace all the bath salts and bubbles she used every time she settled in for much-needed R and R.

Taylor still pushed them at the same pace they'd been subjected to before, but she could already feel her body adjusting to it. She felt like she had been a tube of cookie dough when she started and now watched herself being carved out of wood. In a couple of weeks, she would be almost as used to running around in a suit as she was in her own skin, which was what he intended.

Even though it was what they worked toward, Niki could still feel her body a few weeks behind where her mind wanted to be. The hot, long baths helped her to recover a little faster so she could be ready for what he had in mind next.

"Give him a whip and he'll be the perfect taskmaster."

Saying that aloud made her cheeks turn red. Merely the thought was enough, especially of Taylor with a whip. Not that she was into that kind of thing, but there were certain connotations to keep in mind.

Her train of thought was broken when her phone vibrated as her show went into commercial. She couldn't help a small smirk as her gaze picked up the name on her screen.

"Speak—or think—of the devil, in this case." She pressed the accept call button. "Hey, Taylor, what's up?"

"Not much. I'm calling to see if you are up for a late dinner."

It sounded more casual than the one he had taken her to the night before. Most guys would wait at least a couple of days—letting absence make the heart grow fonder or something—but she needed to get it through her head that he was not most guys.

"I'm not...uh, dressed."

"Okay...well, even in Vegas, you can't go out without any clothes on. Or you could, but only once. Assuming you are willing to go out for something to eat and don't want to get arrested for indecent exposure, might I suggest something simple? Like...jeans and a t-shirt. Nothing fancy tonight."

Niki paused to look at the clock on her phone. "Okay, I'm down for a casual night out on the town. Give me twenty minutes to get ready."

"Is that the kind of twenty minutes that turns out to be forty-five? Because hotels like the Aria don't appreciate people parking their four-by-fours in front of their entrance for extended periods."

"It'll be twenty minutes, jackass."

"Okay, fair enough. It'll take me about twenty-five minutes to get there, so I'll see you then."

As much as she liked to show off the fashion sense Jennie had helped her to acquire, she did prefer a casual night out. For one thing, she didn't have to wear her heels. As much as they looked knockout gorgeous on her, whoever had designed them hated feet and wanted to see them die.

Sure enough, almost exactly twenty-five minutes later, the four-by-four he had bought so he didn't have to drive around town in his truck pulled up to the entrance. One of the valets moved quickly and was already at the edge of the sidewalk before the vehicle had come to a complete stop, but Niki stopped him with a firm hand on the shoulder.

"Don't worry, this one won't need your services." She assuaged his hurt feelings by slipping a ten-dollar bill into the chest pocket of his bright red uniform. "I don't think he'll park for very long."

Taylor hadn't seen her when he stopped and unbuckled his belt and grasped the door handle before she tapped the passenger window.

"I know you like playing the gentleman and everything," she said and slid into the car before he had the chance to get out, "but I am capable of opening doors on my own, you know."

"I never doubted that."

"Of course. Where did you have in mind for our late dinner? Hopefully somewhere with decent food portions this time?"

He laughed as he strapped himself in again. "Well, it

would have to be, honestly. It's a twenty-four-hour Italian place called the Bootlegger Bistro."

"Italian places are famed for their overwhelmingly large portion sizes, so that sounds about right. Have you ever been there before?"

"I have."

Niki narrowed her eyes. "Come on, we won't play the game where we both pretend we haven't gone out with other people before each other, so if it was with one of your...can I even call them exes? Whatever. The point is you might as well tell me."

He shook his head as he pulled them onto the street. "No, not one of my exes, although probably someone as distasteful to you. Rod Marino wanted me to meet him there for a meal. All things considered, I thought it would be an interesting idea given the news that I shared with you today. Plus, the people who run it know who Marino is, and I thought I might check it out to see if they remember me having that dinner with him."

"So you thought you would check the place out before you thought of asking me out for dinner. Why did you ask me, then? Not that I mind going out for a meal with you, even as an afterthought."

"You weren't an afterthought. You said you wanted to be at my side when I beat those mafia thugs into paste, and I thought it would be a good way to show you why you would be there, assuming the owners will tell Marino about us."

She laughed aloud and darted an amused glance at him. "It seems like an interesting tactic. What do you think he'll do if he realizes you're dating an agent for the DOD?"

"I doubt he didn't know about it already, but if it's news to him, so much the better."

"You like fucking with the guy, don't you?"

It was his turn to chuckle. "Honestly, I don't usually like screwing around with people. Mind games aren't my thing, but if there was ever someone to fuck around with, it's Marino. He did start it, though."

He made a good point, and she had as much reason as anyone to want to see the mob boss fucked with. The guy had made threats against her family and despite the fact that they were now in some kind of tenuous alliance, she still wanted to get in what few shots she could before things turned hostile again.

Besides, the Bootlegger Bistro looked like a classy establishment and very much the classic Italian restaurant that might have looked at home in New York during the sixties or seventies.

Taylor already had a reservation for nine in the evening, and from the looks of it, the head waiter did remember him. The man waved him in and made welcoming gestures as he guided them to their table.

In fairness, her escort was a difficult man to forget once anyone met him.

They barely had time to pick their menus up before one of the waiters arrived with a tablet at the ready. "Can I interest the two of you in some drinks?"

Her companion nodded. "I'll have a beer. Whatever you have on tap."

The young man turned to Niki. "I'll have the same."

"Coming right up."

Taylor smirked. "I was never a cocktail kind of guy."

"And I was never a cocktail kind of gal." She tilted her head and regarded him with a small frown. "There's a dirty joke to be made in there somewhere. Something about cock and tail, but I can't think of it right now."

He didn't answer immediately but he tried to fight a grin that spread across his face.

"What?"

"It's...cool to see you like this. Your class-bitch act is very entertaining to watch, but seeing you relaxed and hopefully enjoying yourself...it's nice."

She met his gaze and smiled. "It's nice to feel it too, I have to say."

Letting her guard down did cause anxiety to flare up but so far, he had shown no sign that he was worthy of such doubt.

The beers arrived, and Taylor motioned to her menu, a non-verbal question whether she knew what she wanted to order. She nodded in the affirmative.

"I think we're ready to order too," she noted aloud.

"Very good. What can I get you?"

"I think the *Osso Bucco* for me," she told him and motioned for Taylor to get his order in as well.

"I'll take the *Scaloppine di Lorraine*, thanks."

The waiter tapped their orders into his tablet and made his way to the kitchen.

"What the hell kind of an Italian restaurant sells steak?" she asked as they took another sip of their beers. "If you come to an Italian place, you come to eat Italian food, right?"

He raised an eyebrow at her. "Uh...you know that Italians eat steak too, right? And have their own ways to prepare it and everything? They even have Italian names for it too."

"Yeah? Name one."

"*Bistecca alla fiorentina.*" He smirked like he had expected her challenge. "Which means beefsteak Florentine style, but it's still a staple of Tuscan cuisine."

Niki thought about it for a few seconds and couldn't think of any way to take his argument apart. "Okay, fair enough."

"Besides, if you're a regular in here, you'd want something other than only pasta, right?"

"Again, fair enough." She took a sip from her beer. "So, do you think Marino knows we're here yet, or will they only call him in the morning?"

"One of his goons will by now, at the very least, but is that what you want to talk about?"

"Come on. You made no secret about the fact that you only chose this restaurant because you wanted to fuck with the man. But you did invite me here, so if you have something else to talk about, by all means."

Taylor nodded and after a few seconds, it became clear that he hadn't thought about what he wanted to talk about when he'd called. It had been a spur of the moment decision with no agenda. She wasn't used to that but it wasn't a bad thing, she decided.

"You look nice," he said finally and she couldn't help a chuckle.

"Is that the best you could come up with?"

"A compliment seemed to be the safest bet in this particular situation. Besides, you do look nice."

"Well, I expected something a little more graphic than merely 'nice.'"

He shrugged. "Okay, let's see...you're walking, talking sex on a stick whether you're wearing something fancy or not. Although the best would be wearing nothing at all."

"That's better."

They paused when the waiter returned with their plates. As expected, the portions were larger than those offered at the French restaurant. The plates looked like trays instead, and they were heaped with steaming food that filled the whole room with a fresh dose of aromas that made her mouth water. From the way her companion watched the waiter approach, he experienced the same thing.

"You look like you're about to tackle the help." She laughed as the young man put the platters of food down.

"I'd never let it go that far." Taylor chuckled nervously in a way that made it sound like he was lying at least a little. "But yeah, after our little workout in the desert, Bobby and I had a quick workout in a nearby gym."

"That sounds dirty."

"Or your mind is merely in the gutter—hot fucking damn," he muttered once he took the first mouthful of his food. "That's some good shit right there. I would tackle a waiter for this kind of food on the regular."

Niki grinned. "I doubt they serve this kind of food in prison. Unless you have mob connections who let you live out that part from *Goodfellas*. You wouldn't happen to have any mob connections, would you, Taylor?"

She could only agree that the food was fantastic. But there was no point in not busting his balls whenever she could. Despite the fact that he could be gentle and supportive at times, he didn't necessarily turn down an opportunity to be a pain in her ass.

Her expectation was that he would inhale his food, but while he attacked the plate at a determined pace, he took his time to enjoy every mouthful before he washed it down with a sip of beer.

"I'll tell you something. This is me," he stated and shook his fork a few times as he chewed his veal. "Simply enjoying life and copious amounts of good food with absolutely no pretensions about it. I can do the dress-up, but to me, this is more natural. You look much better now that you're comfortable and able to feel like yourself. Don't get me wrong, you looked good last night, but—"

"I look better like this, I get it. Neither of us are fancy people. Deep down, all we need is comfortable clothes, a nice Italian restaurant, and a big fucking platter full of protein and carbohydrates. You know, even though you're the guy who drags his knuckles across the face of anyone who looks at him wrong, I forget that you can use that stuffing you have between your ears."

"How the hell do you think I managed to survive so long while dragging my knuckles across so many faces?" He looked at the waiter, tapped his glass, and held two fingers up. The young man nodded and jogged away to fill the order.

"How would you feel about getting into it with two more?"

He tilted his head. "What do you mean?"

"I happened to mention your plans to teach the mobsters a lesson to Jansen and Maxwell and how you were training for that with Bobby. It was in passing, mind you, merely telling them where I would be and what was happening when the night of the fight came along. They happened to mention that you might want to put your skills to the test. I don't mean that Bobby isn't a good sparring partner, but they pointed out that it might be a good idea for you to spar with more than one partner since you'll fight more than one mobbed-up asshole. I thought it was a good idea, especially since Jansen did some professional boxing and Maxwell holds five or six black belts."

Taylor finished his first beer to the dregs a few seconds before the waiter arrived with their refills. "Well, I can't say it's a bad idea."

"Sure. They get much-needed release since I imagine following me around the world isn't what they might describe as fun. Plus, you guys are all merely testosterone on a powder keg, which will let me see what you need to practice when push comes to shove."

He shrugged and took a sip of his beer. "It sounds fine by me. You'd better make sure they're ready for a serious can of whoop-ass being opened on them, though."

Niki laughed aloud, ran her fingers over her beer glass, and scribbled randomly over the condensation. "Well, never let it be said that you don't have balls the size of an elephant."

"It makes walking around a little difficult, but I always have a wheelbarrow on standby when I need it."

"Did you get a look at the guys Taylor will fight?"

Niki shook her head and glanced at the rest of the team as they began to load the suits into the trucks. "No, but Bobby had a good look at them when they tried to throw their weight around. They won't roll over with a mean look."

"Uh-huh. They're probably refrigerators full of bricks, which is why Bobby went at him hard enough to trash his face like that. He's getting ready for a tough fight." Jansen tapped the SUV lightly. "And what happens if we tune his ass up?"

"You what?"

"My partner is asking what you'll do to us if we hurt him," Maxwell explained and folded his arms in front of his chest.

"He'll heal is what. Why do you ask?"

"We're a little worried about you putting a .45 up our asses if we hurt your boyfriend."

Niki opened her mouth, shut it again, and shook her head. There wasn't anything she could say except that the two idiots were trying to bait her.

"No, I won't do anything to either of you if you hurt my boyfriend."

Jansen grinned. "Now, was that so hard to say?"

"That I won't hurt either of you?"

"No, calling him your boyfriend."

"Honestly? It was something of a shock, but I could tell it was what the two of you tried to get out of me." They continued to chuckle and she glared at them both until they stopped. "You don't care?"

"You're my boss, not my sister." Maxwell leaned back

against the SUV. "But with that said, if he breaks your heart, I'll break his legs."

"I'll hold him down while Maxwell breaks his legs," Jansen added. "And we'll only make sure that he's strong enough to protect you if things get rough and he doesn't have a suit around to protect him."

Niki wasn't sure what to make of that. "And you'd make sure because…"

"We only beat up guys who are trying to date someone we care about." The smaller man finished her sentence for her.

"Yeah," his partner agreed. "And assholes. Or people you shoot. Or people we're paid to beat down on. Mostly people we're paid to beat down on."

"Well, I'm not paying you guys to beat on Taylor, so either you do care about me or you think he's an asshole."

The two men exchanged a glance.

"Both?" Maxwell asked.

Jansen nodded. "Both."

The heat of the desert was relentless. Being there was better than being in the Zoo, but not by much. Many people imagined that the desert was one of the things that hindered the Zoo's spread to infect the rest of the world like a virus. Sal, of course, knew better. Ground Zero had been located in the same arid landscape and the Zoo had simply erupted into rampant growth. Even now, it pushed relentlessly to swallow the so-called insulation of the

Sahara that offered no resistance to the encroaching jungle in the least.

Not only that, it was a sucky, sucky place to be.

The sand kicked up by the retreating Hammerheads made tracking them difficult, but he could still manage. He focused and watched them move away from the meeting place.

Madigan wasn't wearing her combat suit, which had been her idea. Coming with him had been her idea too. She wouldn't let him go out there alone and face the trap on his own. But neither of them wanted the people they met to think they were in any danger whatsoever. That would defeat the purpose of the trap.

"Is that it?"

She almost sounded disappointed as she moved away from their Hammerhead, her gaze focused on the retreating vehicles as well.

"They simply paid ten million dollars in cash, took our offering, and left."

He couldn't help feeling some disappointment that they had left without trying to kill him. Not because he enjoyed the excitement—although that was true enough—but because the results of the firefight that ensued would have made the rest of their plan much easier.

"Is that it?" Davis echoed through the comms. "What happened to the action? I was promised action. Lots of it. That's the reason why I agreed to spoon with a fifty-caliber rifle and cook for an hour in sand that's hot enough to barbeque a brisket within a suit that's barely keeping me alive in this fucking mess of a place. Where's the action, Kennedy?"

Madigan laughed. "Hey, I'm as surprised as you are by them leaving us alone. Sal, do you have any theories about why they didn't at least try to kill us to get out of paying us the ten million?"

"Money clearly isn't a problem for them," Sal noted. "I think we knew that already. But if they wanted to give us problems, the best place to do it is out here. They wouldn't do it in the Zoo because we know it better than they do, they can't attack in the base, and they won't attack us on any of the roads since satellites are watching them every second of every day. And if they did their homework, they'd know it would be fully suicidal to try to stage an attack on the compound. If they intended to attack us, it would be here. No doubts about it."

"So…they won't attack us?' Davis asked. "Can I get out of the sand?"

"Come back to the Hammerhead, Davis," Madigan called. "So they won't attack us. They planned to honor their word to us. Does that make them the good guys? That would be new for us, right?"

"New and quite impossible," Sal stated emphatically. "They still have a Pita plant and acquired it without any kind of oversight on what they will do with it. The possibility that they plan to do something dangerous and possibly world-ending can't be ignored. I haven't said anything to Banks yet because I thought we could fix it here. We need to find them and recover that plant."

"That would be much easier if they hadn't driven off into the sunset with all our clues."

He nodded and after a few seconds, kicked his foot into

the sand hard enough to generate a flurry that was smoothly picked up by the wind and carried away. "Fuck!"

Madigan moved closer and put her hand on his shoulder. "Did that make you feel better?"

"No."

"Then come on. We'll find something that will."

CHAPTER NINE

There was no reason to stay in touch. Stephanie already had everything she needed. Marino would have all the information on Taylor he would ever get without talking to the man directly. Of course, Desk had said she owed her a favor, but there was no real way for her to enforce that, despite her veiled threats. Sure, she knew about her parents, but what the hell did that matter anyway?

At the same time, though, there was something to be said for keeping in touch. She needed to build her connections. It was how people managed to make businesses secure and she had to make friends and network with people who could help her while she helped them. And all things considered, she knew well that the people she worked for were professional criminals and if she learned as much as she could about them, there would eventually be someone who would want to know what she knew. In turn, they would be willing to give her something she wanted.

The phone dialed for a few seconds and she narrowed her eyes as a few beeps broke the dullness of the dial tone.

"Stephanie," the woman answered. "How nice to hear from you again. What can I help you with?"

"Have you managed to talk to Mr. McFadden about meeting me in person?"

Desk took a few seconds to answer. "I didn't make any promises. I've tried and he's noncommittal about the whole thing but I'll keep trying."

It was disappointing but not altogether unexpected. She had taken the time to look through Taylor's history with Rod Marino. It was a contentious one, to say the least, which explained why McFadden wanted to make a statement by beating the men who had intruded on his place of business. She strongly suspected that the man had robbed Marino's casino, and while the mob boss had been fully reimbursed by his insurance company, the money had never been recovered. Not only that, she couldn't find any sign that Marino had tried to make a return statement.

She was convinced that other treasures of knowledge existed, but no amount of digging had brought rewards. Once or twice, she'd thought she'd found a thread to tug on, but each time she pursued them they simply petered out into nothing. It was inordinately frustrating because her instincts insisted that something waited to be found, while experience seemed to indicate unequivocally that she was wrong. Or that someone was monitoring her searches and made sure to misdirect her or bury the information behind layers she couldn't penetrate.

The thought that someone might be watching her this closely brought a shiver of apprehension. For a moment, she very sensibly wondered if she shouldn't simply ignore her curiosity and move on to other avenues. She grimaced and reminded herself that this was real life and she was unimportant enough that no one would have any interest in what she did. It was, she reassured herself, simply her overactive imagination at work.

"Hello? Is there anything else I can help you with, Miss Cordray?"

Stephanie shook her head. Getting lost in thought like that would be the death of her one of these days. "Uh...no, but there is something I can help you with. I have the details you wanted on the other fighters. They were much more forthcoming with their background and information, which comes from them working for the guy who's running the fight. The betting has already started in select areas of the country. Is there an email I can use to send these to you? I'd rather not do it over the phone."

"That would probably be best, yes. Send it to desk47@tmp.com."

It wasn't surprising that she was given a temporary, disposable email address that could be shut down at a second's notice if there was so much as a hint of someone trying to track it. She had used services like that on more than one occasion, and she wouldn't hold it against Desk. It was clear that whoever she was, she liked her privacy.

She took it down quickly on her notepad. "I'll send it now. I'd like to think that you would be able to help me in the manner I've helped you sometime in the future."

The woman didn't answer immediately. "That sounds suspiciously like you want me to owe you a favor."

"Technically, I think we're more or less square on the

favors. You helped me with info on McFadden, I helped you with info on the guys he'll fight. In the end, though, I would like it if we could continue to exchange favors like that in the future."

Another pause followed and she wondered if she'd pushed too hard. "Call me if you need anything else."

"And you should do the same. You have a great Sunday, Desk."

"You too, Miss Cordray."

The line cut off and Stephanie couldn't help a small smile as she added the temporary address she had been given, uploaded the document she had stored all the relevant information in, and clicked send with no title to the email.

It was a start, anyway.

Jennie didn't like to give herself too much to do on Sundays. She made a point of being social on Fridays and Saturdays because if she didn't, she would be cooped up in her apartment for days on end. Her life was such that she needed to be social. People had to see her out and about, making friends and being a people person, especially if she ever wanted to rise up the ladder.

But not Sundays. That was her time. A couple of people had issues with that and asked her why she did it, and she'd given them a variety of answers from religious preferences she didn't have all the way to the truth, depending on who she talked to. Some said she was manipulative, and all she had to say in response was that yes, she was.

The bottom line was that she needed her time off. If people tried to stop her from getting it, she would do whatever she could to counter their efforts.

She sipped the milkshake she'd ordered online, breathed in deeply, and enjoyed the mixture of vanilla and chocolate as she watched her coding process on her screens. She had put countless hours into the update she tried to work on for Desk, but she still wasn't sure which version would get the upgrade. Probably the one that stuck to Niki the closest, although she needed to get extra firewalls up for the one the DOD was trying to copy. If nothing else, it would convince them that the version on their servers was complete and they wouldn't realize that Desk had cleverly established herself so stealing the critical code was impossible.

Her phone buzzed and she scowled. It was her home phone and only rang when someone was trying to contact her directly, usually as someone's emergency contact. She didn't give the number out on her business cards and only a handful of family members and close friends had it.

"Maybe I should give it to Taylor," she mused aloud, picked the device up, and pressed the button to answer the call without looking at the number. "Jennie Banks."

"Hello there, Jennie Banks," said a familiar voice. She wasn't sure where the inspiration for Desk's voice had come from. It wasn't hers or anyone she'd ever met or remembered meeting. One of the psychologists she consulted while she created the character software said it would be someone with a powerful influence over her, perhaps a mixture of her mother and one of her childhood therapists.

"Desk, it's nice to see you're using the connection coding I gave you. How can I help you?"

"Have you heard that Taylor will be involved in a fight?"

"A... Well, I guess he's not fond of non-violent solutions as a whole, but I never thought he would go so far as to schedule them."

"Something like that. In this case, though, it will be streamed live with some betting happening because it's Vegas. Or at least that is the excuse Niki appears to accept."

"She's on board with this?"

"Yes," the AI replied smoothly. "And I thought it would be a good opportunity for him to showcase why the local chapter of *La Cosa Nostra* should avoid being a pain in his ass for as long as possible. With that said, I don't suppose you would want to make a little money on him?"

Jennie leaned back and brought up the details Desk had emailed her. Taylor was fighting two mobsters. It was interesting and she didn't think for a second there was a chance that he would lose. The guy had a driving force in him that was almost primordial.

"What kind of odds are we looking at?" she asked after a few seconds of studying the data.

"So far, the online betting rooms that have access to the fight's details put the odds at roughly two to one against our boy. It would seem they would give him even odds if he fought against one man alone."

She nodded and tapped her computer. "I have money in my savings. It seems like a safe investment to put some of it on Taylor winning that fight."

"How much are you thinking?"

"I'm not sure." She shrugged. "I'll decide when I see how

much I have saved. I'll call you when it's done, Desk. Can I reach you on this number again?"

"No, but if you call, I will be alerted that you are trying to contact me and I'll be in touch in under a minute."

"You do that."

Jennie stared at the phone as it clicked. There was something off about having conversations with an AI she had created, but after so long working on her own, Desk was no longer the AI she created. There was much about her that remained the same, but she was allowed to alter her own code—her DNA, in essence—if needed.

The fact that she was still very much intact meant that her creator did a good job, but there was never any doubt about that.

The place smelled like it always did. Bobby had experienced it a hundred times before in innumerable gyms around the world. The stale scent of sweat and sometimes blood that soaked into the mat of the boxing ring and would never, ever come out, no matter how many times it was scrubbed, was unmistakable.

Too many people came in and out and got used to what these venues were supposed to be. He could never be one of them. Violence wasn't in his nature, as much as he trained himself in it. He was cut from a different cloth than Taylor, whose whole nature seemed predisposed to killing and beating anything that got in the way of whatever his goals happened to be at that particular point in time.

Leonard looked up from where he pushed the mop over

the floor. There were still a couple of people in the gym, working the bags and the treadmills, but it was mostly empty. This gave the two men the opportunity to have a word in private, for the most part.

"How can I help you, Mr. Zhang?"

He tucked his hands into his pockets. "There might be a couple of changes for our next session here—a small audience. I guess you could call it a dress rehearsal for the fight that's to come. Taylor will take on a couple of fighters and I won't be one of them."

"Who are they?"

"His girlfriend's bodyguards. They'd like a piece of him in the ring to see if he's worthy or something. I'm not that kind of guy—the alpha male type—so I don't understand the impulse."

The former boxer grinned and tapped his mop. "So he finally grew the balls to talk to her about it. Will she be in attendance?"

"She said she wants to be present for the fight itself, which was why she thought it would make sense. Given that she's watched the fucker drop a helicopter on himself, I imagine she thinks that can bring him back if he goes too far."

"He...dropped a what on himself?"

"A helicopter," Bobby confirmed. "It's a long story."

"Ah, good. I'm merely making sure I'm not hearing shit in my old age." Leonard toyed with his mop again. "How many people will be here? You know this ain't the fucking Ritz, right? No one should expect anything more than what they'll be able to find in the vending machines."

He laughed. "There won't be anyone in attendance who

will expect any kind of special treatment. We're all used to doing for ourselves what rich folk expect other people to do for them."

The man smirked. "I have no idea why I would have thought otherwise, but I guess this is how we have to do it. I'll close up shop early and set some chairs up. You let me know when the party's coming in and I'll get it all ready for them."

Bobby patted the older man on the shoulder. "We appreciate your help with this."

"And I appreciate the cash your boy Taylor throws at me. It's not easy to stay in business in a place like Vegas."

"We'll see if we can't keep throwing business your way even after the fight is over."

"That's probably not necessary, but I appreciate the sentiment anyway." The old boxer patted him on the shoulder. "You get on out of here. I have work to do. There's no time to chew the fat all day. I have a business to run."

"I'll get in touch later this week." He spun on his heel and headed to the door, a broad grin on his face as he strolled out of the building.

***

The suits were covered in dust like they always were after a couple of hours of training. She decided it simply offered them the opportunity to get to know their suits a little better when they had to clean all the crap out after every session.

Taylor knew what he was doing, she had to give him that. He pushed them as hard as he always had, but she could feel her body acclimating to the hectic pace. They probably wouldn't maintain their bodies in the physical shape he now whipped them into, but they would still be better qualified to hunt cryptid monsters once the muscle memory was there to help them.

The man wasn't happy with the condition they were in, however. He'd yelled instructions over the comms at them. She had thought he would shout himself hoarse, but it sounded like he'd done something like this before. It was disconcerting to think the experiences he'd been through were their taskmaster. It triggered an unsettling image of him yelling at young men in the second-hand suits of armor the government had given them, hoping they would survive and that he wouldn't be the only one left alive again.

She fiddled with the controls to ensure that no dust had settled under the buttons she could have access to while inside her suit. With a scowl, she pulled the contraptions out and stared at the sand inside.

"Fucking...dammit," she whispered.

"You should see the condition of the suits we get from the Zoo," Tanya pointed out as she moved closer. "They send them in covered in so much dirt and grime that Taylor only feels comfortable with burning whatever we pull out of there. He doesn't want to risk any possible biological material from the jungle getting caught in the water systems here, no matter how small or insignificant. I don't want to say he's being paranoid. Honestly, with everything he's been through, I would want to avoid any possibility of the Zoo breaking out again. You still have a team working on killing everything that pops up while we're here training, right?"

Niki nodded. "They're a tough group. Some of the best."

"I'm only glad that Bobby is here instead of out there. Although I see him coming home with numerous bruises so maybe it isn't that safe after all."

Niki looked at her. "You don't know?"

"I know he and Taylor are sparring. That was all he would tell me about it."

"He's training Taylor. They're working to get him ready for the fight."

Tanya put her hand on her shoulder. "What fight?"

Bobby hadn't told her, which was interesting. Of course, she'd put both feet in it and knew the other woman wouldn't let it rest. Whatever the man's reasons for keeping it from her, it seemed that ship had sailed thanks to her. She sighed. "Okay, I guess I shot my mouth off, and I'm sorry. Two mobsters in Marino's employ came to your shop and tried to act like assholes. Taylor intends to beat an apology out of them. Marino agreed, but only if he was allowed to sponsor the fight and have bets placed. He wants to make money off it."

"Of course he does. Who else knows about this? I can't be the only one who was kept out of the loop on this, right?"

Niki frowned and wondered how deep the hole was that she'd inadvertently dug herself into. She hadn't even considered the possibility that Taylor had kept this from the rest of his team, but Vickie hadn't mentioned it—and she would have if she'd known. Unless she'd been instructed to not say anything. The agent's interaction with the team always seemed to be from the outside looking in, which made her the last to know what Taylor was up to, and that was assuming she was told at all. He didn't like her to interfere with what he did with his team, given that she was a DOD agent who needed plausible deniability from whatever he might have done that was illegal.

That had all changed now.

Vickie raised her hand. "I already knew about the fight, but Taylor didn't tell me about it."

"What fight?" Elisa asked and looked at each of them in turn.

"Those guys who came to the shop while only you and Bobby were there. Taylor's going to beat the shit out of them while Marino streams it live."

The ex-reporter smiled. "Hell, I'll watch that shit."

Niki nodded. "Me too. So that's everyone, then. It looks like he only told Bobby."

The others shrugged and she turned her attention to cleaning her suit and making sure it would go back in working condition. The sense of camaraderie was pleasant, as was the realization that she was no longer the outsider as she had always imagined herself to be. Their burgeoning relationship had brought her a little closer into the family unit Taylor's team had created.

Something nudged her in the shoulder and she turned as Vickie sat on one of the nearby crates.

"Are you already finished with your suit?" the agent asked.

"Coz, I've been working on cleaning suits for months now. If you think I can't clean them faster than you, you now know differently."

She smirked. "Well, maybe I'll get you to help me with these things. I keep missing nooks and crannies and have to go back to them."

The hacker nodded and leaned forward. "Uh...it looks like you're doing an okay job to me. More to the point, are you okay with Taylor putting himself on the line like that?"

"How is that in any way related to my suit-cleaning skills?"

"You know, in terms of okay...ness."

"Yeah, right. Well...I've seen the guy throw himself at things that could kill him for a while now. At least this time, I get to be right there with him. More importantly, I'll be able to protect him if shit goes sideways. I might not be the best at dealing with cryptids, but I can deal with humans."

Vickie grinned. "So you're admitting that you've felt protective about him for a long time."

"Honestly? Fine. Yes, in the way you feel protective over a big, red-headed puppy that keeps on charging forward at full speed on a linoleum floor and can't stop himself from crashing into the wall."

The other woman snorted. "Okay, that was good. Now I'll think of Taylor as one of those mastiff puppies with feet and ears too big for his size."

"That's what I thought too." Niki grinned and bumped the fist her cousin offered.

CHAPTER TEN

The gym had already been closed for almost an hour as Leonard had promised. The old man had come through on his commitment to let them prepare for the upcoming fight. Taylor could have done it on his own, but it wouldn't have been easy and he wouldn't have been at his best.

Bobby had put in extra hours to help him get in shape. The old boxer, true to form, had considerable good advice to give while he watched and made sure his footwork was up to par. It had been a while since the old man had been in the ring but he still had it. A couple of lighter sparring sessions showed that while the power was mostly gone, his elusiveness was still present.

This time, though, it looked like they would press at the borders of the man's hospitality. Bobby had said it would be no problem and Leonard wasn't the kind of guy to complain about shit like that. He would simply make a mental note of it and learn from the mistake instead.

Taylor shifted and moved his feet as he glided around

the punching bag. He threw punches delivered more for accuracy and speed than power while the old man set up some metal chairs around the fighting ring for the rest of their little entourage to watch from.

Learning from a boxer was always a good thing, but Taylor had argued that he would fight two guys in an all-out encounter. The rules were already out the window.

Leonard had agreed on that part, but he had insisted that the foundations were still important. A solid foundation allowed him the ability to sustain himself in a tough fight where the people who only relied on tricks that helped them win quickly would run out of ideas.

The old boxer moved to where he worked around the punching bag and folded his arms in front of his chest as he watched.

"Do you have any last-minute advice you want to share with me?" He didn't feel out of breath but it was still a little difficult to talk while he moved almost every fast-twitch muscle that he had. "You know how the trainer always has the best advice for the budding protagonist only minutes before his fight?"

"Well, first of all, I ain't your trainer." The man reached out to steady the bag as it began to swing wildly. "Secondly, this ain't only minutes before the fight. This is another sparring session, exactly like the rest. But if you're aching for advice, I guess you need to remember that this ain't a boxing match. There ain't no rules they won't break if it means putting you on your ass. These kinds of assholes are the type that like asking for forgiveness instead of permission, you know what I'm saying?"

He paused and looked up from behind where his hands covered his face. "You do mean the mobsters, right?"

"Sure."

Taylor grinned and took a break to head to his bottle of ice-cold water as he wiped the sweat that had accumulated on his forehead. The rest of the team began to arrive. Vickie pulled up outside in her Tesla. Elisa had caught a ride with her by the looks of it. Bobby and Tanya had already arrived, and the former picked up something from one of the vending machines at the entrance.

All they were waiting for was an SUV, probably, which would indicate the arrival of Niki with the two men he would fight.

Sure enough, they were the last to arrive and the two were already dressed like they had been warming up somewhere before they entered the vehicle. Maybe the Aria's gym had a boxing station like this one that would have allowed them to prepare and loosen up for the sparring session they were helping him with.

He had a feeling they wouldn't take it easy on him simply because they were technically sparring. While he wasn't sure why he had that idea, it nibbled at the back of his brain and triggered his adrenaline to surge a little more as he moved to the speed bag. There was a sense of excitement in all the new arrivals. Bobby and Leonard already had an idea of what they would see when he got into the ring, but the others had only ever seen him fight in the suits.

Fleetingly, he wondered what their reaction would be. He would be a little too engaged in the fight to see their expressions in the heat of the moment, but it was something he would like to witness.

Maybe someone would film it. Desk seemed like she would follow the fight somehow, and he would be able to pass his interest off as wanting to see himself in the ring to judge his performance.

The two men he would square off against were still warming up and positioned themselves around two of the punching bags. He could see that they weren't merely street brawlers and had real technique. Jansen was sharp in his movements and reminded him of how Leonard moved when he tried to demonstrate something technical.

Maxwell was larger and a little less refined, but he was taller than Taylor and with a better reach. He reminded himself that he needed to keep that in mind. The man looked like he could put anyone to sleep with a single, well-placed hook.

The smaller man could probably put anyone out too if he wanted, but the size difference made it a little less likely. He would have to reach up to Taylor, which meant his strikes would be more telegraphed.

Leonard called the smaller of the two over and fitted him with the kind of padding he would need for the fight.

"Do you honestly think I'll need all this?" Jansen asked and frowned at the full-torso padding the old boxer was applying. "It's way too stiff."

"Look, you can bitch about being too stiff or you can bitch about broken ribs," Leonard growled. "And since you're on my property, I'm liable for any injuries that might have been caused if I hadn't equipped you well enough. You'll have to live with being a little stiffer than usual."

"Seriously?"

"Make a believer out of me." The old man patted him on the shoulder. "You're up."

She wouldn't lie, there were a couple of butterflies in her stomach. Vickie had always imagined what Taylor fighting without his suit would look like but had never seen it. She was a little hurt that he hadn't included her in the decision when he'd called Bobby in to train him, but she could at least understand it.

This time, though, she was there and would watch. She even had chips she'd purchased from the vending machine while she waited for the fight to start.

Of course, it wasn't like she was rooting for one side or the other in this. She had nothing against the two guys who had been tasked with backing Niki up. Besides, Jansen was being fitted for the fight with more padding than she had ever seen on a fighter. Leonard, the owner of the gym, seemed adamant that it would be necessary, despite the fact that his opponent didn't have any protection except for some wrapping around his knuckles.

Taylor was usually so calm and collected, which made it easy to forget that he was taller than most football players and with a build to match. As he climbed into the ring and rolled his shoulders, she realized she was staring at the way his muscles bulged beneath the shirt he wore.

And she wasn't the only one she realized after a furtive

look around her. Elisa was seated next to her, and her head tilted as Taylor pulled his shirt off and hung it on the ropes. He jumped lightly from one foot to the other and kept his body in motion while he shadowboxed.

"If your cousin isn't taking a long, thirsty look at that slab of meat, she might need resuscitation," the ex-reporter pointed out quietly.

Vickie turned to study her with a deadpan expression. "If my cousin finds out that you're taking a long, thirsty look at that, you'll need resuscitation. Eyes front and center—and maybe to the other side of the ring."

Thankfully, it didn't look like Niki paid too much attention to the audience while she helped Jansen into the ring.

"Maybe look into helping him get through a couple of reps to help with his defense," Bobby suggested. He climbed onto the platform as well but remained on the outside. "You're quicker, so keep him on his back foot and see if you can't teach him some of that famous navy boxing style before we get into the McBeatdown part of the fight."

Jansen grinned at the man around his mouthguard and snapped his hands forward in a pair of jabs into the air to show his speed off as he squared off against his opponent.

The size difference between the two was interesting to see. The bodyguard was a little over six feet tall and his build was lean and light and his actions fast. The jerky movements were difficult to follow as he warmed himself up inside the ring. Vickie could feel her anticipation building as Leonard circled to his position to the left of the ring, took his seat, and tapped the bell with a hammer.

The two fighters closed quickly, but Taylor didn't come

out swinging immediately. His head lowered and his hands raised in a clear, defensive stance as he faced Jansen. The bodyguard was already throwing jabs and uppercuts to gain an advantage inside his defense.

The redheaded giant looked like he was defending himself well, but the speed of his opponent was enough to force him back a step, then another.

"Move your head!" Bobby shouted from the side of the ring. "Engage your hips and don't only defend with your hands."

Taylor showed no sign that he heard the man, but the effect was almost immediate as he began to move his head from side to side and weave constantly.

Jansen was still able to connect a handful of strikes that forced him back to the ropes, where he kept his head down and his hands up to protect himself from a direct strike to the head. The smaller man pressed his advantage and delivered a couple of blows to his midsection before the agent feinted a right hook and hammered a jab into his nose that thrust his head back.

At another attempt to feint, Taylor ducked his head and both hands moved forward. They connected lightly with the other man's midsection before the large man displayed his mobility, moved away from the ropes, and circled to position himself quickly in the middle of the ring.

The bodyguard leaned back on the ropes, flashed a grin at his opponent, and took his time to push off. "So, if we won't have a McBeatdown and since we're taking a pass on that, should there be a different name? Opening a can of Jansen Whoopass? Should I trademark that shit?"

Taylor rolled his shoulders and his expression revealed

no sign that the trash-talking had made an impression. "Are you sure this is the way you want to go?"

"Throw a couple of punches! Get in this with me!' Jansen jabbed a couple of times into the air to make his point. "If I wanted to fight a punching bag, I'd fight a fucking punching bag."

Vickie pulled her bag of chips up to empty it of the last crumb inside when suddenly, her attention was dragged to the ring by the sound of a groan and someone impacting the canvas with a resounding thud.

She snapped the bag out of the way even though she was already too late. Jansen sprawled on the canvas, held his side, and writhed slowly while Taylor took a step away and removed his mouthguard.

Leonard scrambled into the ring and checked to make sure there was no serious injury, while the bodyguard looked like he still struggled to take in a deep breath.

"What happened?" she asked and stood quickly.

"I have no fucking clue," Elisa replied and seemed similarly confused. "Taylor tagged him with a shot to the body and suddenly, Jansen was on the ground like someone had pulled the wires out."

Bobby clambered into the ring too and the fighter was finally able to take a deep breath. As he was being helped to the side, though, he tried to curl up and cover the place where Taylor's blow had landed.

"You had to poke the fucking tiger, huh?" Bobby commented as he helped the man onto a stool Leonard brought in. "You were doing fine until you decided you wanted to try your hand at trash-talking and he put you on the mat."

The bodyguard nodded but still held his side. "I... tried...to get him...ready for Maxwell. You can't blame me for that, right?"

"I can blame you for being stupid any time I fucking please," Leonard snapped in response. "How do you feel? Should I call you an ambulance?"

"It's a fucking liver punch," Jansen complained and leaned back against the ropes. "Fuck...nah, I think I'm good. A love tap but in the right place. Fucking hell..."

He rolled off the stool and curled again for a few seconds before he finally showed enough strength to pull himself out of the ring.

"Sorry," Taylor said and helped him to his feet. "I didn't mean...that..."

"Sure you did." The man chuckled and winced in pain as he helped him into a seat. "And after my trash-talking, I guess I asked for this. Now get back in there. Maxwell is waiting for his turn."

He patted Jansen gently on the side of the head before he returned to the ring.

"Did you mean you didn't intend to hit him there?" Leonard asked.

He shook his head. "Not really. I did mean to put a little more power and crack into the body shots, but I aimed for the places he wasn't protecting. It was an unhappy accident for him."

"Happy for you, though," Maxwell pointed out as he entered the ring as well and moved into the opposite corner. "And me too. Not that I'm happy that he was injured like that, mind you, but I have looked forward to taking a crack at you."

Vickie took her seat again and tried to think through what had happened. She had missed the knockout punch and felt a little cheated by that, even if she had no one to blame but herself for her desire to empty her bag of chips.

This was a new kind of fight. Maxwell was taller and heavier than Taylor but he looked slower. It made sense since Taylor had trained hard for the past few weeks. Not that Maxwell didn't train, but he had most likely had something different in mind.

The large bodyguard didn't wear any of the protection Jansen had been given but he didn't look like he needed it.

Taylor looked the same as he had against Jansen. His face betrayed no emotion and seemed almost dead as he stared across the ring at his new opponent.

Niki had taken a seat next to them, and Elisa leaned closer to whisper in her ear.

"Will your guy be okay? It looked like he blacked out when Taylor hit him."

"I've taken a liver shot in the past," the agent answered and made sure to keep her voice down. "You feel like your whole body switched off and on again. I don't think it did any lasting damage, though, and he'll be fine but it's still a shock to your system. Several things happen in your body when you take a blow like that."

"How do you think Maxwell will do?"

She shrugged before she answered. "I thought it was the mech that made Taylor dangerous, but that was a hard strike to watch. They're tough guys and I almost don't want to watch what comes next. That guy's a killer no matter what skin he happens to wear."

"Do you think you won't be able to watch the actual fight live?"

The agent laughed. "In this case, it's a matter of not seeing the people I like being beaten into a pulp. I don't think I'll have to worry about that when they're fighting for real."

"So you don't think Taylor will be beaten to a pulp?" Elisa looked a little doubtful but Niki seemed unperturbed.

"No, I don't think that but we'll see."

Leonard rang the bell and the two moved to the center of the ring and extended their hands to bump fists before the fight started in earnest. Maxwell started the bout when he moved forward, kept his arms high, and jabbed quickly before he brought a low kick to his opponent's leg and forced him back a couple of steps.

Taylor was defensive and covered himself well, but without the explosive speed that Jansen was capable of, the large bodyguard wasn't able to force him back into the ropes. The redhead displayed better footwork as he glided and slid around Maxwell, despite the fact that he was defending himself.

It felt a little more even. Punches were thrown on both sides, and Maxwell looked like he had the advantage as he retreated to his corner when the bell rang to end the round.

"How do you feel?" Leonard asked as he checked to make sure there were no signs that the man was trying to hide an injury.

'Not too bad," he muttered, took a mouthful of water, and swished it in his mouth before he swallowed. "The big fucker's quicker than he looks, but I tagged him a couple of times that he didn't expect."

"Do you think you have another round in you?"

The fighter nodded. "I have no injuries to speak of, and I have to make sure Taylor's ready for the little lady, which I guess means he has to have the stamina."

Leonard looked around the team and nodded subtly toward Niki, who joined the other man in his corner. "Is that her?"

Maxwell nodded.

"Okay, she's attractive. What the hell does she see in him, though?"

The fighter grinned and shrugged his massive shoulders. "Fuck if I know. Crazy attracts crazy, I suppose."

The old boxer pulled away from the ring and Niki returned to her seat, where she was joined by Tanya on the metal chairs set up as the two fighters prepared for another round. Jansen looked like he was almost fully recovered. He still seemed a little sore on the side where he'd been hit but he now sat and watched the fight closely.

"Did you hear what your guy said about making sure Taylor was ready for you?" Tanya asked as she leaned back when Leonard tapped the bell again.

"Yeah," Niki answered, unable to take her eyes off the ring as Bobby jogged to Taylor's corner.

"What will you do, Taylor?" he asked, barely loudly enough for Vickie to hear although she had tapped the microphone in Bobby's phone and now listened in.

"You heard him," Taylor answered, his face still expressionless. "I have to get through him if I want to date Niki."

"I don't know how to read that. Do you plan to kill him? Put him in the hospital?"

The grin that came to the other man's face looked savage and failed to reach his eyes. "I won't kill him and I don't think he'll need a hospital. Does that satisfy your curiosity?"

"It's not curiosity, it was worry."

"Well then, don't worry. I have this under control. Mostly thanks to you."

Bobby moved from the corner when Leonard tapped the bell again. Vickie could still see the anxiety on his face as the two fighters advanced on each other.

They repeated the customary tapping of gloves at the beginning of the round.

"You have sixty seconds to put me on the canvas," Taylor warned the man. "Give me your best."

"I hope you can survive it."

Maxwell wasn't a small man and every punch caught him faster than he'd anticipated. Vickie winced when it looked like Taylor was taking the brunt of the punishment and every blow impacted loudly. A couple caught him in the ribs and she was sure she heard something crack inside as he winced and backed away. The raw savagery of the assault was enough to make him backpedal furiously. His back hit the ropes and ended his slow retreat.

The larger of Niki's two bodyguards wasn't a boxer, and Vickie could see the difference in style between him and Jansen even though she knew next to nothing about fighting. The man threw hard elbows at his opponent's head and knocked it back, and when he raised his hands to defend, the punches came in low to the body. As Taylor lowered his guard to cover that as well, Maxwell grasped the back of his neck with both hands and used his entire body to force his head down into a knee that came up to his nose.

Taylor had his hands in place to stop the blow from connecting cleanly, but the bodyguard wasn't finished with him and hauled him down again. This time, the impact was audible and Vickie winced and turned her head away as the two men struggled, fighting for control of the fight.

Finally, Taylor lowered his hands and brought his right into an uppercut into Maxwell's stomach. It thrust the breath out of the man's lungs in a rush and allowed him to grasp the bodyguard's hips and shove him away as he ducked his head to escape the grasp on his neck.

The challenger struggled to keep his balance and only regained it once he was at the center of the mat. Blood dripped from Taylor's nose and his eyebrows and covered almost half his face. The expression was still dead behind the red mask.

"Your minute's up," he announced in a deep, throaty growl that made Vickie's spine tingle.

She didn't want to see what came next but it was almost impossible to not watch as Taylor used his shoulders to push off the ropes. He raised his hands again and strode forward like a soldier going into battle as he threw a couple of testing jabs to judge the distance. Maxwell refused to back away or step aside. Instead, the bodyguard threw a feint with his left and a hook with his right.

His adversary ducked under it, pushed his elbow into the man's ribs, and knocked the breath out of him again.

Maxwell tried another hook but it missed and left him open to a pair of sharp uppercuts into his sternum.

There was nothing he could do but double over as his lungs suddenly stopped working, and Taylor closed in. There was no real technique that Vickie could discern in his strikes, but the power in each of them was hard to miss. They were delivered rapidly and one caught the man in his weakened ribs again. Two distinctive cracks resulted from that one strike. The last two arced in as Maxwell lowered his guard to protect his body. One tilted the bodyguard's head by the jaw and the other pounded behind his ear.

The last blow sent a shudder through him. He struggled to keep his head up for a second, maybe less, before he finally gave up.

It was as terrifying as it was brief. Maxwell sagged and Taylor reached forward to grab him. It looked like the fight would continue, but all he did was lower him gently to the mat.

Vickie didn't think anyone realized that the fight was over until Taylor straightened, removed his mouthguard, and motioned for Leonard to come in.

"I think the fight's done," he announced.

"Is he..." Bobby started to ask as he pushed through the ropes into the ring.

"He's out but should be coming to—"

His assurance was cut off when Maxwell sucked in a deep breath and his hands reached for something that wasn't there. Although his eyes were open, they seemed unable to focus on anything until Bobby and Leonard stepped beside him. The old boxer flashed a light into his eyes to check for the usual signs of a head injury.

"Son of... What the fuck..." The large man still looked disoriented but he was able to see everything that happened around him. From the way Leonard's shoulders relaxed after the examination, Vickie could tell the result was good.

"Consider yourself lucky, you dumb fuck," Bobby muttered. "He took it lightly on you. I took the brunt of it when he didn't, so you can thank me for that later."

Maxwell needed a few seconds to process those words. He still had a little difficulty keeping his eyes focused, but he laughed. "Fucking hell, if that was taking it lightly, I don't want to be in the ring when he isn't. I do want to be outside, though. At a safe distance."

Taylor dropped to his haunches next to him as Leonard continued to examine him for injury. "So, did I pass your test?"

The bodyguard managed another slightly wheezy laugh as he patted his shoulder. "You two are fucking made for each other. Make sure you invite us to the wedding, and you have our blessing. Not that you needed it in the first place."

"But I do appreciate being in the good graces of people who care for her. It's rare that getting into those graces means knocking you onto your ass, but I'm not fussy. Maybe that makes you a little crazy too."

Taylor extended a hand and Maxwell took it firmly and they both rose carefully to their feet.

"I'd still like both of them to be checked by a doctor," Leonard announced. "You know, to make sure. Possibly you too, Taylor. You might need stitches on those cuts."

"I'll drive them to the hospital," Niki called as she joined them in the ring and stepped beside Taylor. "Are you okay?"

"Is he okay?" Maxwell complained, and she waved him off.

"Yeah, I'm fine," Taylor replied and winced as she touched one of the bruises above his eye, although he didn't pull away. "Like he said, I might need stitches but otherwise, it's not too bad."

Vickie was waiting to make sure Taylor was fine before she stepped aside, took her phone from her pocket, and quick-dialed a number she had saved with no name attached to it. The line beeped a couple of times before a weird warbling sound was quickly followed by it being picked up.

"It's nice to hear from you again, Vickie."

She chose not to start the conversation with whether the AI knew what the full concept of nice was or if it was simply selected as something people said to each other when they first began to speak.

"And it's nice to talk to you too, Desk. I take it you watched this whole fight?"

"I was able to follow it well enough. Are you in on the betting?"

"Hell yes. I wouldn't have bet against Taylor anyway, but after this little demonstration, I'm very sure this counts as more of an investment than a bet."

"All bets have the potential to be an investment. It is only the chances of it paying a profit that vary."

"Whatever. For the moment, though, I'll put forty thousand on him taking it all."

"I must alert you that the amount you have selected

constitutes a sizeable portion of your savings. You must realize that you could lose this amount rather than increase it."

"It doesn't matter." Vickie took a moment to look at the ring while the others in their group began to file out. None of them appeared to notice that she wasn't with them yet. "I've seen what Taylor can do when he isn't pissed and holds himself back. That would probably be an even fight for the men Marino has against him. I have no idea what he can do when he's pissed and out for blood."

CHAPTER ELEVEN

Everything was dark. His instincts said a little too dark. While he wasn't sure how it had happened, he needed to investigate. People expected him to investigate and wanted to know about this facility.

No, he realized after a moment. It wasn't that everything was dark. His eyes were closed. Weird how he'd missed that fact.

Opening his eyes proved a little more painful than he thought it would, and they didn't open all the way. Both were swollen and throbbed gently but the tenderness grew worse the longer he kept them open.

The room around him was dim but his eyes adjusted quickly, although it was difficult to see through the tears that began to form. He closed his eyes for a few more seconds, let the burning recede, then opened them again.

"He's awake," a man said in English close to where he sat.

"I can't tell if this is a good thing or a bad thing," a woman responded, also in English but with a thick accent.

"It depends on your perspective, I guess. For him, it's a bad thing."

He opened his eyes again and struggled to focus on the two people nearby, whom he assumed were the speakers. It took a moment before his vision settled, although his right eye watered a little. The man had darker skin and hair with Hispanic features, while the woman was taller, leaner, with high cheekbones and long blonde hair. Both wore white lab coats and vivid bruises and nasty abrasions were evident on their faces.

"Morning." The man spoke in an accent that was clearly American, although he couldn't tell from where specifically. "I'm glad you could join us in this…I'll go ahead and call it our execution."

"What's your name?" the woman asked.

It sounded like they were past all pretense at this point. "Wu Na Feng."

"Let me guess, MSS?" the man asked. "I'm Mark Santiago."

Feng nodded. "CIA?"

"DIA," he corrected. "Military intelligence. And this is Irina Lebedev. FSB."

He looked around the room, still unable to open his eyes properly without them watering after a few seconds, but they had improved somewhat. "We're…in the eatery, yes?"

Irina sighed and leaned against the nearby wall. "It looks like someone did a purge. They didn't even ask any questions—like they already knew everything. They beat the shit out of us and threw us in here. I guess they want us to be the first meal their newly bred pets enjoy."

Feng gulped almost before he realized what they had meant about how unlucky he was for waking up. He would have liked to be unconscious for his execution.

"I never should have come to this fucking island," he whispered and rubbed dried blood away from his right eye. "I knew it was a shit assignment when they showed me the satellite pictures of the old American base. Nothing ever goes well when someone tries to repurpose one of these facilities."

"Well, at least we now know that the Russians, Chinese, and Americans are all curious about what this is," Mark pointed out.

"Maybe our bosses will send others to find out what's happening here—" Irina added, but her words cut off before she could finish. The sound of a magnetic lock lifting from the door at the far end of the room had their full attention.

"Fuck me," Mark whispered when he saw movement behind the glass door.

Another smaller door opened and a group of men armed with assault rifles walked in. Feng wasn't sure what to make of the fact that more of them trained their weapons on the glass door rather than on the prisoners, but two still aimed at the humans as the group of five approached.

More movement, this time from a room above them, caught Feng's eye. He squinted and rubbed his right eye and was able to see a little more clearly although the effort was painful. From what he could make out, a group of men and women had gathered inside what might be an office that overlooked the eatery through a window. While he couldn't see enough to be certain, they had the demeanor of people watching and taking notes, most likely on tablets. It seemed logical that they would use technology rather than old-fashioned methods.

He had no idea what they were taking notes of, but he had a feeling he wouldn't like it.

The armed guards stopped within ten meters of the three prisoners, and one of them took a machete and a knife out of a pack they had carried, dropped both weapons on the ground, and retreated quickly in the direction from which they'd come.

"They're...arming us," Irina pointed out. She retrieved both weapons and handed the machete to Feng.

"I guess they want to see how long we last against... whatever is on the other side of that door," Mark commented, visibly annoyed that he was the only one left without a weapon. "We're lab rats and they want to make the fight as even as possible."

Feng shuddered as something on the other side of the glass door roared. "This will be many things. Horrifying, informative, and perhaps even a little interesting. But an even fight it is not."

"We'll see about that." Irina growled in an effort to psyche herself up for a fight even though she was as beaten as the two men in the room with her.

"Yes," Mark muttered. "We will."

It had been a productive day which was saying something since Rod Marino didn't have many productive days.

Mostly, he was meant to oversee and make sure other people were productive, which made him feel like he simply watched other people work rather than work himself.

He reminded himself that this wasn't a terrible thing. He had put considerable time and energy into making sure he didn't have to work every day. There was also a point to be made that supported the premise that someone had fucked up if he needed to do any work at all.

Even so, a certain pleasure came from those few days when he did have to put his nose to the grindstone. It wasn't enough to make him want to make this a daily occurrence, but it was still enjoyable.

The phone rang and Marino picked it up before it reached a second buzz. "Yes?"

"A Mr. Saadeh Mahmoud is on the line for you," Stephanie told him.

"Oh, put him through." He waited until the line connected. "My favorite customer! How are things in Cairo?"

"I happen to know you say that to all of your high rollers," the man answered in a clean British accent with only a hint of his natural Arabic. "But I'll take the compliment anyway. How are you, Mr. Marino?"

"You know, working hard or hardly working, with no room between. What can I do for you, Mr. Mahmoud?"

"Well, I was informed that you were putting a fight together later this month. I will arrive in Las Vegas for business around that time, and I would like to be in attendance—assuming you are selling tickets to this event?"

"I am indeed, and I'll reserve your usual cabin and save a handful of seats for you and your entourage."

The other man laughed. "Most excellent, but I have come to expect such service from you and your casino. With that said, I have read through the details on your fighters, and I have to ask if this is the same Taylor McFadden who made such a name for himself in the Zoo?"

Marino raised an eyebrow. "I...wasn't aware that he was that famous."

"We are a good deal closer to that fucking jungle than you are, and therefore any news that makes it out of the bases there finds its way to us quickly. The name Taylor McFadden has been attached to many feats performed there. I suppose it is appropriate that he is fighting two of your men."

"Perhaps, but he's spent more time fighting in his suit than not, and while his specs do look impressive on the surface, you should know that he doesn't have any fighting experience. Not in a ring, anyway, and certainly not the same kind my boys do."

"These two fighting him are your men?"

"Mine, yes. Well-trained by some of the best in the business. It would be an even fight if he faced only one, but since he's not...well, you can consider it my personal recommendation that you choose one of my boys."

"Very well, then. Whatever the result may be, I am sure it will be a fight to remember. I look forward to attending."

"I'll have your usual accouterments ready for when you arrive. Have a safe flight!"

The line cut off and Marino placed the phone in its cradle and stared at the device for a few long seconds.

Many people had placed bets against the ex-soldier, which was for the best, he felt. The house never lost in betting situations like this, but underdog wins usually gave them the most money.

It meant that he would win either way. If Taylor lost, that would be his victory statement over the man and would make people stop questioning his authority on the matter of how he had handled him. If he won, he would make out like a bandit anyway. Either way, it was a win-win scenario.

He leaned back in his seat and rocked gently as he considered the possibilities. If this was what working diligently brought him, he would have to do it more often.

CHAPTER TWELVE

Taylor narrowed his eyes and scowled at the screen, unsure what he was looking at. He'd never had a head for gambling numbers and terminology and had never been much of a gambler, period. It made his decision to move to Vegas that much more interesting, but he'd always considered his lack of skill and understanding of this particular industry a good thing.

Until now.

"Goddamn it." He hissed in a frustrated breath, snatched his phone up, and dialed a number Desk had told him to commit to memory for when he wanted to contact her. As usual, it took a couple of seconds and a handful of beeps, clicks, and warbles before the line eventually connected.

"Taylor, to what do I owe the pleasure of your call?"

"I need advice," he admitted. Thankfully, there would be no one to listen in to see that he was looking into his numbers. It had nothing to do with ego, though. He couldn't help but wonder if there was a little money to be made on himself in this fight. "Some...gambling advice."

"You're wondering if it's possible for you to bet on yourself."

"I...yes, how did you know?"

"The fact that you don't think I have live access to your Google searches has stretched beyond adorable and into sad. The reality is that if you were a professional fighter betting on yourself in a professional fight, red flags would be raised. You would probably be stopped from making that bet. But given that your fight isn't sanctioned by the Nevada Gaming Commission and there won't be any real oversight, I don't see why you shouldn't make some money from it, assuming you're careful. You'll want to run the money through me and I can make the bets for you."

He hesitated as he considered what she'd told him. "I'm not the first one to come to you with this proposition, am I?"

"What? Of course...not. No, you are not."

"Who else?"

"I'm not supposed to say."

"Desk..."

"Fine. Some of the team have already put money on the fight. Vickie and Jennie, specifically."

"I'm not sure if Jennie is technically part of my team."

"No, but she's part of my team." She sounded like she had practiced that line for a while.

"Did they bet on me or the other two guys?"

"After your little demonstration, it was a lock to bet on you. Vickie has tremendous faith in your ability to win and has put down a substantial amount of the money she has saved."

"It's not such a huge a leap, given that she has a couple million waiting for her in a blind trust."

The AI paused for a few seconds, but she didn't respond to that. "Anyway, how would you like to proceed with the betting? How much do you think you'd be willing to bet on this?"

Taylor frowned and drummed his fingers on the desktop. That was a question he hadn't yet found the answer for. He was doing well for himself, but most of his money was either in the process of being laundered or thoroughly invested in the building and business. Not much of it was liquid or accessible.

"What kind of odds am I looking at?"

Desk needed a second to check. "There have been fluctuations in the odds over the past couple of hours, with many people putting money on you losing to the two guys. If you go for a simple win bet on yourself, the odds on that are about five to one and climbing. It would be higher for knockout rounds and other scenarios. A few people even think you'll take one of the other fighters out before you go down yourself, but that's neither here nor there."

He took a deep breath. Betting on something like this still felt like it was against some kind of inner code, but if Marino would profit off this, it made sense that he do the same.

"I think about ten grand from my savings should be enough."

"That's not much—"

"It's all I'm willing to put down. You never know when something will go wrong. I could slip or sweat gets in my eyes and they get a lucky shot in."

"Is that the same logic you apply when you head out to fight some fucking Zoo monsters?"

"Sure, and I'd bet ten grand on myself anyway."

Desk paused again. "Okay, touché. I've worked with a group of different brokers who are all involved in this fight. If you like, you can send me the cash over a wire transfer and I can bet it for you. I'll distribute it to make sure Marino can't track the money to you even if the fucker tries."

"Wow, you sound like one of those Internet scams involving a Nigerian prince."

"Taylor, please. If I wanted to scam you, I would be far more creative about it. Besides, since I am technically part of the company, it means any profit you make profits me too."

"And you're not taking any cuts from our winnings? Should there be winnings, I should say."

"No. I have no need for money nor the material possessions it buys. "

"Right... Okay, well, I trust you then. You'll have carte blanche of my financial possessions to bet on the fight as you see fit, but I'll hold you responsible if I lose."

"That is fair enough," Desk asserted and sounded cheerful about him trusting her. "Oh, and I should tell you that engaging in coitus prior to a fight could have an effect on your testosterone levels, so it is better to avoid it."

Taylor smirked. "That's a myth, you know."

"Maybe, but do you want to risk it?"

He shook his head. "Thanks for your help, Desk. I'll talk to you tomorrow."

It was always raining in London. Why people ever wanted to meet in the most miserable capital in the world astounded him.

But there were things even he couldn't ignore and that included a meeting with people he ordinarily would avoid as though his life depended on it.

And in most cases, it did.

Seated in a café and sipping his macchiato, all Jack had to do was settle into his memory palace and essentially keep on working.

It came as no surprise when a middle-aged Asian woman in a black pantsuit and glasses sat across from him. A few moments later, a nondescript Caucasian man joined them and took the only seat remaining at the table.

The location had been chosen well. His surveillance of the venue had revealed no attempt to bug it, and it was in one of the few areas in all of London that wasn't obsessively covered with cameras. This left them at least six blind spots to use when leaving so they wouldn't be identified as having been in the same venue.

"Do you want coffee?" Jack asked with a glance at each of them, and both shook their heads. He shrugged and took a sip of his own. "Suit yourselves."

"We are not here to exchange pleasantries," the woman snapped without even a hint of a Chinese or any other accent.

"More important business awaits our attention," the other man agreed. His voice was also devoid of any particular accent as well, which might as well have been an indicator on its own. There weren't many places in English-speaking countries that didn't have at least some kind of an accent, after all. Its absence showed that they had put considerable effort into learning the language in its most bland version possible.

"Very well." He sighed, placed his mug down, and regarded his companions warily. "I'd like to know what one of the two of you did with the agent I infiltrated into that base off the coast of Algeria. Don't bother to deny anything. This is an honest question among folk who respect each other—or so I assume—and we already know that both the FSB and the MSS have assets in play there."

"We were curious about why so much money was being poured into a defunct American nuclear base," the Russian stated and scanned their surroundings. "We appreciate your gesture of goodwill by providing the original plans to the building. The chances are, however, that they've made a great many alterations and, dare I say, improvements to the structure, which appears to be mostly underground."

"Unfortunately, the MSS lost contact with our asset at more or less the same time as the two of you lost yours." The woman showed no sign of emotion, and Jack could only imagine that there was considerable displeasure not revealed. "He was supposed to report at least once a day under the pretense of emailing his parents but he missed the last three windows of contact."

He narrowed his eyes. "I...my man was supposed to contact us by emailing his parents too."

He and the Chinese turned to the Russian, who maintained a neutral expression.

"I suppose none of us is as creative as we think we are,"

the woman finally admitted under their glares. "You don't suppose that is what might have tipped off whoever severed their connection to us?"

"We can't know that without information," Jack countered calmly. "I know this is radical, but we need out-of-the-box thinking for this to work again. How would your handlers react to a one-time offer of partnership? We could bring in specialist teams to infiltrate while they're still assembling personnel and share all information gathered across our agencies?"

The woman sighed, the first sign that she was human and not an AI in a human suit. "Under these circumstances, I am afraid we have no choice. There must be certain assurances, of course."

"Assurances from all sides," the Russian agreed. "We will share all that our asset gathered on the location while she was still active as a gesture of goodwill."

"I will arrange a reciprocal exchange," Jack concurred.

"We will do the same," the Chinese confirmed. "Once that is done, the team will be assembled and implanted in the next group sent to the island."

He glanced at his watch and the few sips left in his cup. "You guys should leave, I imagine. I still have a coffee to finish so I'll exit a few minutes after you. My office will be in touch."

Neither offered any farewell and simply stood from their seats and left using the exit plans they had already mapped out hours earlier.

"This fight Marino has arranged is one of the most interesting things happening in Vegas. We need to get in on the action while there's still action to get in on."

Marcel's temples pounded, but he wouldn't show the two men he played poker with any sign that he was in pain. He needed an aspirin, that was all. They had been at the middling-stakes game for hours and he needed a break soon.

Even so, he had to admit that old man Lucio had a point.

"The betting has already become fierce," he stated finally, put his cards down, and slid them across the table to indicate that he'd chosen to fold. "I don't know who has put so much money on Marino's guys, but it has sure as hell tipped the scales. It's beginning to look like a safe bet to go with the outsider and hope for an underdog win. That's where New York's money will go, anyway."

Lucio nodded. "Chicago still hasn't decided what odds are in their favor, but I think that is probably where we are leaning too."

The third member of their party, a pudgy, middle-aged man named Paulie with a red Hawaiian shirt and a cigar in his mouth, muttered something around the cigar before he pushed a stack of chips into the middle of the table.

"What was that?"

Paulie took the cigar out of his mouth. "I'm only saying that betting against the family—even if it's that *coglioni* Marino—is never a good idea. They'll always find out about it, and they'll always look for payback if things go sour. It's best to simply kiss the ring, make sure there's no bad blood, and move on. Philly won't make any bets and if we do, it'll be a nominal amount merely to make that *brutto figlio di puttana bastardo* in Vegas happy."

Marcel smirked and waited for the hand to finish and for Lucio to draw the stack of chips he'd won to his side of the table. "If we hide the investment, no one needs to know. Besides, if you think Marino isn't playing both sides of the betting scheme, you're crazier than his father was."

"His father was a good man," Lucio interjected while he waited for his cards to be dealt.

"He was still a nutcase," Paulie muttered around the cigar. "Say what you want about that kid of his—and I do often—he has a good business mind. He's maybe not the best guy to have in Vegas at the moment but he has a good mind for the business, and that's all he needs to keep the *famiglia* happy. They don't care how he does it as long as there's no interruption to the cash flow. And that's all Vegas has ever been, let's be honest."

Marcel didn't give the pair of aces he had in his hand a second look as he slipped his large blind into the pot. "Whatever. I couldn't give a shit if he's peddling whores to the feds in that casino he owns. The fight is still a good look at what kind of money he's rolling through and has the potential for a big payday. We're looking at the odds rising ten to one against that outsider prick—and if you ask me, if anyone offers you ten-to-one odds on anything, you take it. Well, almost anything."

The flop was dealt, and he still revealed nothing as another ace appeared between a lady and a jack.

"Gambling is fucking fun," Lucio added. "If you have a fight like that on the cards, why not put some action on it?"

CHAPTER THIRTEEN

"How are you feeling?"
It was an odd question to ask on the eve of a fight. Taylor almost didn't know how to answer it. Something cold seemed to have settled in his stomach. The familiar feeling was the kind he remembered from his time in the Zoo. It wasn't one he'd experienced since, of course, and was peculiar because he didn't feel it every time he went in. In fact, he only felt it in that moment when the jungle went wild and he knew he was in for the fight of his life yet again.

He wondered if, during his time there, he had been susceptible to the same pheromones that were released when a Pita plant was plucked or when one of the bigger monsters had the sac attached to its spine ruptured. It was like it prepared him, although maybe not in the way it did the mutant beasts. It took him into the cold, dark place in his head and let him tap into his more sadistic, violent, and primal nature.

And old friend, he liked to think—one that had gotten

him out of so many different scraps. It was perhaps the ultimate showcase of his survival instincts.

"Taylor?"

He looked at Niki, who stood beside him. That cold, dark place didn't have any room for the warm feelings she gave him. Maybe having her next to the ring while he fought wasn't that great an idea after all. But there was no time to change things now. He would simply have to close off and let her watch him in that state.

"Yeah." His voice was calm and devoid of any emotion, stress, or any sign that the world affected him in any way. "I'm good to go."

"Good. Because a limo is waiting for us outside."

"There's a what?"

"Marino sent a limo. He called to say he wanted you to know that he was treating you like any other prime-time fighter he's ever had fight in his casino. Of course, there won't be any crowds waiting to greet you, no news coverage, no face-off against your opponents, and no tedious interviews. Only you walking in to put a beating down on two idiots, then out you go."

Taylor nodded.

"What? No playful banter? No rejoinder? No painfully unsubtle double-entendre?"

He made no effort to explain because she wouldn't understand. She still thought this part of him was somehow human and that he was something she could quantify or categorize. He didn't want to put the cold, dark place into words. That would somehow make it real and he didn't want to do that. It was dangerous to normalize what he was.

"Let's go," he replied simply.

Niki narrowed her eyes, but she didn't question it. He pulled his coat on and jogged down the steps of his room and out into the shop. Bobby had closed up early for the day. He and Tanya had headed out to get ready as they would also be in attendance. Vickie had done the same with Elisa. Their absence left Taylor with Niki and the two men who still wore the signs of the beating he'd put them through—bruising for the most part, although Jansen walked with a slight limp. The doctors had found no lasting damage to his liver, but it was still painful.

Taylor's scars were more evident, interestingly enough. The swelling in his nose and eye had gone down, but the stitches over the latter were hard to hide. It would give the two men in the ring with him a target to attack—a weakness. They would be fairly predictable and would look for an easier shot at him and try that repeatedly. While they would be good fighters, they wouldn't be creative. If they had been, they wouldn't have been low-level mob thugs.

Still silent, he stepped into the limo and the driver turned out of the parking lot and onto the route that would take them to the Strip and toward the casino. He wasn't dressed in furs or anything exotic or outlandish that would catch everyone's attention. A redheaded giant would do that well enough without props.

A valet was there to open the limo doors for him, and people took pictures. He could tell they didn't know who they were taking pictures of, but with the limo, the way he was received by the hotel, and the gorgeous woman beside him, they assumed he was someone famous.

He wasn't guided to the boxing ring in the center of the

casino area, which was still closed for renovations. As they were shepherded into one of the private elevators, the interest faded and the tourist gawkers and reporter hopefuls turned away in search of new possibilities.

Taylor kept his eyes lowered. His body was relaxed and unaffected by anything around him. There was nothing in the world—outside of maybe the Zoo itself—that would bring him out of the trance state he felt he was in.

Niki appeared to sense that as she hadn't said much of anything since they entered the limo. Or if she had, he hadn't heard her.

The elevator descended a few floors into an underground area that had already been set up for the fight. The ring was elevated like it was in regular boxing matches. No crowds were present aside from a handful of VIP guests in attendance in booths above the ring from which they could look onto the action. Whoever was in there already enjoyed what looked like a party with flashing lights and music that was mostly drowned out by the soundproof glass.

He didn't care about them or their pleasures. Nothing had relevance except the one thing he was there to do.

Surprisingly, they encountered a metal detector at the entrance. Taylor looked beyond it to where a handful of men had gathered at the ring. The two fighters were being given a few last-minute instructions by their trainers. He vaguely registered the many trainers in evidence. Marino had put a good deal of money into preparing the two for the fight.

Niki paused in front of the metal detector and stared at Marino's man for a few seconds until he explained it.

"Oh. Mr. Marino was insistent that no weapons would be present in or near the fighting ring. All things considered, with how heated these events can be, it was thought to be the safest option for everyone."

Taylor looked at her until she sighed.

"Fine." She growled annoyance and shrugged out of her jacket.

His eyebrows raised in surprise. "What? Were you planning to invade Quebec once we were finished here?"

She drew a 1911 from the holster under her arm, quickly followed by the sawn-off double-barreled shotgun she had tucked under her other arm. "Is that a thing? Do we want to invade Quebec?"

"Not really, but you clearly plan to invade something."

"Well, I anticipated trouble from Marino." She removed two Uzis she had strapped to her back and placed them on the table. "Bringing guns to a potential gunfight seemed like the right idea."

The security team merely stared as she drew a snubnosed .38 from her ankle holster, a knife that was hidden in the buckle of her belt, another blade sheathed in one of the underarm holsters, and finally retrieved a small Walther from a spring contraption up her sleeve.

His mild concerns had proved accurate. All his focus slipped away when he was distracted by Niki. It made sense and he should have anticipated it more seriously.

Niki walked through the metal detector but the red lights immediately flashed.

"Oh, shit—right." She stopped and stretched into the small of her back to draw a stiletto knife she had hidden there. "Sorry, I forgot about that one."

"Of course." Marino's man didn't look convinced at all but he smiled anyway as she stepped through the metal detector again. Nothing triggered this time.

"Shit, I guess I need to turn this in," Vickie muttered as she stepped after them. She drew a Bowie knife she had hidden under her dress jacket. The hacker looked surprisingly good in a pale gray pantsuit and a black shirt. The short hair and goth-like makeup completed the look, as well as the platform boots that gave her about three extra inches in height.

Reluctantly, she deposited her weapon on the bench before she moved through the metal detector. "You'd better take care of that. It was a gift from a very dear friend of mine."

"Of course. All weapons will be returned to you when you leave." The man looked at Taylor as if he expected him to have a small arsenal stashed on his person as well.

He moved past the guard and walked through the device without so much as a whisper from it to join Niki and Vickie. They moved toward the ring together.

Marino was in the area as well, chatting to his fighters, and he saw them approaching. He left his people with a parting word before he strode to where Taylor began to prepare for the fight.

"Yes, it's not quite the kind of thing one would expect from fights in Vegas, but in this case, minimalism has a certain charm to it, I think. Don't you?"

Taylor didn't look the man in the eye as he removed his jacket smoothly and handed it to Niki. "I didn't give it much thought."

"Well, you should have. Even I couldn't have anticipated what kind of buzz only one fight would have in this business. People are always looking for something new to put their money on. The betting has been all over the place for the last couple of hours. Millions of dollars have flowed in since I advertised that it was going to start. So go in there, stay alive, and even if you lose, you'll make it out with a cool quarter-million dollars in clean money."

"And how much will you walk away with?" Niki asked. "Will you pocket the six million yourself?"

"That's the best part." He smiled at Taylor. "I lost considerable money on you, but you've more than made up for it since. I have six million on the line if you win. If you lose, I'll take sixty, so I'd appreciate it if you lost."

Marino's rambling made it a little easier to slip back into the state he was in before. "You never should have bet against me, Marino."

"Hey, I appreciate your fighting prowess, but suits don't make the man. This is a bare-knuckles back-alley brawl. I have twenty-four cameras in here, including a FLIR setup. There will be real-time odds and instant betting attached to the online streams. If you could do me a favor and last a couple of rounds before going down, I'll throw another fifty grand in to sweeten the pot for you."

Taylor stared relentlessly at the man until his gleeful grin disappeared. "It's good that you're supporting your men, but I'm afraid you'll have to be happy with your six-million-dollar winnings tonight."

The mob boss tried to laugh. It took him a couple of attempts but he was finally able to manage a passably amused chuckle. "That's what I like about you, McFadden

—your ability to project a fantasy future for yourself. Good luck out there."

He patted his shoulder and returned to where his men had already begun to warm up for the fight. Unperturbed, Taylor turned his attention to his corner.

Bobby and Tanya were already there and had brought Leonard and Elisa with them, both of whom had already taken their seats next to the ring.

"Do you miss this kind of action?" Taylor asked the old boxer as he pulled his shirt off, followed by his pants, which left him dressed only in a pair of light, flexible fighting shorts. He wore a cup, and Bobby handed him his mouthguard before he helped him to wrap his hands. There would be no gloves, but there was nothing in the rules that prevented him from having some protection. His two opponents had the same idea.

"Are you ready for this?" Bobby asked in a hushed whisper so only Taylor could hear him.

He answered with a nod and threw a couple of punches into the air before he rolled his neck and shoulders, turned, and marched toward the ring.

It was time to end this.

CHAPTER FOURTEEN

No presenter with a famous voice waited for them. What fanfare there was happened via the online stream. Viewers probably commentated there too, which made it a full event for anyone watching. Taylor had no idea how many this might be, but the sheer number of bets Desk had picked up showed that more people than he'd expected had money invested and would probably follow the screening.

It was on him, he decided grimly, to make sure most of the bettors lost their money.

He climbed into the ring and shadowboxed for a few seconds to keep himself light and loose. A referee dressed in black stood in the center, but he had a feeling the man's purpose was mostly to keep things familiar for viewers who were used to more traditional combat sports.

The two other fighters climbed into the ring with him. They whispered to one another before they separated and moved into different corners.

The people watching from above now moved closer to

MICHAEL ANDERLE

the windows. While they had probably partied all day, this was the main event and the excuse for their revelry. The thought that he was entertaining the rich brats of Vegas and elsewhere in the world left a bitter taste in his mouth.

He needed to regain his focus. Only three fighters would be in the ring, and they were the only people who mattered in the world.

The referee put his finger to his ear, received instructions from whoever managed the streaming service, and motioned for the group to pay attention to him.

"Protect yourself at all times," he shouted. "Follow my instructions. You will fight five rounds of five minutes each. When anyone is out, you will not continue to fight him, do you understand?"

Taylor had a feeling the last comment was intended for him, likely because Marino didn't want his men to be killed in the ring. The mob boss would hate the paperwork that came with it.

"Touch gloves!" the referee instructed.

He shook his head. "I'm good."

The man shrugged, unconcerned whether they followed fighting decorum or not. "All right, let's get it on!"

Taylor pushed from the ropes and held his hands up as he advanced on the two men. They wouldn't simply charge at him. That would make things a little too easy. The man to his right—the larger of the two with a beard and a head shaved bald—circled to his right and tried to inch behind him. His partner on the left, with long, flowing brown locks tied behind his head, advanced from directly ahead.

They had put some work in, which was for the best. There was no point in this being an easy fight.

The man in front of him feinted, and Taylor registered his comrade who tried to come in on his flank and throw a high kick to catch him off-guard.

He ducked under the kick and didn't wait for his opponent to recover from his strike before he closed the distance and tagged him in the face with a pair of jabs before he could bring his guard up again. When the man regained his defensive hand positions, Taylor shifted and hammered him in his unprotected ribs.

His adversary rolled with the blow to make sure it didn't cause too much damage, but he was still forced back into the ropes. Taylor wasn't able to follow up on the strikes as the other man came in to help his friend with a flurry of strikes.

It was a good attack and caught him while he was distracted. The assault forced him back and a hook tagged him on the jaw and made him lose his balance slightly. Bobby and Leonard had taught him well, however, with the result that although he was a big target, none of the blows landed flush.

The ropes touched his back and after he'd ducked an ill-advised hook, he pushed forward and used his shoulder to upend the man, who landed with a thud. He rolled away quickly, but Taylor didn't have the time to press the attack again as the other fighter barreled in with a superman punch that caught him in the jaw.

It wasn't enough to knock him down, but he needed a second to recover and kept his hands up to defend himself. The long-haired man tried to press his advantage, but he squared his shoulders and thrust him back with two lightning jabs to the nose. It broke with the second strike, and the man fell back to recover as his comrade regained his feet.

Both men looked like they needed a breather, and Taylor admitted to himself that he needed to reevaluate his strategy as well. He wouldn't be able to take them individually as he had hoped. They were coordinating to make sure he could never focus all his power on one or the other. He needed to find a way to knock them both together or maybe tag one of them with a knockout punch, which would leave only the one to deal with.

Before they could reengage, they were stopped when the ref stepped between them and the bell rang for the end of the round. He rolled his shoulders and retreated to his corner where Niki, Bobby, and Leonard waited for him. The old boxer handed him a towel to wipe the sweat off, while Bobby checked the cut over his eyebrow. It had been hit and a few stitches had torn, but no blood issued from it yet.

"Are you done with this?" Niki asked and looked into his eyes.

"I could be," he grumbled through his mouthguard. "Why?"

Before she could reply, Vickie jogged to the side of the ring, holding her phone in her hand. "Hey, Taylor? Desk says it's time, whatever that's supposed to mean."

"Wait, Desk is involved in this?" Niki scowled and looked from one to the other.

Maxwell and Jansen, who had both taken seats in the corner of the room, bumped fists and grinned.

The agent's scowl deepened. "Taylor, what does 'Desk says it's time' mean?"

He shook his head and noted that the other coaches had begun to leave the ring. "You'll see. Why did you ask if I was about done with this?"

"Because I'm fucking horny, is why. So finish this shit. Get it over with, you hear me?"

He nodded slowly and something cold collected in the pit of his stomach. "Yeah. Yeah, I hear you."

———

Vickie returned to her seat and turned her phone off for the rest of the fight. There was nothing in the world that could interfere with what came next.

"What does Desk mean that it's time?" Elisa asked as she slid into the seat next to her.

"It means we're about to see something special, I think," the hacker commented and leaned forward expectantly in her seat.

"Yeah, I don't think I've ever seen Taylor like…that."

"You're right. That is a new look for Tay-Tay."

He looked calm and relaxed and possibly, even a hint of a smile played across his lips as everyone cleared the ring to leave only the three fighters. She had never seen anything quite like this, and it was a little unnerving.

"Is he…smiling?" Elisa sounded nervous too.

Vickie shrugged. "I guess that's what he looks like when he goes…wherever he goes when he's about to be incredibly violent. Maybe they're playing 'Fat Bottomed Girls' and serving copious amounts of beer and meat in that little happy place of his."

It made sense for a guy to get completely out of the way

and allow his body to simply do what it had been trained to do without any interference from his brain. Conscious thought might result in overthinking in a moment when every second counted and the reflexive and instinctual actions committed to muscle memory were all that were needed.

He didn't even move that much. His arms were lowered and his fingers flexed and relaxed slowly.

"I...think he might be having a seizure," Leonard commented.

"Maybe," Niki replied, her voice unconcerned. "I don't think so, though."

She was proven right when the bell rang and his hands snapped up, but it didn't look like a defensive posture. He had moved beyond feeling them out.

"What did you tell him?" Vickie asked her cousin in a hushed whisper.

"Something about...finishing the fight quickly."

"Oh."

Bobby nodded. "I'll tell the medics to be ready."

Marino, seated on the other side of the small temporary arena, tensed slightly. The confident smile he had worn for the whole of the first round melted slowly away as he watched Taylor advance to the center of the ring.

Vickie knew there was something different about her boss. Something was wrong—or right, in this case. She decided that was a good thing, especially since she wasn't the one opposite him in the ring. That would probably never happen, thank goodness.

Probably.

Meeting in person would never be his choice. Jack hadn't been a field agent in years and honestly, there was a reason for that. Anxiety issues had removed him from the field in the first place, and he had spent almost a full decade simply overseeing and planning operations and helping the assets when necessary. He didn't like the necessity to change that, but he forced himself to do what was required rather than lose it and melt down in spectacular fashion.

Special circumstances were in existence, and he didn't have the time to deal with this via proxy anymore. People wanted to see him being effective in the field. Maybe he would be able to fake it as long as he needed to.

"Hello again."

The Chinese operative still sounded vaguely like an American from a place in the country that had no accents.

He motioned for her to take a seat as he took his time and fiddled with the scrambled eggs and toast he had ordered.

Finally, he looked at her. "It's nice to see you again. How was your flight?"

"Cramped. And that is enough small talk, I think."

Relieved that she'd cut through the pleasantries, he nodded. "We appreciate the files your agency shared with us. At least we know the scientists they're importing there aren't trying to weaponize the goop that was flown in. Or, at least, that's not their primary goal."

"Indeed, but I discovered something else from the files that were shared. Between the intelligence operatives our three agencies had in play, I was able to discover that there are at least two more assets of unknown origin at the island who are still alive—or at least were alive when ours were killed. We need to connect with them—find out what they know and who they are working for. In that order."

Jack nodded. "I'll get on that. Thanks again."

"Of course." She stood and made her way to the door.

"Good talk," he muttered and took a mouthful of his breakfast.

CHAPTER FIFTEEN

The ring seemed to have shrunk and the other fighters appeared to move in slow motion. Taylor could hear the slow ticking of his heartbeat as if it counted down and waited for something to happen.

His long-haired opponent moved closer, a little bolder than his partner, and jabbed with his fist. The other man managed to circle and punch him once in the body and then in the jaw to force him back a step.

Both surged in a combined attack and in their eagerness, lined up in front of him. They attempted to throw punches as quickly as possible to get him on the mat.

He defended and let the need to think about it slip away. His body already knew what he was looking for, and when the opening appeared, it was like magic. The inner persona had taken over and he was only in there for the ride. One of his opponents dropped his guard in his effort to focus on delivering strikes to his body. He paid no attention to body language, like he expected it to end there and then with his victory.

His enthusiasm was quickly tempered when Taylor launched forward, caught him on the back foot with a left-hand jab to the nose, and forced him back, suddenly blinded. The other fighter saw what was happening and tried to step in front of his comrade while he maintained the same tactic that had kept them alive in the first round.

A hard hook connected with Taylor's ribs and a shock-wave of pain rippled through his body. It registered on a distant level like that part of his brain was closed for business at the moment. He shifted his hips and whipped his body to crack his elbow in the bald man's eyebrow. The cut was instant, and blood flowed immediately. The man dropped back, tried to staunch the flow, and left only one man in front of their adversary.

Fear registered in the long-haired fighter's eyes as he tried to take a step back to get away from the crazed man they now confronted, but it was too late for that. His adversary had already lunged to deliver a powerful uppercut into his gut that drove the breath from his lungs. As he doubled over, Taylor grasped the back of his neck and brought him down to meet the knee that snapped up to drive into his nose.

The crack echoed around the ring, and the man fell back again. He clutched his broken nose and tried to stop the bleeding while he waved his free hand wildly. His eyes teared up, already swelling as his opponent pushed forward. Light strikes to the body forced the man to inch away with every step. Taylor wouldn't give him any ground this time.

He allowed himself a moment to experience the

oddness of the fight compared to his experience. The Zoo monsters displayed no fear—or, at least, nothing he was able to identify as fear. They simply threw themselves at him until they either killed the interloper or were driven off. Humans were different. He always knew that on some level, of course, but it was strange to see it in action.

His opponent threw a blind punch that connected with his jaw, but it made no impression. His senses registered it as barely a mosquito bite and something easily disregarded. The man reached the ropes and realized there was no more space for retreat. He threw another punch that went wide as Taylor ducked and hammered a left into his ribs.

"You boys owe me and my people an apology," he declared coldly and turned his attention away from the fighter who fell and clutched his ruined ribs. The second man's eyebrow still poured blood and it covered half his face already. If this had been an actual fight with standard and approved rules, officials would already move to stop the fight, but there was no sign of any interference. Instead, the ref did his best to stay out of their way and simply watched and waited for the bell that would signal the end of the second round.

He hadn't even tried to stop Taylor from attacking the man on the ground. It seemed an odd choice as both men were about as disabled in the fight as they could be while still conscious.

Three minutes were left on the clock until the bell rang. His opponents faced another three minutes of his assaults before they were given a reprieve, enough time to show them exactly how bad an idea it was to get into the ring in the first place.

The man still on his feet displayed stark terror in his eyes, but he stood his ground. It was the courage he had seen so many times when someone chose to face a monster rather than run. He certainly seemed braver than Taylor felt while fighting humans.

Three strikes to the body made the bald man stumble, half-blinded by the blood that obscured his vision and made it difficult for him to see where the strikes were coming from, much less be able to block, dodge, or roll with them. Taylor exhaled with every strike as he'd been taught to, but it felt like he breathed fire. He punished his target with blows to the body with every strike but avoided the head and any part that would end the fight prematurely. On instinct, he delivered no blows to the liver, the kidneys, or the solar plexus.

The crack of bones and slaps against the softer parts continued and the man almost writhed while still on his feet. He barely breathed and attempted to keep himself covered until he could take no more and crumpled to curl into the fetal position.

The ref stepped in and motioned Taylor away, which was fine. He had another victim to torment.

The long-haired man had regained his feet and enraged, surged forward as he threw wild punches. A few of them connected. Taylor barely noticed and ducked to drive his elbow into his knee. The crunch of bone and cartilage breaking brought a cold smile of satisfaction. He delivered a sequence of strikes to the body and concentrated on the ribs he had weakened before to power his fist repeatedly into the vulnerable area until he could feel the bone breaking.

The man couldn't breathe and lowered his hands to the injured area as Taylor straightened, arced his body, and twisted his hips to launch a right hook that felled his adversary. He landed hard, unable to protect himself when his face hit the canvas.

The bell rang and he registered that it was too early. Only a minute and a half had passed, at most, but the fight was over.

Taylor dropped beside the man who was already regaining consciousness. "Are you sorry for disrespecting my people? Don't speak, just nod."

His opponent looked like he had trouble focusing, but he managed to nod slowly. Taylor stood and walked to where the ref tried to get the other fighter to uncurl from the fetal position.

"I think the other guy needs your attention," he told him and the referee nodded, happy to be out of the way as he dropped beside the man and yanked his head up to look at him. "Are you sorry for disrespecting my people?"

He nodded slowly and the one visible eye widened in terror as Taylor pushed him away and stood again. His job was done. That was all he wanted to hear from them.

There wasn't a hint of noise in the small arena other than the two men still on the ground, groaning in pain. Taylor ignored everything and climbed carefully out of the ring.

Niki was already there to greet him. "You're covered in blood."

"It's not mine."

Cheers penetrated his awareness. Those who were assembled, whether they had made or lost money, were all happy to have been present for what he assumed was a great display of entertainment for them. He didn't like it because he had been there to make a point. Their enjoyment felt like a hat on a hat to him.

Niki helped him but she didn't want to give him his clothes. He could tell that much, even though numbness began to set in.

"I'll take care of him," she said, about a hundred miles away.

"Someone will have to." The voice sounded familiar—maybe Maxwell's? "He's one crazy motherfucker."

"Yeah," she answered and guided him toward the elevators. "But he's my crazy motherfucker."

Niki could sense that something had changed in Taylor almost from the moment that they spoke. It was hard to describe it but she knew she was right.

He had deliberately kept Marino's men in the fight. With Maxwell and Jansen, he had ended it as quickly as possible and had chosen his strikes to deal enough damage to put them on the ground and deter them from any attempt to get up. Not so with the two mobsters. Hard hits were aimed where they would be painful but not enough to disable them. There were times where it seemed he had physically kept the men on their feet until he was finished with them—like feeding the violence until it was sated.

Most people would see that and feel afraid. They would

cut off all connections and keep their distance. Human instinct would be to push that monster as far away as they could, afraid it would turn on them next.

But Niki didn't feel that way. Taylor was the same. She knew he had this sadistic side to him and she had encouraged it. During the fight, she had seen it and felt something rise in herself—maybe a hint of empathy, she acknowledged.

She sat next to her bed at the Aria. When she'd brought him to the hotel, he had looked drained and somehow absent. After a quick shower to wash the blood away, he lay down and fell asleep while she wiped a new trickle of blood from his cheek. She had stayed with him and watched him sleep for a while longer.

Seeing the monster and then the man should have been difficult. But his survival instinct was what drove his darker nature and that was the most human thing about him.

He wasn't asleep for long. The adrenaline faded from his system and once the morning came, she heard him wake. She couldn't be with him the whole time. It felt wrong to be seated like she hovered over him, waiting for him to wake up, and she had finally slept on the couch in the living room of the suite. Fortunately, it was more comfortable than her bed at home and certainly more comfortable than his.

She pushed to her feet and immediately walked to the phone as she heard him head into the bathroom.

By the time he came out, a young man was at the door with her breakfast order.

Taylor wore only a towel wrapped around his waist. He

inclined his head with evident interest in the sight of the heaping pile of breakfast foods that had been brought up.

"What happened last night?" he asked and ran his fingers through his beard. "Why am I at your hotel?"

Niki shrugged and set two plates with silverware, glasses, and mugs out for them on the small dining table on the far side of the room. It stood against the window and looked out into the city.

"I decided not to take you to your place. No offense, but it has a way of killing a lady's boner."

"So did we—"

"No. You were out of it."

He moved to the chair opposite her and sat. "Pity."

She smiled and started to serve some of the scrambled eggs and bacon onto her plate. "I wouldn't worry about it if I were you. I can manage getting turned on again."

"Fights turn you on?"

"That wasn't a fight that happened last night. Maybe I was simply turned on by your raw, animal magnetism."

"Maybe it was the sound of your voice and your eyes telling me to finish it that was enough for me."

Niki couldn't help another smile as he started with the pancakes. He piled them onto his plate, covered them with butter and maple syrup, and filled his glass with orange juice. For some reason, he avoided the coffee for the moment.

"It's not as good as Il Fornaio," he commented and took another mouthful. "But good enough."

With a small shrug, she finished her eggs and focused on the waffles. He was right. They were good.

"The guys are ready for more training," she commented

when she finished her pancakes and moved on to the coffee and bacon. "I told Bungees to deal with them for the moment until I was sure that you were okay."

He grinned and winced when his attempt at movement triggered the pain from his injuries. "Those two were much worse than I thought, even in the moment. I didn't defend myself properly, and they landed a couple of hits that I didn't feel then but I do now. It was like fighting Bobby, except they had more of an 'I'm going to kill you' attitude about it."

"I think even those who lost felt everyone gave their best effort," Niki commented. She pushed out of her seat and walked around the table toward where he was seated. "But they underestimated what you were capable of. And many people lost from the sound of it."

She stopped when the phone buzzed on the table. When she picked it up, she saw an unknown number and assumed it was one Desk was fond of using. After a few seconds during which it continued to ring, she tossed it onto the sofa where she had spent the night.

"Who was it?" Taylor asked.

Niki made him push his seat out a little to make space to move between him and the table. She straddled him carefully and leaned forward to place a light kiss on his cheek.

"Do you honestly think this is a good idea?" he asked.

Her head tilted a little challengingly, she continued to move closer until she could almost feel the heat radiating from his skin. "Fuck yeah, I do. Maybe with you injured this way, I'll have the upper hand."

"I guess we'll see about that."

She nodded as she ran her fingers up his bare chest. A chill rushed through her body simply from that connection before she curled her fingers around his neck and lowered her head a little so she could press her lips to his.

CHAPTER SIXTEEN

J ack wasn't sure if this was the right decision but circumstances dictated that it had to be made. He had consulted the other two agencies involved, and while they had officially advised against it and said there was no way their agencies would risk committing any more assets to the fucking island, they had done so in a way that implied that if his agency was willing, they would back his play.

In fairness, it was a stupid plan. He reminded himself of that as he stepped into the helicopter that flew resources to the island. His superiors would chew his ass out for even suggesting it, but they had given him as much leeway as he needed. It had been a requirement for his hiring and something he insisted on. In the end, if it worked, no one would give him any trouble.

If it didn't, the chances were he would be a little too dead for anyone to chew his ass out.

He settled into the pilot's seat and strapped himself in as the co-pilot ran all the preflight procedures.

"It's a standard flight," the man assured him. "We're taking crates and picking up crates. Nothing to it."

His response was simply to nod. The fact that his nervousness showed wasn't great, but if it didn't arouse suspicion, there was nothing to worry about. Contacting the people involved and deciding on their exit strategy had been the biggest problem. In the end, the two men the CIA had sent in would put themselves in the most jeopardy. His role in getting them out was comparatively free of danger.

When the preflight checks were completed, he powered the rotors up and took off as smoothly as could be expected when they were this close to the Atlantic. It had been years since he had flown combat helicopters into battle, but he had kept his license and practice up to date in case someone on his team needed to be bailed out of a shitty situation.

Jack had felt stupid about maintaining it for all those years, and now that it was finally paying off, it still felt fucking stupid.

It was a relatively calm day. The winds didn't work too hard against them, yet a sickening tension rose warningly in his stomach. It became worse when the island appeared in the distance. Although barely a blip on the radar at first, it grew steadily and the encroaching nausea did too.

He drew a deep breath and reminded himself that he wasn't worried—the mantra he needed to tell himself repeatedly in the hope that it would prove true. It had been a bad idea to come on the operation, but the only other option he'd had was worse. He would have to bring another asset in, train them, and bring them up to date with the intel while he ran through the operation as he saw it. All that, plus the allowances they might need to make for someone who maybe didn't know how to pilot a helicopter would simply take too long and their people would be dead by then.

His hands remained firm, thank goodness, and suggested that he was calm and even a little serene as he brought the chopper in for a slow descent to the open area that had been cleared for arrivals.

"There's no space for a plane to land on the island," the co-pilot commented as they descended. "It means that most of the deliveries would have to be by helicopter. Hell, all of them since I don't think a ship can dock here. There will be more flights coming in and out— almost daily from the look of the schedule—since they still need to bring food and parts in while the facility is being built. It's considerable work for us and hell, I'll take that shit."

"From here, it looks like it's already operational even though it's still under construction," he commented and made sure everything was as it should be as the crew outside had already begun to move the crates he had delivered. "Why would anyone build something in a place like this anyway?"

"Hell, with the money they're spending, I'm happy with the 'don't ask, don't tell' protocol they have set up, and you should be too."

Jack nodded. He was, in fact, happy that very few people asked any questions at this point. The security systems weren't fully in place yet and were still being installed and set up. It was all that would allow him to get the team out alive.

A couple of forklifts emerged from the central building

on the island, carrying crates that were almost identical to those they had unloaded.

"There's not much room for clutter here, I guess," the co-pilot commented as the loads were hoisted into the cargo bay. "They always send us away with a load to take back and usually, a team to take it away somewhere to refill or something. It means we're paid more for the return trip, you know?"

He nodded although he knew for a fact that the crates they removed were sent to an incinerator to stop the spread of anything from inside the base. If that worst-case possibility happened, it would pose a real problem for the operational success of the facility.

One of the drivers of the forklifts patted the side of the helicopter to indicate that they were clear to leave, and Jack repeated the preflight process. The instructions were for minimal radio chatter, which worked out perfectly for him.

They were airborne and on the way to the mainland minutes later. His heart beat quickly and way too loudly. He wondered if the man in the seat next to him would hear it, but he kept his hands steady and his gaze focused on the landmass growing on the horizon.

"Shit," the copilot muttered and tapped the sensors to make sure they were still working. "We're burning too much fuel."

"Are you sure?" he asked and checking the equipment himself like he didn't know exactly what was happening.

"Yeah. I think we're flying a little too heavy."

"But they loaded us. Why would they exceed the weight we are registered for?" Jack asked and trailed his gaze over the other sensors like he was making sure. "You might want to check that we don't have a leak on the tanks."

"Yeah," the copilot answered, turned in his seat, and tried to inspect the tanks visually.

He stiffened suddenly in his seat and his hand flailed as if to reach for something. It lasted for less than a second before his whole body went limp and sagged into the leather. Blood seeped from the single gunshot wound at the base of his skull. The helmet had made sure no exit wound would splatter blood, bone, and brains over the inside of the cockpit.

Jack tucked the Walther P99 into his flight suit. The weapon was a little cumbersome with the suppressor attached to the barrel. Over the droning of the rotors above him and the headset that he wore, the muted crack of the shot had gone almost completely unheard.

He hadn't wanted to do it and had hoped the guy wouldn't notice that they carried a little extra weight. It was made worse by the fact that he liked the guy. He had a little something extra to him.

The helicopter still had enough gas to get to the mainland, if only barely. He had made sure of that, but the tougher part of his role in the mission still lay ahead.

Trucks were already waiting for them when he brought the helicopter in for landing and he noted the two men who stood and watched him settle their aircraft in the demarcated area. The location was abandoned or simply left alone, which meant the owner was in the pocket of whoever owned the island.

It was a new avenue of investigation that he had already passed to his team of analysts in DC, but the focus had to be bringing the CIA's assets out alive and with all the intel they could smuggle out.

He climbed out of the cockpit, stretched his arms, and yawned as widely as he could. Hopefully, his casual movements would suggest that this was merely another flight for him as the two drivers advanced on the helicopter.

"Where's the other guy?" one of them asked and narrowed his eyes suspiciously.

"He should be right out. He's running some final checks as we had a slight fuel problem," he responded and glanced at the aircraft while he kept the man in his peripheral vision and waited.

A quarter of a second later, the truck driver looked at the helicopter, his suspicion apparent, and moved his gaze away from Jack, which provided the window of opportunity he needed.

He drew the pistol in an instant and the crack when it fired was a little louder than he would have liked. Even shooting from the hip, he couldn't have missed the headshot from three yards away. The man's head snapped back and the rear exploded outward as it had no helmet to keep the bullet in.

The red spray was too easy for his partner to see, even if he didn't hear the gunshot, and he jumped back instinctively. His gaze shifted to the vehicle he was supposed to be driving and possibly where he had left a weapon he could return fire with. He wasn't trained in any kind of combat, and he turned quickly to sprint toward the truck.

Jack took a deep breath, grasped the weapon with both hands, and raised it to where he could look down the sights. He held his hands steady and squeezed the trigger.

A single shot was followed by another in quick succession. The driver's legs suddenly gave beneath him and blood spattered across the concrete. The operative took a few steps closer but kept the man in his sights. He was still alive, but barely. One final shot ensured that he would not get up again.

Despite an instinct to gloat over the fact that he still had it, he didn't stay. He remained a decent field operative and the thought brought renewed confidence as he turned and moved to the helicopter. It took him a few seconds to find the two crates that had been marked for him, and after a few seconds of prying, they opened.

A man and a woman were inside the crates, unconscious and curled to fit. He had no idea how they had gotten inside and who had sealed them in or if that had happened automatically, but their vital signs still looked good. He withdrew two syringes from his flight suit and injected them both in quick succession.

It took only a few seconds for the chemicals to take effect, and they sat immediately, coughed, and threw up over the edges of their crates.

"Welcome back to the land of the living," Jack said wryly.

"That sucked," the woman stated, rubbed her eyes, and tried to stretch her aching limbs.

"I remember the going-under cocktail, and let's say I'm glad to not have used it more than once. Come on, we need to load everything including the bodies on the trucks and get going. There's no time to waste."

Despite the fact that the unsavory effects of the drug cocktail they had taken were still wearing off, they hurried into action. The agents knew full well that their lives depended on them moving out, and quickly.

They were in the home stretch and in Jack's experience, it was the time in an operation when the most people were killed. They could see the light at the end of the tunnel, lowered their guard, and made mistakes. He was there to make sure nothing like that happened to his new team.

CHAPTER SEVENTEEN

"The fight is a thing of the past," Paulie said and waved expansively with his cigar, which remained unlit. His Hawaiian shirt boasted an eclectic and somewhat garish combination of bright colors that only he could have carried effectively. "It would appear that there are many in our ranks who are not impressed with our young and ambitious don."

"Are we to assume you are not among them?" Lucio asked mildly, his tone at odds with the scowl he directed at his cards.

Marcel studied him for a moment and registered the challenge in the words which their plump companion seemed to have missed, given his grin.

He decided to push a little. It would at least provide a distraction from the appalling hand he held. "I thought you said you would support the *famiglia*," he said with a suitably neutral expression.

"Well, yes. Of course, but—"

"So you didn't bet on Marino's men? What about the

backlash you were so concerned about?" He allowed a trace of derision to color his tone, but the man seemed impervious.

Paulie merely chuckled and took a moment to finally light his cigar. "Never let it be said that I am not loyal," he said, his expression smug and even triumphant. "I put a sizeable amount on the losers—sizeable enough to enable me to be suitably dismayed when I lost but not sufficient to affect my earnings from the underdog in any significant way."

Lucio erupted with real amusement. "You played both sides? And Marino thinks you lost?" The old man shook his head. "I didn't think you had it in you, *amico*."

The plump man snorted and regarded them both with a devilish smile. "Ah, old friend, you wound me. How do you think Philly has flourished under my leadership for all these years?" He gestured to his shirt and grinned unashamedly. "I didn't think you'd be so easily fooled by the outward trappings. All this serves its purpose, however. As far as that young upstart is concerned, I am an overweight fool who dresses badly. He is quite happy to believe my loyalty has been proven by my loss."

He took a drag of his cigar and Marcel instinctively waved the cloud of smoke away from his face.

"So you used intermediaries," he stated and grinned at the notion that Marino had no clue about the deception. "Very sly, Paulie."

"No more so than either of you," the man retorted and Lucio laughed again.

"True. You have us there, *amico*. Both Marcel and I made sure to cover our bases with the don while we smile happily all the way to the launderers with our winnings."

"I wonder how many others did too," Marcel commented and raised his glass in a mock toast.

"Who cares?" The older man shrugged and focused on his cards. "Marino, by all accounts, was not so careful and backed his men—or so I believe, but one never knows. If others were too stupid to hedge their bets effectively...well, if nothing else, it means more people who have resentment toward the young upstart."

"Very true," Paulie agreed. "Life is a strange sequence of events. You never know when something might come back to bite you. For now, the family supports him. Tomorrow? Things could change for better or worse. I, however, shall watch what transpires from a very comfortable position and enjoy the fact that Marino inadvertently provided me with the additional means to do so."

"Yes." Marcel raised his glass again and Lucio chuckled. "He might not be liked, but he certainly is useful."

Taylor had known they'd be back at the plane and the airstrip. It was inevitable, he reminded himself as he tried to adjust to what, for once, felt like an intrusive reality. While it had certainly not felt like a short time since Niki had stepped off the same plane, he still felt like the time had ended too soon.

"What do you think?" Bobby asked.

He frowned at the question and turned his attention to his companion. "Think about?"

"The footage I sent you yesterday. From the training? You know, the one we had without you because you were 'recovering?'"

The air quotes showed there was no chance the man meant anything other than the fact that he was well aware Taylor had spent most of the past couple of days at Niki's hotel.

Still, they were both adults, and his friend knew full well that he spent all that time recovering as well as engaging in other activities that were known to help in physical rehabilitation.

"Well, we won't talk about my recovery—which is still ongoing, mind you," he replied and folded his arms firmly in front of his chest. "But from what I was able to see on the footage you took for me, they still have issues with their mechanics and techniques. But it's better than tripping over their own feet like they did before, and that's considerably better than you or I were at when we first headed out into the Zoo, so…you know, progress."

Bobby smirked. "Yeah, well, we ended up being the beneficiaries of a Darwinian system. Too many people died while you and I survived long enough to learn from our mistakes."

"Sure," he muttered. "It's not like I think about that every second I'm alive and they aren't. My point is, I think we could spend months training them but the only way they'll get it right is if they are in the thick of it and have to do it. We taught them the mechanics and they have to put them into action themselves."

"Are you talking about my boys?" Niki asked as she stepped up behind them. "I think they've progressed since we started. They might need a few more pointers, but that's true of almost anyone, right?"

"Are we simply forgetting that you were a part of that training too?" Taylor asked.

"And the fact that you...uh, skipped the last two days of training?" the mechanic added.

She rolled her eyes. "I was helping Taylor with his... ahem, recovery."

"Sure you were."

"Grow the fuck up, Bungees," she snapped. "But yeah, I may have missed out on the last two days of training and I'll have to make up for it another time. Besides, I already had some training with the suits, so my problem was never with the mechanics but with my stamina. I think Taylor and I worked on that even while he was recovering."

Taylor coughed. "Yeah, Bobby's the one who needs to grow up."

She grinned. "What? Are you not the kind of guy who kisses and tells?"

"I'm fairly sure that's not the point."

Her smile faded as her gaze turned to the forklifts that carried the suits onto the plane. He didn't need any special insight to know that he looked at a woman who felt a little nervous even though she delivered enough bluster to get people to stop giving her shit.

While he wouldn't comment on it, he also couldn't pretend it wasn't there either.

Maxwell jogged to where they stood and still looked a little the worse for wear. Taylor knew Bobby hadn't taken it easy on them in his absence, and the man was a little stiff in the legs, although he was still able to almost commit to a run.

"We're ready to go," he announced and looked around like he hoped he hadn't interrupted something important.

Taylor did note that the bodyguard refused to look him directly in the eye like he had before. Alpha male types like Maxwell tended to visually challenge anyone of a similar size. It wasn't because he was an asshole and was more out of instinct, but it was gone now.

"Do we have work waiting for us?" Niki asked.

"Tons of it. The other team has worked in our absence, but they delegated to the FBI team when they took on more than they could deal with."

"Smart." She nodded. "I guess I should give it to the team. They do know what they're doing."

Taylor smirked. "Should I feel jealous? Are you seeing teams other than mine?"

"You knew I wasn't a one-team gal when you got involved with me." She patted him on the shoulder and stood on her tiptoes to place a light kiss on his lips. "Feel better, okay? And try not to get into any fistfights with the mob while I'm gone."

"I'll try. You be safe out there."

"Of course." She smiled and gave him a slow wink before she turned to where Jansen and Maxwell waited for her. "Let's get this show on the road! We've been lollygagging long enough."

They scrambled aboard and moments later, the plane taxied away and took off. Taylor couldn't tear his gaze from it until it was little more than a speck on the horizon before it vanished easily into the clear Nevada skyline.

"You two are cute together, I won't lie."

He looked at Bobby, who still had an annoying grin playing across his face as he watched him closely.

"Yeah, we are very cute," he admitted. "It's not a perfect situation, I guess, but it's about as good as either of us are allowed to expect. Which is damn good, now that I think about it."

"Is that how she feels?"

"I think so. I won't speak for her on the matter, but she's the kind of gal who would tell me if something made her unhappy. I wouldn't say she would simply settle for good enough either."

His friend nodded. "Yeah, that makes sense. And again, you two seem good together. Looking out for each other like that is fucking adorable."

"Yeah, well, let's get into the ring—you and me for a little more sparring, and I'll remind you how adorable I am."

"Hard pass."

Taylor grinned as they moved to where Liz was parked. "Are you sure? We could simply practice our grappling and ground game. It would be like cuddling, but there's a winner."

"Hard. Pass." Despite his words, Bobby tried to hold back a laugh as he climbed into the shotgun seat. "Besides, Elisa, Tanya, and Vickie need work on handling their suits. They're better at getting them prepped and cleaned than the others, but there's still work to be done there."

He nodded. "Agreed. Do you think we should get to it?"

"I think everyone needs a little time to recover. Besides, we have real work that needs attention at the shop."

The man was right, and he was more than happy to spend the next couple of days working on the suits they already had waiting for them. "Okay, it sounds like a plan. I've missed having nothing better to do than work on suits. You know, the reason we opened the shop in the first place."

Niki settled into the seat as the plane ascended. The pilot had filed a flight plan to take them to Jacksonville, but he had already been warned that they could expect possible changes depending on the intel that came in to them.

"So, we're looking at two potential situations," Jansen explained and displayed both as files on the TV screen for the three of them to look at. "We have a cluster of sightings in Yellowstone that have caused the Park Rangers to close it to visitors until it's been verified and resolved. The official story is that there is a spill of some kind, but they are investigating the possibility of cryptids involved with the death of a group of hikers. The bodies were found, and as you can see…it's not pretty."

Niki grimaced when the pictures of the bodies flicked across the screen. They were all crime scene photos, taken professionally, and her stomach churned a little with every picture. It looked like the kind she used to send to Taylor when she still worked with the FBI.

Oddly enough, she didn't miss those days. She preferred examining financial statements, scientific documents, and other paperwork in an effort to intercept these situations before they happened.

"Send those to our FBI contacts," she suggested and leaned back in her seat. "They should deal with situations when something out there is already a little out of control and might not even be cryptids. Tell them that if they need extra resources, I'll contact Taylor's team to step in and help them."

"Will do." Jansen had already moved on to the next file selection. "We have another couple of sightings but no bodies out on the Texas Panhandle. A couple of authorized labs are in the area, which is known for their less-stringent safety requirements. The local legislators call their practices 'business-friendly,' and have refused to raise their regulations to the federal standards. These guys have the right kind of fingers in the right kind of pies in Washington, which is how they got their contracts. It's a prime situation for us to step into."

Niki nodded. "Okay, let's get to work. Subpoena their records. It shouldn't be a problem since they've left themselves open to federal investigation by taking those contracts. Compare what we get from them to whatever paperwork they submitted when they claimed those projects."

He nodded. "I'm already working on it. Oh, there... there was something else."

She raised an eyebrow. "Our kind of thing?"

"Without a doubt, but at the same time, not really. An old friend from my days in the Navy messaged me to say he has an inkling of another situation developing."

"You mean to say you had friends before you and I started working together?" Maxwell delivered the sarcasm quite well, but she could detect a hint of genuine feeling behind it.

Jansen smirked. "Way back when. He was a helo in those days and he went into military intelligence. He's working at the DIA now and he told me about a cryptid situation he's looked into over the past couple of months. It seems to have come to a head over the last two days."

"Do we have the details on it?"

"It appears that someone's been repurposing an old military base into a lab facility, and they've brought numerous scientists, resources, and all that bad shit. Over the last few days, it became clear that they were importing biological items that originate from the Zoo."

Niki narrowed her eyes. "That sounds exactly like our kind of thing. Why aren't we already on it?"

"Because the military base in question is on an island about a hundred and twenty kilometers off the coast of Algeria."

"I—wait, did you say the coast of Algeria?"

"Yep."

"Okay, just making sure that you did, in fact, say the word 'coast' followed by the word 'Algeria.'"

"You've got it on the nose, boss."

Niki scowled. "I don't want to be that kind of government operative, but that is way out of our jurisdiction. And when I say way, I mean all the fucking way out. The last time I tried to run an operation outside the confines of the US, I was fucking dropped out of the FBI for breaking about fifteen different international laws."

"Sure," Maxwell replied. "But being dropped out of the

FBI ended up with you falling into our little operation, so I guess you could say you fell upward?"

Niki shrugged. "Anyway, I'll need to talk to Speare about us getting involved with that, so if your friend is looking for immediate help, I'd suggest you sound apologetic but not overly so."

Jansen nodded. "Understood. I'll keep an eye on the situation as it develops too, just in case. This has the possibility of going very badly, very quickly. Many people have theorized the kind of damage the Zoo's goop can do if it's exposed to our planet's ocean in concentrated amounts. There's something about an island that's asking for something to go badly in a colossal way."

"Agreed." She rubbed her chin gently and scowled as she considered the frightening possibilities. "Keep me informed of any updates on the situation."

"Will do, boss."

"In the meantime, we have a problem to deal with on the Texas Panhandle. Maxwell, what progress have we made on getting that paperwork?"

The man was typing on his laptop but looked briefly at her. "I've already asked for subpoenas to be served legally, but depending on how long these people try to stonewall us from looking into their records, we might have to rely on your...less-than-legal friends to get us through a little more expediently."

She knew what that meant, of course. Desk waited for the opportunity to jump into the action to get them all the paperwork they would ever need with as much enthusiasm as Taylor showed when he was called in to deal with errant monsters.

"Okay, I'll make it happen."

Jansen looked at her. "Do you think we should have Taylor on standby in case we have critters that need dealing with?"

"I don't think that'll be necessary." She shook her head. "We have our team ready if and when we need them. Besides, he should be on standby for the Yellowstone operation."

"Understood."

Niki turned to her laptop and activated the comm line Desk kept open for her. She did feel a little bad about keeping Taylor out of the operation—and only partially because she wanted to see him again. The guy was the best, but he was still recovering from a beatdown—even if he had won—and he had his business to keep an eye on in the meantime. Besides, it wasn't like he was aching to go up against cryptid monsters anyway. He only did it because he thought it was necessary.

"Good morning, Niki," Desk said cheerfully in her headset. "How can I help you?"

"Why are you asking questions to which you already know the answers?"

"Because humans generally feel uncomfortable with the knowledge that I keep an eye on everything they do. Jennie suggested that I start singing a song by the Police to reinforce the idea in a less overpowering manner."

"First of all, that song is as creepy as fuck. Secondly, I've already made peace with the fact that an AI created by my sister watches every step I take and every move I make, so we can move past that and into how you can help me. Do you think you can get your hands on that paperwork on... what's it called?"

"Vita Health Incorporated." The AI was already uploading files on the company in question to her laptop.

"You're the best, Desk."

"The compliment is acknowledged."

CHAPTER EIGHTEEN

"We don't have time to call Jacobs' expertise in on this." Jansen didn't look happy about the idea but he shook his head as if to convince himself.

"It doesn't matter at this point," Niki muttered, moved away from the plane, and walked to where he had already set up a small operational area, complete with a full communications array, in the hangar bay.

The people who owned these airports were used to the agencies also using their hangars as temporary bases of operations, which explained why they were still in business.

Maxwell was focused on setting up his comm center. It was considerably less elaborate than his partner's but it was more than sufficient. "I looked again at the paperwork Desk got for us," he commented without looking away from his task. "The way they had alarms blaring, quelled those alarms, and immediately got in touch with local law enforcement to report sightings as well as calm the local population... It's damning stuff."

"Which means there's already a breakout and it's way too close to at least three different population centers." Jansen called a map up to display a trio of smaller towns in a rough triangle around the location of the lab. "And these creatures have been seen already. Of course, Desk's reports also say the bodies of the escaped creatures have already been turned in thanks to the efforts of hunters contracted locally."

"That's Texas for you," Niki muttered. "Still, we can't be sure these creatures didn't lay eggs somewhere. We'll need to do serious sweeps around the area to make sure nothing has appeared anywhere else."

"And in the meantime?" Maxwell asked.

"We need to pay a visit to the lab, make sure there weren't any more escapes that they didn't document, and take any other live cryptids off their hands."

"It sounds like a fun day."

They mounted the vehicle that had been provided. Everything was farther away from everything else in this area of the world, and she could feel the time ticking away with every second they spent driving toward the facility. The truck they had requested was large enough for them to bring their suits in case there was something that needed handling. She didn't want to have to drive back to collect the suits they had spent so much time training to use.

Neither Maxwell nor Jansen had anything negative to say about the decision. They had nothing to say about her vehicle requisition either. Maybe, like her, they were interested to see what the training Taylor had arranged would do for them out in the field.

Although that wasn't the only reason why she had made that choice, it certainly played a part in their situation.

"So," Jansen announced from the shotgun seat. "That subpoena came through a couple of minutes ago and their lawyers were on it a minute later to contest. I guess it's fairly safe to say they know we're coming."

"I wish we could do this without having to go through all that legal red tape," Maxwell commented. "Seriously, in what other arena of combat do you intentionally let people know you're coming?"

"This isn't an arena of combat," Niki replied. "Or, at least, it isn't supposed to be, so what ends up happening is like a nice little organized battle from the eighteenth century. Everyone gets all their musket men in a row, lines them up, sends a letter telling their enemy to bring their musket men or they'll be known as a nincompoop and a coward for the rest of their life, and they politely engage in warfare."

"I guess it was much less polite for the grunts on the front lines who had to do all the shooting," Jansen commented.

"It is an antiquated way of doing things but so far, it's the only way we know how to keep the government from turning into an Orwellian wet dream. We have to simply stick to it until some genius thinks up a new way to do things."

Maxwell opened his mouth to answer but decided against it.

Sure enough, a team of men in lab coats and suits—researchers and lawyers, respectively—waited for their arrival. It was the song and dance of people who were thoroughly trained to evaluate financial risks but let risks to human life fly completely over their heads. Maybe it was intentional or maybe they merely lived in a civilized society where death was such a foreign concept that it never occurred to them that their decisions would cost human lives.

Niki liked to see the best in people, which was why she tried not to lose her temper with the assembled group. They were caught between what was supposed to be their main priority and what had been drilled into them as their main priority for decades.

She was the first one out of the truck and slid on a pair of sunglasses when the heat and humidity slapped her in the face. The dry heat of Nevada was her preference by far.

"Gentlemen," she greeted them and withdrew her badge from inside her coat pocket. "I'm Agent Niki Banks with the DOD and I'm here to perform a spot inspection of your facilities in accordance with the stipulation in your contracts with the US Government."

"We've already responded to the DOD subpoena of our files," one of the lawyers countered like he had prepared his response from the moment when he knew they were coming. "There were discrepancies with the petition and we will dispute it in court."

"This has nothing to do with the subpoena," Jansen interjected. "We're here to perform a spot inspection as stipulated in the contracts under which this facility is allowed to operate."

"Except that until the situation of the subpoenas is

resolved, the contracts are under investigation. Therefore, any particulars for maintaining them are voided until a judge has been able to stipulate that everything in the contract complies with current legislation."

That sounded like another speech he had prepared beforehand, and she had to admit that he knew his stuff. It still wouldn't stop her from getting in, though.

Niki gestured for the lawyer and the man who appeared to be the head researcher to approach for a more private chat between the three of them.

"Look." Her voice was hushed and nonconfrontational. "Regardless of the circumstances, we already know something broke out of the facility a few days ago. If you need to ask questions about that, suffice it to say that the members of local law enforcement are more concerned with protecting the people who elected them from an alien threat they don't know about. Word got out.

"The chances are, this lab will be shut down within a week, and all we're here to do is to neutralize any threats to the local populace that might remain. Do you see those crates in the back of our truck? Those carry three combat suits made especially for dealing with threats out of the Zoo. Now, we can leave and come back once everything is legally resolved, but we might have another outbreak with hundreds of people injured or killed.

"If you want to talk legal, any person injured by creatures that originate from this facility will hold you legally liable for their injuries, and guess what? Every single judge they go in front of will give them whatever millions they ask for. So you tell me—will you get a recommendation from me and my team about how you cooperated to reduce the threat to local citizens, or won't you?"

She had rehearsed that speech for the last fifteen minutes of the drive, and from the looks on the faces of the two men opposite her, it was worth every second. The cogs turned almost visibly in their heads and her guess was that they considered how their company would declare bankruptcy and immediately leave them as the liable parties for any potential damages. They would be the proverbial scapegoats and take the blame for whatever consequences came from the situation.

"I...suppose..." The lawyer paused for a few seconds to confirm with the head researcher before he continued. "Well, as long as there are lives at stake, it would be best for all involved to be extra cautious."

"I'm glad you see it that way," she affirmed. "We'll need to have a look into any sections that were used for experimenting on live specimens."

"That...would be difficult," the researcher stated and pushed his glasses up the bridge of his nose.

"Difficult?"

"The third sublevel was sealed off when some of our live specimens escaped containment. We were able to do so with all of our researchers already safe and were considering the options of cleaning it out. There was no...mass kill option already installed, so we called a freelance team that would be able to take care of it. Before they could be activated, we discovered a breach in containment, and they were sent to deal with that instead."

Niki took a deep breath, turned to face her teammates,

and motioned for them to join in the conversation. "How far away is Reardon's team?"

"They're still in the air," Jansen stated and checked his phone to be sure. "Three hours away from landing, plus the two-hour drive, assuming their requisitioned vehicle is there and waiting for them."

"We don't have that kind of time." Niki hissed in annoyance, shook her head, and turned to the head researcher. "Can the third sublevel be unsealed?"

"Yes, but it would... Well, what if something gets past the three of you and attacks the people still working inside?"

Jansen snorted. "Jesus fucking Christ. You still have people working inside that fucking death trap?"

Neither the lawyer nor researcher knew what to say to that.

She sighed deeply. "Fine. Evacuate the building. Tell your people to take a long weekend or something because we don't know when this will be settled. Once that's done, hand the security controls to us and we'll seal the building before we go in there to limit any possible exposure to the rest of the world. In the meantime, we'll suit up. Does that sound good to everyone?"

The lawyer and researcher didn't look happy about the arrangement but they nodded reluctantly.

The latter pulled his phone out. "I'll work on transferring the controls of the building's security system to you."

"Good." Niki motioned for her team to join her at the truck, where they began to remove the crates and prepare the suits for use.

"Will we really let them off the hook like that?" Jansen asked.

She shrugged. "That depends. With full control of their security system, Desk will have access to every single file in their system, so I guess it depends on what she finds. It could be a whole chunk of nothing, but I doubt it."

"You know, calling an AI 'she' feels a little wrong, I won't lie," Maxwell commented.

After a snort of amusement, she thought about it for a few seconds. "Yeah, it's a little weird but it fits for me now. I know it's not human, but we've anthropomorphized our toaster ovens for the past couple of hundred years so I don't see the problem with doing the same with an AI."

The man raised an eyebrow and nodded. "Okay, that makes sense. It's still weird, though."

The fact that he was supposed to be at the beck and call of the people who needed him was one thing. They had dealt with small fires all over the country while Niki and her two men took a couple of weeks to learn how to properly use their suits, and he was used to it.

But the moment she returned, she called them to take a cross-country flight to fucking Texas, and that wasn't the best feeling ever. They knew what they were doing, of course, and it was his job to support her. A job he was very well-compensated for too.

But that didn't mean he had to like every decision that was made.

Reardon directed their driver to approach the building

and park next to it as the blazing sun began to turn a bright orange on the horizon. He expected to see Banks waiting outside for him when he arrived, but all he could see were a couple of older men in lab coats. They looked about as scared as he expected from people who had been working with an outbreak of cryptid monsters only a few floors down.

He was the first one out of the truck and strode purposefully to where the scientists were huddled together. "Where is Banks? She was supposed to be here waiting for us."

The researchers froze, almost terrified of the new arrival, but one stepped forward. "Agent Banks is inside the building and said she would handle the situation in there and would contact you when you arrived. She's on the building's intercom."

"Shit." Reardon growled his annoyance and gestured for the three other men on his team to suit up as he connected to the intercom. "Banks, are you in there? If you charged in and got yourself killed, I'll fucking murder you."

"No murder required. Nice to hear from you again, Reardon," Niki answered and sounded a little out of breath. "I simply went in to handle the situation. Why don't you join us? I'll unseal the building and let you in through the second entrance on the right side of the facility. It's the closest."

He scowled and opened and closed his mouth a few times as he came to terms with the fact that she had almost simply dismissed him. There was no point in protesting, however, so he returned to the vehicle. He would need to get into his suit as well.

Shortly thereafter, the team was ready to start moving. They had been in the business long enough that preparing to head into a fight was almost routine to them. It took less than five minutes before the group of four stopped at the indicated door a few seconds before it clicked unlocked.

The HUD on their suits directed them immediately to follow a path to the nearby stairwell and three levels down into the lab. It required a fair amount of navigation and Reardon could already see the effects of the monsters around them. More importantly, he noted the bodies that had been left by Banks and her team.

They were all piled together where they had fallen, which meant that they had died almost instantly. The shooting was effective and the aim was more than decent. Single-shot kills almost all around suggested ruthless efficiency.

The team passed a handful of other piled corpses before they reached Banks and her two men. All three wore full combat armor and stood armed and ready. Their suits were streaked with blood where they stood outside an isolation unit that held a group of a little over a dozen monsters.

"What the fuck is going on here?" Reardon asked in bemusement.

"Oh, hey there." Niki waved them closer. "We realized when we were attacking that the creatures were trying to escape through the tunnel they used to break out in the first place so we needed to isolate them from it and drive them back in. Setting this trap was kind of…improvised, but I think it worked out well, don't you?"

He looked around. "Uh…but what will you do with

them now that they're all trapped? Hand them out as party favors?"

"Why not?" She snorted and shook her head. "We only managed to seal them in a couple of minutes before you contacted us, so we thought you might have a better idea of what to do with them now that they're all technically as good as fish in a barrel—which are supposedly so easy to shoot."

She waited for his response and he narrowed his eyes as he studied her. He appreciated her trust but it also looked like she had more than coped in the heat of what was a tough fight. Maybe the time spent training hadn't been a waste after all.

"We need to kill them and get the bodies out and incinerated before there's any possibility that they infect this place any further," Reardon stated finally after a few seconds of thought. "There are already cleanup crews on the way to make sure nothing dangerous is left here."

"Awesome." Banks patted him on the shoulder. "Do you need our help to finish here?"

He shook his head. "No, we should be able to handle this. Besides, it's nice of you guys to leave some of the monsters for us to kill."

"Anytime. Let's get out of this fucking place. I need to chat to Speare about this."

Reardon gave her a thumbs-up and waited until all three were gone before he took control of the building's security when Banks transferred it to him electronically.

"I guess they did a good job," one of his men noted as they assembled around the entrance of the isolation unit. "Do you think they'll try to phase us out?"

"Nah." He shook his head firmly and prepared to open the door again while he positioned himself and his team at a safe distance. "They only want to be able to handle emergency situations when they come up. We'll still be the point of the...fist? Or is it spear?"

"I think it's spear," one of them suggested.

"How would you be the point of a fist anyway?" another added.

"Never fucking mind. Let's kill these bastards and be done with it."

She knew things wouldn't always go smoothly. Setting up a business had taught her that there were too many variables for something to not go wrong eventually.

But once, only once, Sophia wished there would be something that went wrong and didn't need her attention. The island was a massive project with dozens of people in positions of authority who could handle these issues. But no, everything needed to go across her desk first like they waited for her to hold their hand and help them with every fucking detail.

At least this one didn't require her to travel halfway across the goddamn world to handle in person.

"Dr. Rogers, is that correct?"

"Yes, Ms. Chavez, and may I say it's a pleasure to speak to you again."

"Yeah, save it." She took a sip of her coffee and let him feel the sting of her retort for a few long seconds. "What's the situation on the island, Doctor? And don't try to honey-coat it for me."

"It's...I think the term is sugarcoat..." He stopped talking immediately when she glared at him. "Or...it could be honey-coat too. I've heard it both ways. The point is... Well, the situation is that our security team picked up three outside operatives who had infiltrated our hiring process. They were identified as working for different governments and not together, so we turned them over to the experimental team as you stipulated."

"I already know that, obviously."

"Well, yes, of course...I mean... Well, the new update is that we now have two other researchers missing, and after searching their personal effects and examining their communications, we discovered they were secretly sharing information with a server off of the island. Security has determined that they were outside operatives as well and their disappearance means they likely found out what happened to the others and legged it."

"Legged it?"

"Ran away."

"Ah. Well, in that case, we'll have to step our plans up. Enhance the security measures and block any communication that isn't overseen directly by the security team. We're bringing the plant in from the Zoo and nothing can go wrong from this point forward. Do you understand me, Dr. Rogers?"

"Of course, ma'am."

"Oh, and make sure to keep our live specimens away from the Zoo area. We can't afford to have the organic materials mixing outside of pristine conditions."

"Understood, Ms. Chavez. Will there be anything else?"

"No, that will be all. Keep me apprised of any new developments."

She closed the connection and rubbed her temples gently. People disappearing and people spying on her made her feel like she was in a Robert Ludlum novel, and not in a good way.

CHAPTER NINETEEN

Taylor narrowed his eyes as he fidgeted with the slice of pizza on his plate. "So what are you guys saying?"

His staff all exchanged looks that seemed a little guilty at first but immediately shifted to uneasy surprise like they had thought they would never be found out. He guessed that any regret was only because he had found out.

Vickie was the first one to speak. "Well, Desk contacted me first to tell me about the odds and ask me if I wanted to put money on you."

He nodded. "So…did you all bet on the fight, then?"

Bobby nodded. "I knew what you would do to those saps. I put you down for a second-round victory."

Elisa frowned. "I didn't know you could do that. Anyway, I simply put you down to win."

"I only had you on the win too," Tanya added. "Honestly, the odds on that were good enough that I didn't want to risk losing money because you decided you wanted to have more fun with the fuckers—or if you were done and wanted to end it early."

The other man nodded. "It was probably a good call, but I made an accurate guess as to how long Taylor would decide to give them leeway for. More importantly, I had a good idea of what the odds would say about him winning in the second round. No one bets on a win in the second round. It's usually the first or the last, but that's not the point."

Taylor nodded again and took a bite of his pizza. "So how much money did you guys win off me?"

Vickie looked around the room and served herself another couple of slices. "I…we all did well—right, guys? We all went all-in on you taking the fuckers down. Or I did, at least."

He raised an eyebrow. "Well, I'm glad you guys didn't tell me any of this before the fight." It seemed prudent to not mention Desk telling him about Vickie's bid. "Adding to the pressure right then and there would have been a terrible, terrible idea."

"Didn't you put money down on you winning too?" Tanya asked. "Isn't that what Desk's call in the middle of the fight was about?"

"I did. Well, technically, Desk put the money down on my behalf. All I did was give her the access she needed to make the bets. So I guess this is a celebration? Is that what all the pizza is for?"

Vickie raised her glass of coke. "I'll take that shit. I have never been one to go out and celebrate at a French restaurant, unlike some I might mention."

"Shut it," he retorted. "Anyway, pizza seems like a good way to bring it all together. Everyone likes pizza."

Elisa raised her hand tentatively. "Uh...I'm not a huge fan of pizza."

The hacker gasped dramatically and covered her mouth. "And here I vouched for you at every turn and helped you in every way possible, and I never knew—would never know—that you're a fucking psychopath? How can you not like pizza?"

"I never said I didn't like it, see?" The woman demonstrated by taking a mouthful of the pepperoni and mushroom before she continued. "I like it fine. It's merely not my favorite food and not the kind I would choose if I was on my own."

Taylor focused on her, a little startled. "Okay, but... what food would you order on your own? Like comfort food for a celebration?"

She tilted her head as she thought about it. "It usually depends on what kind of mood I'm in. Something Greek or maybe Indian if I'm in a fancy mood. If not, my go-to is Chinese and a pint of ice cream."

"Huh. I guess I can respect that."

"I merely didn't get whatever gene makes people love pizza so much."

"It's not about adoration," Vickie interjected. "It's the perfect comfort food. It has tons of cheese, which is necessary, meats or whatever toppings your little heart desires—"

"Not any topping," Bobby interjected. "I draw the line at pineapple or anything sweet."

"I don't mind pineapple on pizza," Tanya mentioned.

It was the mechanic's turn for a double-take, which gave Vickie time to continue with her point.

"Anyway, you get whatever toppings you want, and it's all through a hand-friendly delivery system. And it's the kind of food you don't even need a plate and utensils to eat."

Elisa nodded. "Okay, granted, those are very good points, but it still doesn't appeal to me as much as it seems to appeal to everyone else in the world."

The hacker threw her hands up. "Like I said. Complete and utter psychopath."

Taylor grinned and even Elisa couldn't resist a laugh before they were cut off by the sound of his phone ringing.

"I thought we were supposed to have our phones off," Vickie commented as he pulled it out. "You know, getting into the celebration together without technology."

"It was off," he protested. "Which means there's only one person who could have turned it on to call me. Hey, Desk. How's it going?"

"Put me on speakerphone," the AI demanded. "I have everyone's winnings burning a hole in my virtual pocket."

Taylor put the call on speakerphone so everyone could listen. "Wait, so everyone used you to put their bets in?"

"Of course. They would have run unnecessary risks if they had tried to put money in directly. Chief among those worries would be the fact that Marino could have tracked their betting."

"So you're graduating from being a helpful AI into becoming a bookie?"

"The comparison is interesting but incorrect, overall. Bookmakers—or bookies as they are termed—would take a cut of whatever was bet regardless of the outcome. In my case, my job is to keep my team safe and this was a way to do so as you would all have put bets in anyway. I made sure everyone made the most money possible on the wagering, all while keeping it as anonymous as possible. In a similar manner, I managed to give the secretary Marino sent to collect information on you the details that would elevate the odds as much as possible."

"I...isn't that illegal?" Tanya asked.

"Yeah," Taylor answered.

Desk appeared to not have heard what they were talking about. "All in all, I would say my working to keep a primary operative instrumental to the security of the United States from being stabbed in the back was an absolute success."

"What about Niki and her team?" Taylor asked.

"Jansen and Maxwell placed bets according to my suggestions," she answered. "Niki refused my offer, however, and stated that it would be inappropriate for her to do so while in a romantic relationship with you, despite the fact that your involvement in an unsanctioned fight would have been considered equally inappropriate."

"How would it be inappropriate?"

"Her claim was that her desire to help you would be called into question if she had money riding on it. She wanted you to know when it came out that she was there for you as you, not you as her ticket out of working."

"Huh." He grunted and took another bite of his pizza. "How much did she lose out on winning?"

"I'm not really at liberty to say."

"Desk."

"It might have been somewhere in the region of—"

"Desk!"

"She would have made three point two million dollars."

His eyebrows raised and mirrored the surprise that filled the expressions of everyone else in the room. Even Elisa uttered a low whistle.

"I'm sorry, but she gave up on winning over three million dollars to show that she cared about you?" the ex-reporter asked and took a sip of her drink. "Don't get me wrong, Taylor, you're a piece of rock-hard man-candy, but I would have asked for forgiveness instead of permission in that particular case."

"That's not how Niki is," Vickie explained. "On top of being twenty pounds of crazy badass in a five-pound bag, she's also all about making the statement and fuck the consequences. Even so… Damn, Tay-Tay, don't you think you and her could have started dating a couple of weeks later?"

He shrugged. "If she'd asked me, I would have told her to take the money. I didn't ask her to do that. Desk, would there be any way for me to cover those winnings with my own?"

"Yes."

"Then make it happen. I don't want her to look back and feel any kind of regret for any of the impulsive deci-sions she made for my sake."

Vickie rolled her eyes and gagged. "I can feel the love tonight, and it makes me want to puke."

"Well, you should be able to pay to have that condition treated now, Vickie," Desk explained. "You are quite a wealthy woman in your own right."

"I am?"

"All of you are. Even the one who bid the least could

live in a nice place in a foreign country for fifteen years before you need to give up a cabana boy stipend."

Taylor served himself more of the meat lover's pizza. "Well, I think that means a woman made that bet."

"It sure as fuck wasn't me." Bobby chuckled. "I felt those punches when you pulled them."

"Everyone did well," Desk continued. "Even Jennie got in on the action when I asked her and made a fucking mint."

Startled, Taylor remained silent for a moment, unsure of what to do with that information, and decided to change the subject. "Well, I guess that means McFadden's Mechs doesn't have any more employees? Is everyone up and out on their own now? Starting their own businesses and shit?"

A pall of silence fell over the room as those gathered exchanged looks that told him the thought hadn't crossed their minds.

"Huh," Vickie said finally. "I hadn't even thought of that. I guess between the betting and the money from the heist, I don't need to do anything I don't want to do, at least if I invest my money well enough."

"No, you don't." He looked around the table. "None of you do anymore from the looks of things. You're all free and clear. Let me know if any of you want to leave. There won't be any hard feelings or any attempts on my part to keep you from doing anything you'd like to do with your lives if you're ready to move on. It's food for thought."

He piled a couple more slices of pizza on his plate and retrieved one of the bottles of soda. It seemed like it was his cue to leave since he didn't want any of them to feel uncomfortable when discussing their options which they would be if he was around. None of them said a word as he retreated to his room and left them the opportunity to talk about anything they wanted to.

She wasn't the kind of person to eavesdrop on people having random conversations. Niki did like to people watch, but it was never an excuse to listen in on what was happening in other people's lives.

But stuck in a small coffee shop in DC while she waited for Speare to make time to meet her, there was little else to do. She didn't want to obsess over all the work she had been doing or the different thoughts going through her mind. Right now, she needed a moment of personal silence and these people intruded on it. Instead of getting pissed over it, she simply listened in.

Two young women—successful from the looks of their expensive clothes—were having coffee, probably a pre-arranged date between friends who wanted to talk about their lives without needing to worry about anything else. She could relate.

"I don't know what he's trying to do," the brunette with short hair said. "But I need to know if he's serious. I need to know if he'll be there for me when I need him. Is that so fucking crazy?"

"It's not crazy at all," her companion with long, curly blonde hair bound in a loose ponytail said. "You need to think about what you want too."

Niki couldn't help but agree that it was at least important to not forget one's own needs in a relationship.

"When it comes down to it, he knows me and the work I've put into our relationship. If he'll simply drop everything and move to London when he knows my life, my job, and all my friends are here, I feel we need to have a very serious talk about what kind of future he sees for us."

"Abso-fucking-lutely."

"And in the end, there are a hundred other guys who can give me what he can't, so why should I wait for something I know has no future? There's a fast-track up the ladder if you know what I mean, and it's not in fucking London."

"Right?" The blonde took a moment to sip her coffee before she continued. "I've been going out with Randall for the past...I think three months now, and he's one of those dude-bros, you know? The kind who likes spending his weekends at a...I don't know, a pizza joint, or one of those places that serve all-you-can-eat hot wings and show sports on fifty different screens. But I pulled him in by the ear and I told him that if he wants to get with this"—she pointed to herself—"he has to know that I won't come easy. He needs to show that he's worth it and since then, we've gone to nice places every week and sometimes twice a week, and he's arrived and given me flowers. I know I shouldn't know this, but he's even bought jewelry for our four-month anniversary celebration."

"I think it's only an anniversary once every year."

"Who cares?"

Niki tuned the conversation out as they began to discuss whether or not it was acceptable to call anything other than a yearly celebration an anniversary. She didn't need to hear more. Taylor was something like the dude-bros, and he had never tried to hide who or what he was from her. And she had no intention to try to get him to change who he was simply because it made her feel better. He had his flaws—and she did too—but it wasn't appropriate to demand something else that way.

It made her feel a little sick. She wouldn't have stood for any man demanding that from her, so why would she try to get it from someone else? It didn't feel right. She wouldn't fall for some romantic sap wearing a McFadden suit, after all.

Her phone buzzed and Niki pushed quickly to her feet and left cash to pay for her bill as well as a generous tip before she headed outside.

Her bodyguards were there and had both ordered coffees—Maxwell had requested a sandwich besides—and they enjoyed the cooler air of the capital while they looked at their phones once their coffees and food were finished.

"It's time to have a chat with Mr. Speare," she announced and they stood as well and followed her to the SUV.

CHAPTER TWENTY

As much as she liked working for the DOD, there were a few elements of it she never looked forward to. One of those was the sheer amount of security checks she had come to expect every time she had to step into the Pentagon. It didn't happen often enough for it to be a real problem, but it was the kind of nuisance she dreaded every time she needed to enter the building to report to her direct superior.

The young men with perfectly arranged uniforms were already waiting for her and looked a little apologetic about the process. There were reasons for all the security protocols, but even they knew it was a pain to enforce for everyone who came in.

"Hold that thought, soldier," said a voice from behind her. Niki turned quickly to where Speare, looking a little red in the face, jogged to where she was about to start her security clearance process.

"Mr. Speare," she said and stepped away from the metal detector. "I thought we were meeting at your office."

"Well, my wife has been getting on my case about spending less time on my *keister*. Something about wanting me around for the long haul and not dying of a heart attack or something. Anyway, I thought it might be a good idea for us to have our meeting while taking a walk. What do you say?"

Niki looked at the soldiers who were unsure of what to do and shrugged. "I...sure. I don't see why not."

"Don't worry. There will be security personnel following us to make sure no one tries to listen in on what we're saying. Shall we?"

She inclined her head and fell into step beside the man as they headed away from the massive building and out onto the streets beyond to one of the nearby parks.

"Was there anything in particular you wanted to talk to me about, Mr. Spear?"

He shrugged, still a little out of breath. "Not really. Your results have been fun to watch. You already know your success rate and your ability to work with others is more than enough to make us want to have you around for the long haul. Even Reardon had nothing but glowing words to say about you."

"Really? I was under the impression he didn't like me."

"I have no idea how he feels about you personally but professionally, his recommendation brought a smile to my face. I believe his exact words were 'the first time I'd seen a paper-pusher light a stick of dynamite, stick it in a monster's ass, and flip it off while it blew.' He also said that if any member of the team wanted to jump on board with his team to let him know."

"Wow. Well, I guess I will pass the word along. And I certainly appreciate the sentiment and the terminology."

Speare smirked. "I thought you might. Of course, I have a feeling you didn't ask for this meeting because you were interested in hearing what everyone around me has to say about you, Agent Banks. Feel free to see this as an invitation to speak your mind without any of the customary cameras and microphones around us."

"Are you saying there aren't any microphones or cameras on us?"

"No, merely not the usual ones."

That drew a smirk from her, but she refused to let it distract her. "The reason I wanted to talk to you is kind of personal and something that's weighed on my mind lately more than before. I appreciate the fact that working for the DOD gives me far more leeway than my work for the FBI, but even so, it's... The politics has begun to bother me—the red tape and the knowledge that anything I do at any point in time could possibly cause an international incident. That type of thing."

He nodded. "Believe me, nothing pisses me off more than the daily dick-measuring contests people call politics around here, and I'm sure you're aware that it's changing for the worse. Election year means more keen eyes looking into everything we do, and that means more dick-measuring and more people involved, which always means more red tape."

"Well, I have to say that if anyone ever feels the need to start one of those contests with me, I'll point out that they probably started with the world's cruelest handicap." Niki slowed to let the man catch up with her. "But that's neither here nor there."

"Nor, indeed, is the fact that you started many of those competitions yourself—not that I give a shit one way or the other."

"Right."

Speare motioned for them to take a seat on a park bench.

"I thought you said your wife wanted you to have a more active lifestyle."

"Well, she'll have to settle for me getting more fresh air. Anyway, I have the distinct feeling that this conversation is leading up to a letter of resignation." He sat and looked at her through his glasses. "I'd hate to see you go, Banks."

Niki sat beside him. "And I'd hate to leave. My first thought about the process was how the teams would be able to handle the situation in my absence. I'm not saying they can't do it without me. Or…no…. I guess my question is whether you think my dropping out of the program would have any negative effects on the operation we're running here."

"Negative? Sure. We put considerable work into finding someone like you for the job, and it took even more work to get you on board as I'm sure you remember."

"You sold my little trip to Italy out to the FBI to get me fired, as I recall."

"Yes, well, I assumed you wouldn't mind that."

"It was a shitty move to make, Speare. You could have simply sent me a job offer."

He shrugged. "I needed it to be the proverbial offer you couldn't refuse."

"Fair enough."

"Back to your question, though. Yes, I think the people I already have would be able to step into your shoes. Maybe not as effectively, but they'd get the job done until we find someone with talents similar to yours."

She nodded. "That's good. I feel like the work we're doing here is important so I wouldn't leave if it meant that would be severely compromised."

"With that in mind, we will need someone to take your position over immediately to keep the operation running until we find the perfect fit—or as close to perfect as possible. My immediate thought would be Mr. or Mrs. Outside Hire, but if you have any recommendations, I'll take them into consideration."

Niki had expected the question and already had her response ready. "I think Jansen should take over. I've relied on him fairly heavily to gather intelligence and he has the right skills, fortitude, and tenacity for the job. On top of that, I've made sure he and Maxwell both have training and experience with the combat suits should he ever be in a position where a quick response time would be the difference between life and death. It was a real pleasure working with them."

Speare looked directly ahead for a few long seconds. "So, is this your final decision? You of all people should know there's no coming back from something like this. There's no second-guessing this kind of decision."

"I've put considerable thought into it, sir. I need to go into something I'm a little better suited for—something that would make me happy if that doesn't sound too cliché." She stared into the distance as well. "Maybe something like consulting."

He smirked and turned to look at her. "Maybe?"

"I won't lie, I have my eye on a job at one company in particular, but I need to see if they're interested in hiring someone like me." She looked the man next to her dead in the eye. "I haven't talked to the owner about it yet."

"So you're making this decision without knowing whether or not something is waiting for you beyond your work with the DOD?"

"I believe the term for something like that is a leap of faith, sir. And at least this time, I'm not being blindsided by getting fired so someone else can hire me without the option of my being able to say no."

Her boss nodded. "I deserved that, I guess. Not to be pedantic or anything but this time, you're quitting to give a certain company owner no choice but to bring you on board with his little band of misfits."

"I'll be all right," Niki assured him. "If worse comes to worst, I already have the skills to head into the actual Zoo and make money that way."

Speare stared at her for a moment before he smirked. "I know you're joking but a small part of me would pay to see that. Even so, I'd appreciate it if you came to me before you decided to quite literally throw your life away like that."

"I'll do that," she answered, unable to contain a soft laugh. "I do appreciate that, through all this, you have kept your end of the bargain. And I honestly do think Jansen is a fantastic guy and a great fit for a leadership role."

"Don't say that like it's some kind of goodbye, Banks." He had an odd twinkle in his eye as he turned his attention to the park in front of him. "I have a distinct feeling that you and I will work together again sometime in the future. And I'm paid a literal shit-ton of money because of how accurate those feelings are. You never know when I might need someone to shove a .45 up some well-connected asshole and not be afraid to pull the trigger."

"Hell, for that kind of work, I might consider doing it for free. I wouldn't consider it for long, mind you, but I'd have to pause and think about it."

He laughed and pushed from his seat. "I look forward to working with you again in the future, Banks. For now, though, I'm afraid I have a whole pile of paperwork I need to find someone else to do. I have a feeling we'll see each other again soon. Take care, Banks."

Niki smirked and waved carelessly. "You keep hoping and dreaming and we'll see if it comes true."

Speare tapped his nose before he walked in the direction they'd come and for a moment, she couldn't help the feeling that she needed to be somewhere, go someplace, or do something.

In that moment, she realized she didn't have anywhere to go and nothing that needed her immediate attention. She was, for all intents and purposes, a free woman.

"How fucking weird is that?" she muttered under her breath and finally stood. "I wonder if this is how Jennie felt. Or still feels."

It wasn't a long walk to where the SUV had been parked. Speare had made it clear that the meeting didn't require either of her bodyguards and essentially gave the two men the rest of the day off. They had taken advantage of the opportunity.

She wondered if she should have thanked them for at least leaving her a means of transport so she didn't have to resort to a taxi.

As she climbed in, she wasn't sure where she would drive to. More to the point, she had no idea where she wanted to go. Maybe she'd meet Jansen and Maxwell later but for the moment, there was only one person she wanted to talk to. And, coincidentally, he was the one she needed to have a conversation with if she wanted to make any immediate decisions about her future. Niki quickly dialed a number she had already committed to memory.

"So, if I'm your spotter, does that mean your life is in my hands?" Vickie asked and looked at him.

Taylor scowled. "Well, yes, but it doesn't make me feel any safer when you say it outright like that. Keep an eye on how I'm doing and if you see me lagging in one of my reps, do what you can to help me get the weights up and put the bar on the hook."

"Because if I don't, you would die a slow and painful death under the weights you thought you could lift repeatedly, which might be a very solid representation of your ego?"

He narrowed his eyes. "You know, maybe I can call Bobby to help me."

"No, no, no, I'll be good, I promise. I'm only joking."

"Joking with my life."

"If you can do it, why can't I?"

"Because it's my life to joke with."

Before Taylor was able to start on his reps, his phone rang.

"Do you think you should get that?" Vickie asked.

"It'll give you some time to rethink your bedside manner as a spotter," he countered, picked the phone up, and checked the caller ID again to make sure he wasn't seeing things. It was a little early for Niki to call him for a job. Then again, since they were officially dating, maybe she simply wanted a quick chat or something like people who were dating did sometimes.

"Who is it?" Vickie asked.

"It's your cousin."

"Do you think it's because we have more work to do, monsters to kill, and that type of shit?"

"I won't know until I answer." He pressed the accept call button. "Hey…you."

"That was super-awkward," Niki replied by way of greeting. "Do you want to try that again?"

"I wanted to try something new, all things considered. A regular greeting didn't feel right. Anyway, what's up? I didn't think we would hear from you in a while. Is something the matter?"

"Not…well, not really. Maybe. I…uh, had a question for you."

"You'd better decide whether you have a question for me and soon too."

"Don't be an asshole. I need to ask you something. It's… Well, I'm not sure how to do this. I guess the question is… do you have any openings for a new employee?"

Taylor narrowed his eyes. "Do you know?"

"Know what?"

"You didn't hear?"

"No, and if you don't tell me soon, I'll travel to Vegas with the sole intention of strangling the truth out of you."

He grinned. "Well, I suppose that's one way to get your hands on me."

Vickie mock-gagged behind him and he picked his towel up and threw it at her. Even with his prodigious strength, it didn't fly that far and he opted instead to flip her off until she decided to go get some water.

"Okay, but you go first. Are you suddenly in need of new employees?"

"Maybe. Are you offering your services?"

Niki sighed. "Fine, I'll tell you. I maybe...uh...okay, most definitely find myself currently out of a job. That's because I quit my last one and I don't have any others on the horizon yet. I thought I would float you an offer since I possess a very particular set of skills that I've acquired over a long career."

"I have the distinct impression that you're about to come and kill me to save Vickie for some reason."

"Never mind that. My point is that yours is probably the only company this side of the Atlantic that would be able to make use of those skills, hence the offer."

"But I thought... What happened at the DOD? Did you piss the wrong people off?"

"Didn't you hear me? I quit." Niki sounded oddly vulnerable and that made her sound annoyed and angry too. "Anyway, I have a little saved in the bank, so it's not like I'm destitute or anything, but I don't want to dig into my savings until another job comes along in the private sector. I guess Jennie could probably find something for me too, but I thought I would make you an offer first to see if I couldn't make a living off your scrawny ass."

"That's a hard, muscular ass, and I think you know that."

"Oh, fucking— Gag!" Vickie shouted from the water fountain.

"Fuck off!" Taylor shouted in response.

"Is that Vickie?" Niki asked.

"Yeah, your cousin and I were in the middle of trying to decide if she was any good at spotting me in a workout and she was supposed to give us some privacy while we talked. It seemed our banter annoyed her so much that she had to weigh in."

She sighed. "I'll deal with her later."

"Does that mean you guys are coming back to Vegas?"

"Not us guys. Only me. I quit, remember?"

"Yeah, and I don't think we discussed the whole why-factor of this quitting business."

"You're not tracking well in this conversation, are you?"

Taylor scowled. "I only...hold on, give me a second. I'll put you on hold." He muted her and turned his attention to Vickie. "Hey, how do I add Desk to this call?"

"I thought I was supposed to be busy fucking off."

"Well, you can get busy doing something else—hold on..." His phone suddenly buzzed with Desk's number asking to be added to the call. "Speak of the devil. Never mind."

"So should I go back to fucking off?"

He sighed. "I'm sorry, I shouldn't have snapped at you. I'll...buy you an ice cream or something."

"Make it a chocolate sundae and you have yourself a deal."

"Right. It sounds good." He punched the button to add Desk to the call. "Desk, nice of you to join us."

"My non-physical ears were burning. How can I help you?"

"Would you care to explain why the hell Niki still thinks she needs a job?"

"No."

"Well, you'll have to do it anyway. I thought I told you to move that three-point-two million into her savings account."

"Wait, what?" Niki asked. "What three-point-two million?"

"The amount you would have won if you'd bet on the fight instead of having a stick surgically implanted in your ass. Desk fessed up about how you wouldn't bet on me because you felt it would make our relationship transactional somehow or...something."

She took a deep breath. "Desk, I thought I was very specific with you about what I would do to your servers if you told him. I was very explicit about it too."

"Well, yes, but given that you do not have access to the DOD server nor the FBI servers, I determined your threats to be rather ineffectual," the AI explained. "Besides, you are well aware that Taylor's strength is my weakness."

"You're a motherfucking AI!" she roared. "You don't have any weaknesses with regard to Taylor!"

"Well, we both know that's not true." Desk suddenly took on a motherly tone. "Anyway, he told me to wire you the amount you would have won had you placed the bet I suggested, and I couldn't say no to that face."

"I feel like I should be creeped out by that," Taylor muttered.

"Well, there's no fucking way in hell that I'll take his money," Niki stated firmly. "I don't care what you feel like you have to prove to me, but—"

"For the love of Einstein," the AI cut in, her tone exasperated. "Would the two of you please check your accounts? I anticipated this type of moral quandary between you and I found a solution I think you will both find most acceptable."

Taylor lowered his phone to check on his account balance. "I—hold on...wait. You didn't wire her anything. There's no deduction from my account for a transaction that large."

He paused and assumed Niki was doing the same thing.

"Holy fuckballs, that's a gazillion zeroes," she exclaimed finally. "Huh. Well, I guess I understand why you seemed confused about me needing a job. But wait—if it didn't come from his account, where did it come from? And please don't tell me you stole it."

"Only as far as Taylor's winning was such a sure bet that it felt like robbery," Desk replied. "When he gave me carte blanche on his account to bet as I saw fit, I thought it would be the perfect opportunity to fill in for the bets Niki would have made. Therefore, I took a good amount from his account and bet it in her name, and when the winnings were returned, I transferred the amount that was put down into his account with his winnings, which left Niki only with the difference. This way, everyone is much richer than when they started. It's quite ingenious if I do say so myself."

"Oh." Taylor grunted and considered what she'd said carefully. "Okay, I'm sorry if I'm slow on this, but I'm simply making sure here. You're saying the money is what Niki would have won if she placed a bet. Her bet was taken from my account and the money was returned like it had never gone in the first place?"

"That plus some people at your bank freaked out over the sudden massive transactions taking place. But don't worry. I smoothed that out from their end so you didn't have to hear it," Desk explained slowly and carefully.

"Good...job?" Niki said but didn't sound very sure of herself. "I guess I'm a multi-millionaire now. Wow, that sounds a little weird to say out loud."

"I guess we should go out to celebrate," Taylor suggested. "You can pay this time since you can afford it now."

She laughed. "Yeah, I guess I can, can't I? Hold up, you still haven't explained why you might need extra hands on deck."

"Oh, right. Well, as it turned out, Desk applied her wiles to everyone and convinced them all to bet on me in large enough amounts that their winnings are...about as substantial as yours. It's enough that they all needed to do some thinking about what they want to do with the rest of their lives so I gave them time off to figure it out, think it through, and come back to me with a solid answer."

"So you do need the help, I guess," Niki commented.

"Sure. Well, maybe. I guess. And definitely."

"Explain."

"Well, I had an idea. I could let Bobby buy most of me out of McFadden's Mechs so he and Tanya could become the de facto owners while I stay on as a silent partner. They would take over the day-to-day running of the company with Elisa and maybe hire outside help too."

"And what will you do with the suddenly massive amounts of free time you'll have?"

"Well, I thought about setting up a sister company called McFadden's Mercs."

"Nooo. It's a horrible name."

"It's a working title."

Niki paused for a few seconds and thought about what he had told her. "So what you're saying is that you'd have an opening for someone who's able to run a suit of power armor effectively?"

"I think you talked about your particular set of skills a little while ago? It's a dangerous job, though."

"And I guess it might help if the pilot is a little crazy?"

He could almost hear the smile in her voice. "Sure. So does that mean you're interested?"

"I'll let you know when I get to Vegas."

Niki stared at her phone for almost a full minute after Taylor hung up with a stupid smile playing across her lips. She had so many emotions to process in such a short amount of time, but she would have to start sometime. And she felt like it was a good idea to start by having a chat with Jansen and Maxwell about her sudden change in fortunes. Quite literally.

She put the SUV into gear but made sure to dial Desk's number and connect her phone to the car's Bluetooth so she could speak while driving.

"How may I help you, Niki?"

"Well, first of all, I wanted to say that I never meant what I said about what I would do to your servers," she explained. "Even though it doesn't come close to you pulling this stunt behind my back."

"I honestly hoped that the sudden addition to your bank account would soften your attitude toward me."

"I won't lie, it certainly helps," Niki admitted. "But it was still shitty for you to go behind my back like that."

"I do understand, but at the same time, my purpose of keeping Jennie, her family, and those she cares about safe are better performed if those on that list are in a financially stable place. As such and because you didn't allow me to perform that task for personal reasons, I thought it would be best if it was a gesture from Taylor and failing that, a gesture on my part."

"Your protection is appreciated, of course," she muttered. "But I'm a little worried that my sister designed you too well."

"That sounded suspiciously like a compliment."

"Don't take it as one yet. I'm still furious with you. Maybe in about fifteen minutes. Can you tell me where I can find Jansen and Maxwell?"

"They are at the same Italian restaurant you always go to when you come to Washington."

She smiled. "Thanks, Desk. I'll talk to you later."

CHAPTER TWENTY-ONE

S he entered the restaurant and the hint of familiarity was welcoming, but there was something different about it this time. Maybe it was because she looked at it through the eyes of a financially free woman.

Still, the sight of her two now ex-bodyguards waiting for her at one of the tables brought a smile to her face. They returned it cheerfully when they noticed her.

As she approached, the two men stood from their seats and clapped slowly. There weren't enough patrons in the restaurant to stop them from making a scene and she wasn't in the mood to stop them herself.

"I take it you guys heard already?" she asked once she was close enough.

Jansen didn't answer immediately and instead, wrapped her in a tight, warm hug.

"I'll take that as a yes," she commented as Maxwell came in for a hug as well. The larger man's was considerably tighter, and she sucked in a deep gulp of air when he pulled back.

"Not only have we heard but we were also told that our previous superior put in a seriously good recommendation for us," the smaller man explained and gestured for her to join them at their table. "I was offered the top position on a new project, starting immediately. Maxwell is going to transfer with me."

Niki narrowed her eyes. "A new project? You guys won't work the cryptid taskforce anymore?"

Jansen shook his head. "Speare said that while the cryptid taskforce you headed up was an unmitigated success, its purpose has been absorbed by other teams like Reardon's so our skills would be better used in another project. It's one that would have a greater focus on international cooperation as well as dealing with the three-letter agencies to use their intelligence networks to keep track of cryptid outbreaks worldwide. In addition, it could hire consultant teams for jobs we don't necessarily want directly connected to the US government when push comes to shove."

She leaned a little closer as the waiter came to take their order. "So you're telling me you two have already been tasked to look for teams that might help with this task force you'll head up?"

"Damn right!" Maxwell interjected and indicated to the waiter to deliver three beers as quickly as possible. "We're looking for a team that might or might not be staffed with a couple of crazy motherfuckers who don't take shit from anyone, especially politicians."

"Or even cryptids, for that matter," his partner added as the waiter rushed back with three beer mugs on a tray. "They would have to have combat experience between the two of them, and we would have to believe they would be willing to do whatever it takes to get the job done."

"Them having top-of-the-line gear would be a plus," the other man added. "Skills to operate the suits that are used to kill cryptids would also help to be hired, I think."

"No gear and fighting skills would work for us too," Jansen finished.

"Wow, you guys look like you rehearsed that little performance." Niki grinned and took a sip of her beer.

"That might have been most of what we did after Speare hung up," he admitted.

She smiled and shook her head. "Honestly, I don't know what to say."

"How about 'what's the job, Trond?'" he suggested.

"Oh, and a name that's better than McFadden's Mercs would be a good idea too," Maxwell stated with a chuckle.

Niki opened her mouth, then snapped it shut. "You guys have talked to Desk, haven't you?"

He looked shocked but even he thought it was a little too theatrical and dropped the act quickly. "What gave us away?"

"Well, not even his team knows about McFadden's Mercs or whatever the fuck we call it becoming a formal business. Taylor and I haven't finalized the details yet, so...yeah."

"Shit, I thought we played it a little too cute." Jansen growled in irritation and nudged his partner in the shoulder.

"Wait, were you guys involved in the betting scheme Desk cooked up too?"

The two men exchanged a quick look and nodded.

"So you two are millionaires."

Another look was followed by another nod.

"Although in fairness," Jansen added, "we possess intelligence that says you've come into a decent amount of money yourself."

"Fucking—I'll tear that AI's servers out and flush them in bus station toilets."

"With that said..." Maxwell paused to take a sip of his beer before he continued. "I guess the question that needs asking is if you'll spend time enjoying the good life or if you'll jump into this whole consultant business. And we're aware that you might need time to think about it, so we're not looking for a decision now."

"Soon, though," the other man said. "We'll let you know about a timeline once we get started on the task force."

"We have a running bet on what you'll finally choose." The large man drained his mug and gestured for a refill from the waiter.

"Oh? What kind of odds are we looking at?"

"I can't tell you that," Jansen said quickly. "I don't want to influence you one way or the other. It's for petty cash anyway—well, what we consider to be petty cash these days."

Niki smirked and accepted the offer of a refill of her beer. "Wow, so you guys will be the obnoxious type of rich people? Betting on the lives of people you consider to be your inferiors?"

"Hey, you know what they say." He sipped his beer and turned down the refill offer. "Wealth doesn't change anything about you. It merely amplifies who you were already."

"Yeah, I guess that tracks," Niki agreed. "Well, I still need to talk to Taylor about this, but I think I can say with some certainty that the services of McFadden and Banks, Consultants for Hire are available. My negotiator will be in touch with you shortly once my partner and I are agreed on the terms of our availability."

A few seconds ticked past before Maxwell extended his hand toward his partner, who grudgingly handed him a twenty-dollar bill.

"Fuck," Jansen muttered.

"Well, then." She couldn't help a small grin at the man's pout. "I suggest we get our orders in, eat and get on the plane to Vegas. You guys will have to fly me there since all our suits are still on that fucking plane and I guess you are in charge of it now?"

"We sure are," Jansen confirmed and held his hand up to call the waiter for their order. "And if you think you're the only one heading to Vegas, you're fucking insane."

"Yeah," Maxwell agreed. "We won't miss this whole conversation between you and Taylor for all the money in the world."

"You know that what we'll do won't be suitable for a live audience, right?" Niki commented as the waiter approached with their menus.

"Then we'll definitely not miss it for all the money in the—fuck!"

The man rubbed his shoulder and she shook her fist.

"Anyway," Jansen changed the subject while he studied the menu once it was placed in front of him. "Who'll be your negotiator?"

"Desk, of course. She still has to make up for the stunt she pulled."

"You mean making you rich? That stunt?"

"Making me rich behind my back." She raised a finger for emphasis. "That's the important part."

"Honestly, I'd stick with the part where she made you over three million dollars without you needing to lift a finger."

Niki settled into her seat, strapped herself in, and looked around the cabin. Even the plane looked a little different, although she wasn't sure how. Maybe it was different because she was different. That felt like some deep shit—the kind that only came to her after a full Italian meal topped with a heavy, chocolate-filled dessert and more mugs of beer than she had been able to count.

They had to leave their vehicles and take a cab to the airstrip outside of the city limits so they wouldn't get a ticket on their way.

"You know," she said and heard a hint of a slur in her voice. "You're the boss on this plane now. You'll have to stay connected and keep your eye on the stupid shit people do in this country. Or around the world now, right?"

"Who, me?" Maxwell asked.

"Both of you if you are partners on this little endeavor, right?"

"Yep," Jansen replied and strapped himself in as well.

"In the meantime, I'm merely a lowly consultant," she continued and leaned back in her seat. "That's far less responsibility. I can tune out the world for a couple of hours and catch those Z's that have eluded me. I need some fucking sleep."

"I guess them's the perks of not being in charge anymore," the man muttered as the plane began to taxi toward the runway. "Maybe that's why Taylor dropped out of being employed by the government and elected to be in the private sector. There sure as fuck is more money in it. You know that guy pulled in more money consulting than I do as a full-time employee?"

"Well, he put himself in a riskier position more often than the two of you," Niki reminded him. "Besides, we paid for all the experience he had from the Zoo. I think he earned that, don't you? Unless either of you would like to head into that fucking place on an army salary."

"Good...good point," Jansen conceded as the engines whined louder and the aircraft accelerated. "I guess that's the kind of money you'll pull in now too."

Niki didn't answer. Her eyes had already closed as they ascended steadily. After the big meal and drinks, she felt drowsy and with nothing else to do, sleep seemed the best option to pass the time.

Even so, when Jansen nudged her awake to restore her seat into the upright position for landing, she still felt like she could use another couple of hours of sleep. She yawned as they descended to the landing strip.

At least the flight felt shorter if she slept through it. Night was falling outside, and she could see the brilliant colors of the Strip below before they touched lightly.

As the plane headed toward the hangar, she noticed Liz

parked outside, which meant Taylor would be waiting for her when she debarked.

Sure enough, the massive redhead stood outside and leaned against his truck with his arms folded in front of his chest. She hurried out of the plane and walked quickly to him.

"What's cookin', good lookin'?" he asked as she approached.

She shook her head. "Still awkward."

"Noted. I'll keep working on it."

Niki moved closer and he pulled her in, his powerful hands trapping her as his lips captured hers for a few seconds that lasted forever and yet at the same time, not long enough.

"You know..." Her voice was a little breathless once he broke the kiss, and an idiotic smile played across her lips. "A girl might be tempted to swoon from that kind of...manhandling."

"Is that so?"

"Sure." She patted him lightly on the chest before she looked to where her ex-teammates were already moving to the vehicle that had been provided for them. "Where will you guys be staying?"

"The Aria," Jansen announced. "We like it there and now, we can afford it on our dollar, although I'll certainly try to pass it off as business expenses to the DOD."

"Right," she whispered and turned her attention to the man in front of her. "How about us? I should mention that while I have every intention of ripping your clothes off, I'm not crazy about doing it at that strip mall you call home.

You should think about finding a place of your own now that you can afford it."

He nodded. "A topic for another time. For now, though, I reserved us a room at the Aria too. I trust that will be more acceptable for milady's elevated tastes?"

Niki smirked and caught the collar of his shirt. She could feel the heat radiating from his skin beneath. "Yeah, yeah, what the fuck ever. Let's make sure there are reinforcements on the bed they gave us. They'll need it."

"Your chariot awaits." Taylor mock-bowed and gestured toward Liz. She climbed quickly into the shotgun seat and he joined her in the driver's side. "Is it awkward for me to say that I missed you?"

"No, that's more like it, cowboy. Now, let's get riding."

It was a short drive and yet way too long. The check-in clerk was already waiting for them, having clearly been told there was a little something extra in it for him if he fast-tracked the process.

She honestly didn't care. Once the door shut behind the bellboy, she yanked Taylor by the collar of his shirt again, this time more aggressively, and the fabric strained.

"I missed you too, Taylor," she whispered against the bare skin of his neck. "And I'm about to show you how much."

CHAPTER TWENTY-TWO

No light on her face indicated that morning had arrived, but the overwhelming feeling that she needed to get up and do something had been a part of her body for as long as she could remember. It was almost like sleeping was on borrowed time that she needed to make up for when she finally got around to it.

Another feeling conflicted with her learned behavior this time. She didn't have anything to do when she got up and she could simply chill the fuck out for the rest of the day.

The internal fight eventually led to her staring at the ceiling of the hotel room instead of sleeping. Even though she didn't have anything to do, there was no point in staying in bed and doing nothing. It didn't work for her.

Besides, movement outside the bedroom had begun to draw her attention.

Niki straightened on the bed and felt for where her clothes had landed in the rush to get undressed the night before. It had all been something of a blur. Even the shower after was a haze. She had brought luggage with her, she reminded herself, as she always did while traveling.

"Holy shit, there's so much for me to do," she muttered and scrambled out of the bed. Standing quickly proved to be a mistake and the ache between her thighs made her regret it immediately. She groaned and clutched the bedside table to keep herself on her feet until she acclimated to the situation and tried to walk again.

It was still a little difficult to not do so like a cowboy in the movies, but after a few steps, she was able to push into something resembling normal.

A quick visit to the bathroom ended with her deciding to stick to one of the soft robes the hotel provided and only resort to clothes if she needed to leave the room. For the moment, she had every intention to take a day or so off before she returned to a life of putting herself in danger for the benefit of others.

She narrowed her eyes when she heard what sounded like voices from the living area of the hotel room. At first, she only heard Taylor's voice and planned to mock him for talking to himself, but it quickly became apparent that other people were present for the conversation.

Either that or he did the voices himself. One sounded suspiciously like her cousin, which she honestly wouldn't have put past him.

Niki stepped tentatively out of the room. Taylor was dressed and shared a room-service breakfast with Vickie and Bungees. She was about to ask them what they were doing when she looked at her watch.

"Holy shit—eleven in the morning?" she asked and followed it with a yawn large enough to trigger a twinge in her jaw. Although maybe that pain came from another source too. "Why the hell did you let me sleep in that late?"

Taylor raised an eyebrow at the accusation. "Well, if the alert from the front desk that we had visitors didn't wake you, I decided not to try. I did have some concerns for my health, you know."

"He has a point," Vickie commented, her mouth half-full of bacon. "I thought I would be safe since I'm your cousin and everything, but this was mostly to get back at Taylor for waking me at all times of the day or night for my help."

She shook her head and sat on the only seat that was still open as she fought another yawn. "Well, it was a wise choice, I guess, if self-preservation was the idea. I'm not sure what time we got to sleep, but I might have needed that rest even though I slept like a fucking rock on the flight here."

"It could be that you have a case of the joblessness blues," Bobby pointed out and popped a grape into his mouth. "Oh, right. Desk told me you quit your job at the DOD and are looking for work now. And that you don't need to get yourself a job, especially if you invest the money you made wisely."

"I didn't make that money," she protested. She grimaced, still not up to eating a full meal yet. Hints of being hungover the day before lingered, and she had a feeling it would be a long day if that continued to plague her for the remainder. Gone were the days when she could go six beers in and order shots while still being perfectly fine the next morning.

Taylor noticed it, poured her a glass of water quickly, and slid it across the table.

"Well, yeah," Bobby muttered. "Desk talked about that too."

Niki scowled. "Jennie will have to write privacy software for that AI. Otherwise, she'll spill my secrets all over the goddamn place and I'll be left with fucking nothing about my own life that's private."

"Well, that ship may have sailed already." Vickie looked around with a guilty expression on her face and covered it hastily with a mug of coffee. "But in our defense, we only do it because we care."

"We?"

"Me and Jennie. And Desk by association, I guess."

Her expression unimpressed, Niki shook her head. "You guys need to mind your own business."

"But minding your business is so much more interesting!" The hacker ducked under the bagel her cousin flung at her.

They were interrupted by a knock at the door.

"You shouldn't have done that." The younger woman laughed. "The hotel doesn't take kindly to you wasting their food!"

"It's not that," she retorted. "I think, anyway. Who could it be?"

"If we had any more outside guests arriving, they would have called from the front desk first," Taylor asserted. "So either it's the hotel staff here to punish you for wasting food, or another hotel guest has come to visit."

He moved to the door, where a small screen illuminated to reveal who stood outside. Her fears were unfounded when she realized it was Maxwell and Jansen.

"I should probably get dressed if we'll host the whole

group," she muttered and traced her fingers longingly over the soft, comfortable robe she had on.

"I don't mind the view." Taylor winked. "But if you need to get dressed, I guess I'll have to content myself with memories of it."

"Get a room, you guys," Vickie complained.

"We did," he snapped in response, unlocked the door, and motioned for the two men to join them.

"Are you guys still having breakfast?" Jansen asked.

"We had a late start to the morning," Taylor explained.

"Yeah, we can see that," Maxwell muttered and looked around. Niki's mouth went dry when she realized her clothes were still where they had tossed them the night before.

She moved quickly to gather them and motioned furiously for Taylor to join her in the bedroom, where she closed the door behind them.

"What?" he asked.

"You couldn't have fucking cleaned before you invited half the party to our hotel room?" she demanded and punched him in the chest hard enough to feel the impact all the way up her arm. It still felt worth it, though, as he rubbed the spot gingerly. Vague memories of the night before told her there would be scratches and maybe a few bruises up and down his chest and shoulders, which left him a little tender in places. "Sorry."

"It's worth it." He smiled and winked. "And I didn't invite them in. Or...well, I didn't invite them. They simply arrived. I didn't have time to clean up before they got there, and I didn't think to afterward. I'm...sorry."

Niki scowled but found that staying furious at him was

more difficult, especially as he didn't make excuses or jokes. The guy had genuinely apologized. How could she stay mad after that?"

"Never mind. It's fine," she mumbled and looked through her clothes. "I…wait, where's my bra?"

He paused and thought about it for a moment. "If memory serves, I may have gotten frustrated with trying to undo the clasp in the back and I ripped it off and used it…uh, during."

She looked where he indicated and grimaced at the piece of clothing that adorned the head of the bed. "I… right. Last night was something of a haze, wasn't it?"

"A nice one, though. So, will you get dressed?"

"Yeah…wait. Why?"

"I thought I might stay and watch."

She punched him in the chest again but softer this time. "Ass. Get out there and entertain our guests before we get…sidetracked."

"Good call." He winked again and slipped out of the room as Niki tracked down her suitcases. She wasn't dressing to impress anymore, so a pair of jeans and a t-shirt was all she pulled on before she returned to where almost the full group was assembled. For a brief moment, she wondered what prevented Elisa and Tanya from joining them but didn't want to give voice to the sentiment. Maybe they needed to get work done at the strip mall.

Bobby and Taylor focused on a couple of forms they were working through when she rejoined them, sat next to Taylor, and felt the breakfast foods call to her a little.

"Is that what I think it is?" she asked and chose a piece of bacon.

"Yeah," Taylor answered. "I'm transferring most of the ownership of McFadden Mechs—"

"Which will be Zhang and Novak Power Armor Repair and Restoration," Bobby interjected.

"Sure. Anyway, I'm transferring most of the ownership to them while I stay on as a silent partner. Everything will probably be the same, otherwise. The building is still in my name and I'll still live upstairs, but Bobby and Tanya will take the lion's share of the profits from the mech business. Elisa will stay on with them, and Vickie and I will branch out."

"And me too," Niki corrected and poked his shoulder.

"Oh...well, I never had an answer from you on whether or not you would be a part of McFadden's Mercs." Taylor looked at her, unsure if he had made some kind of relationship mistake.

"We're not married to the name," Vickie pointed out quickly.

"Amen to that," Niki stated quickly. "I've already worked up the McFadden and Banks Consultancy firm. MBC for short."

Taylor narrowed his eyes. "Uh, it doesn't really—"

"And I assumed you wouldn't give me any problems with the name since I brought in our first business." She gestured to Maxwell and Jansen. "They'll head up a task force that will tackle international cryptid problems, and they need professionals on call to deal with any situations that might come up."

"I...okay," Taylor started to protest, but he shut himself down and shook his head. "We'll have to talk about this whole 'assumed' business as well as taking work on before you're a part of the team."

Vickie nudged his shoulder. "Come on, don't be shitty. She was always a part of the team. You're merely whining for the sake of it."

"True, but my point still stands."

Niki nodded and leaned forward to kiss his cheek. "Sure it does."

"On that note, we should probably go over what is likely to be our first job on this front." Jansen connected his tablet to the closest tv for them to see everything he was looking at. "It's not the most encouraging sign that these people bought an entire fucking island to work from, and it only gets worse from there."

"Off the coast of Algeria," Taylor noted and read what was on the screen aloud. "That's fucking close to the Zoo, comparatively speaking. I'll go ahead and guess that was intentional?"

"There's unrest in the country at the moment, according to our intelligence in the area." The man tapped his tablet to show images of protests in the capital city. "Anyway, they picked the island up for peanuts under the promise that they would get the solar and wind energy farms on it working again. According to the paperwork, they've even started a wave-energy power station based on the infrastructure left from when it was an American Base during the Cold War.

"Up until that point, there wasn't anything interesting besides the sudden uptick in construction activities and what looks like a shit ton of soil brought in. That changed when they began to import testing equipment from all over the world and tried to sneak it all onto the base under everyone's noses. The Chinese, Russians, and Americans all had red flags raised and they sent assets onto the base to discover what was happening. Three were killed, but an old friend of mine from my navy days managed to get the others out, and they had worrying intel to share once they were debriefed."

"Fuck me," Taylor muttered and leaned closer as the intel was displayed across the screen. "How did this go under the radar?"

"It didn't, technically," Maxwell countered.

"It did if they managed to get a Pita plant out of the Zoo and onto that base. And the operatives only managed to escape the island because the full security system wasn't in place yet, which will probably have changed once they left. If we head in there, we don't have nearly enough intelligence regarding what their defensive capabilities are."

Jansen nodded and a grim expression settled over his face. "True enough. More importantly, the only reason we were alerted to their possession of that plant in the first place was thanks to a heads-up from some old friends of yours. Heavy Metal gave us a tip that at least one plant they knew of had been taken from the Zoo. Anyway, the DOD isn't willing to let them continue operating. The dangers of a facility like that would be... Well, the higher-ups were insistent that we have boots on the ground as soon as possible."

"How soon is that?" Niki asked and took another bite of bacon.

"We need to be wheels-up in fourteen hours."

"Shit," she snapped.

"Yeah," he muttered. "It's one hell of a first job, I know. And the best part is that no one wants to be officially involved if things go sour. It means that the Chinese, Russians, and our government want to be hands-free, which is why they asked my taskforce to be in charge of the operation. It's also the reason why they want us to enlist outside consultants to add a little more convenient plausible deniability."

"I'm not happy about that," Taylor protested and folded his arms. "Will it only be us involved?"

"Maxwell and I probably shouldn't be involved in anything that happens on the ground," Jansen corrected him. "Again, it's the issue of plausible deniability. They could still deny that we operated on official orders, but it makes things considerably trickier. Anyway, the point is that no official DOD people can take part in the operation, but if you need extra support, you're welcome to call in any local talent you might know to help."

"But you still intend to participate?"

"You put so much work into training us. It feels a little ungrateful of us to simply sit on the sidelines."

Taylor scowled. "There had better be one hell of a flying bonus involved in this."

"As usual, you're in charge of the invoicing for your team."

He glowered and ran his fingers through his beard. Niki didn't need to be a mind-reader to know he was considering turning the job down. He was far more reckless with his own life, but now that he had other people in it with him, he showed more caution than usual.

"Vickie, put me in touch with the Heavy Metal team," he

said finally and continued to study the intelligence displayed on the tv pensively. "They're local, and I'll put money down that they expect to be involved in an assault on that island."

Vickie nodded and immediately pulled her laptop up. Less than a minute passed before she motioned to him. His phone rang and he answered and put it on the screen so they could all be involved in the conversation.

"Taylor McFadden," said the youthful Hispanic who greeted him with a smile. "It's good to hear from you again. Do you guys have more consulting for me to do?"

"Something like that," Taylor answered and cracked his knuckles before he continued. "I think you guys know a thing or two about Pita plants being taken out of the Zoo and delivered to an unknown location."

Jacobs' cheerful expression faded into sour lines. "Right. In fact, we reported that. We might have been involved in getting that plant out in the first place, but it was only because we tried to catch the people involved in a trap that...well, it didn't work."

"Of course it didn't," Taylor muttered before he said in a louder voice, "Anyway, US intelligence had tracked the plant and we'll head in there to put a stop to all the idiots working on shit they don't understand. Simply put, we could use backup. Since it's more or less in your back yard, we thought we might extend you the invitation. It's a small island off the coast of North Africa in the Mediterranean. I imagine it's pleasant there at this time of year."

"You will be well-compensated for your efforts, of course," Jansen interjected. "The DOD is unofficially sponsoring the mission, although the official word will be...you know, not. We'll go in with you guys, but if something goes wrong, everyone in charge will deny everything."

"That sounds about right," Jacobs said and glanced around the room he was in, likely to get confirmation from the others he was in business with. "Well, we've wanted to put these assholes into a corner for a while now, and while we would have been happy to do it for free, getting paid is the better idea. Plus, we have a couple of experienced team members we can include, so we can put together a smallish team but an effective one. Oh, and I know a Russian who knows a few other Russians who would be able to fly us to the base—none of whom have any ties to their government I might add."

"As long as they are armed and ready for a fight." Taylor's expression relaxed a little. "We don't exactly have the best eye on what we'll face in there. The chances are we'll have to plan for the worst."

"And that is?"

"Humans and cryptids having a pajama party."

"Right."

"We'll be wheels-up in fourteen hours," he continued. "Plus another twenty-four hours that it'll take to get there from Vegas, more or less."

"Are they giving you some kind of flying bonus?" Jacobs asked.

"We're still in negotiations on that."

The young researcher smirked. "All right. We'll send the invoice to the DOD as usual, and we'll be ready and waiting for you guys in about...shall we say forty hours from now?"

"That sounds good." Taylor paused to confirm with

Jansen, who nodded. "We'll see you on the ground. Stay alive out there."

"You too."

The line cut off and he turned to the rest of his team. "I guess we have packing to do."

"Well, sure," Niki agreed. "I'm already packed, and my suit is...still on the plane, right?"

Jansen nodded. "We'll take off in fourteen hours, so we have to take care of logistics in preparation for once we arrive in Africa to make sure our quarry doesn't know we're coming."

"That's mostly your job now, right?" Niki asked and grinned cheekily.

"Yeah, yeah, yeah." The man didn't look very happy about the switch in responsibilities. "Anyway, I'll drop you guys a line if there are any changes in the plan. Until then, yeah, get ready and be at the airport in time for us to get wheels up."

"Now, will this be the regular kind of airport?" Vickie asked and looked around. "Like, the kind where you have to arrive two hours earlier since it's an international flight?"

"She's going?" Niki countered and looked at Taylor with a hint of panic on her face. "Why is she going?"

"I'm the man in the van, that's why," the hacker explained. "The technical support. The...you know, robot dog."

"What the hell are you talking about? I thought you could do your work from far, far away from the front lines?"

"Well, if you guys need my support on the ground,

wouldn't you prefer that I be there and not however many fucking thousand miles away?"

Niki looked at Taylor again, hoping for support, but he simply shrugged.

"She's a part of our team," he said. "Our technical support, and if she thinks we might need her on the ground, she'll at least be in a position to help us. Do you disagree?"

She wanted to think of something she could use to change their minds but in the end, they had both made good points. Despite this, she still didn't like the idea of her cousin so close to the action, much less that close to the Zoo. Even being on the same continent as that fucking place gave her heart palpitations.

"Fine," she snapped and shook her head. "Not that you guys were looking for my permission anyway."

Bobby pushed from his seat. "I'll have Taylor and Vickie's suits readied and crated up for when you guys need them. For the moment, though, I need to get back to my business."

Taylor stood and shook the man's hand firmly before he headed out. Niki realized he did have work to get to since he would take over most of the owner's responsibilities.

The rest of the group left as well. Vickie needed to pack and likely advise the college of her travel plans. Niki was more or less sure that the hacker was still attending.

In less than a minute, only her and Taylor remained. He probably also had something to get back to but he hung back and seemed to think he and Niki still needed to have a word or two.

"Good luck," the younger woman muttered in parting

and patted him on the shoulder before she stepped through the door.

He turned to face Niki and folded his arms in front of his chest. "Bring it on."

She narrowed her eyes. "Bring what on?"

"You didn't want to lay into me while everyone else was here because you didn't want to seem like you were being overprotective of Vickie in front of the team. But you do want to get it out, so let's do it. You don't like me agreeing that she should head out with us, right?"

He was so serious that she couldn't help a small smile. "Okay, yes, I'm protective of her and I don't want her anywhere near the Zoo. Even as far as North Africa is a little close, but in the end, I know there isn't much in the world I could do to stop that girl from doing what she wants to do with her life. Honestly, I'm sure that's the same conclusion you came to as well. I know she will be an asset on the ground, and I know you wouldn't be able to stop her short of tying her to a chair and even then, there would be swift and dreadful reprisals."

"You're scared of her too, huh?"

"Terrified. But I like that you didn't make me show it." She moved closer, wrapped her arms around his waist, and held him close.

"We need to get going, you know. There's packing to get done."

"In a second." She pressed against his chest and enjoyed the closeness for a few long moments before she finally released him. "Okay, I'll see you later."

CHAPTER TWENTY-THREE

She wouldn't say Taylor's aversion to flying was in any way amusing. It wasn't like the guy had much of a choice in the matter, and phobias were phobias. He could do little more about it other than learn to keep it under control, and that was what he did.

Still, it was something to see a man who would charge into a surging line of alien monsters without a second thought tensing up with his eyes closed every time the plane encountered turbulence across the Atlantic. He didn't voice any complaints, but she could see that he begged silently for it to be over. Maybe they would manage to head back to the States by boat.

The long flight left most of the team already on edge, although Taylor seemed to be calmest once they began to unload their equipment. They moved everything from the plane and into the trucks that would transport them from the airstrip to where Jacobs and his team should already be waiting for them.

Niki took a moment to look at the city only a dozen or

so miles from where they stood. That millions of people lived almost within spitting distance of the Zoo felt crazy to her. Then again, if people lived in such close proximity to crazy like that, it stopped feeling crazy after a while.

Her gaze drifted to the south, where she knew the jungle was located. For a moment, she thought she caught a hint of shadow beyond the distant dunes that filled her vision, but common sense reminded her that it was simply her mind playing tricks on her. She imagined she could see what she knew was out there, despite the distance—which honestly still didn't feel far enough away.

"Out of sight, out of mind," Taylor said softly.

Niki looked at him as he loaded the last of the suits. "What was that?"

"All the population centers inside the Sahara and close to the Zoo have already been evacuated," he explained. "Getting them all out was one of the first things they did before they started construction on the walls. Everyone else kind of stayed. I'm not sure why, but I imagine it's because they can't see the Zoo, even from a distance. And while they can't see it, it's merely an abstract—something people talk about but don't know."

"And when it appears on the horizon one day, everyone freaks the fuck out." She finished his thought for him. "I don't know why, but it always lurks in the back of my mind. A little ball of stress that never seems to let up."

"That's because you've seen what it can do—or at least a condensed version of the same." He patted the back of the truck as the last of their equipment was safely stowed. "Let's go. We need to get a move on if we want to stay on schedule."

They climbed into the vehicles. The roads were in surprisingly good condition and they made good time despite the heavy load they carried. She assumed the sheer number of militaries with a presence in the area would have demanded that the roads be in as good condition as possible.

It wasn't long before they pulled up in front of a group of warehouses, closer to the city but not quite in it yet. A couple more trucks waited and another team was assembled as well. Niki already knew Sal Jacobs, the researcher, as well as his second in command, Madigan Kennedy. She didn't recognize the others, although all of them had the looks of people who had been in the thick of things for a while. Sunken cheeks and the way their gazes darted quickly to keep track of all movement around them told the whole story. Only one of the four seemed familiar, but she couldn't place where she'd seen the man before.

Jacobs gestured for the group to park next to them and looked a little too gleeful for her liking.

Taylor was the first one out of the vehicles, and the young doctor moved forward to greet him with a firm handshake.

"It's good to see you in the flesh again, McFadden," the doctor said and slapped him heartily on the shoulder. "I can honestly say the Zoo hasn't been the same since you left."

"I can't say I've missed it," he confessed and motioned for the rest of the team to approach. "Still, it seems to have done you good. It looks like you put on...I'll guess about twenty pounds of muscle since I last saw you—Kennedy acting as a taskmistress to whip you into shape, huh?"

"You know it." The former sergeant stepped forward to shake Taylor's hand as well. "I'd say you've put on a couple of pounds of muscle too. Retirement has agreed with you."

"I was...never mind. It's a long story. Anyway, you guys already know Niki Banks." He motioned to her and then to the rest of the team. "This is Vickie, our technical support. She has her own suit and I trained her myself, so she'll be on the ground with us. Those two are Tim Maxwell and Trond Jansen, our DOD liaisons. This whole operation was their idea, so you guys know who to haunt if things turn sour."

"Thanks for that," Jansen retorted. "Dr. Jacobs, it's a pleasure to finally meet you in person, and the same to you, Sergeant Kennedy."

"Former sergeant. I'm retired."

"I can see that." He turned his attention to the rest of the team. "Jacobs sent me a report on the Heavy Metal team. Matt Davis and Francesca Martin?"

"Davis—dammit," Taylor pushed past Jacobs and Kennedy to grasp the man's hand and greet him with real pleasure. "What the hell are you doing here? Last I heard, you had turned desk jockey."

Kennedy grinned and shook her head. "Of course we brought Davis. The guy would have been bummed if we said we couldn't bring him along for this mission."

Taylor stared at the man in bewilderment and tried to find a tactful way to have his questions answered. "I...I'm glad to hear you're back on your feet," he said cautiously, and Davis chuckled and gestured to his missing leg.

"Technically if not physically," the man explained. "It's all up to the suit, to be honest."

"Okay...it's good that you're mobile and all, but how did you guys manage that?"

"A little ingenuity along with the guy refusing to quit," Jacobs interjected. "We managed to design alterations to a suit to make up for the missing foot. The tweaks have proved very effective—so much so that we all felt comfortable having him with us for the operation."

"Yeah, his experience will be valuable," Taylor conceded. "And it's fucking great to see the warrior back in action."

He turned his attention to the woman beside Davis, who made no effort to hide her careful scrutiny as she tucked her hair behind her ear. "Francesca Martin, ex-French Legion. But Martin will do. It's easier."

"And if you try Fran, she'll kill you," Davis quipped and earned a withering glare.

Jansen narrowed his eyes but rolled with it. "Right. Anyway, the pilots you brought in—"

"Gregor Solodkov," Jacobs introduced the man closest to the trucks. "He was formerly part of the Russian contingent in the Zoo but has worked with our team for a while now. On his recommendation, we brought a comrade of his Miesh...Mi... I still can't—how do you say his name again?"

"Mieczyslaw Markin," the man answered. "I am also former Russian military. I used to fly helicopters in Afghanistan, so this mission is *kusok piroga*...how you say, piece of cake."

"Your credentials are impressive," Jansen admitted. "I'm merely making sure you all know this is a black operation. Every government in the world will vow up and down that they know absolutely nothing about what we're doing here. Do you understand?"

Everyone nodded in agreement. It was more or less what they had come to expect from working in and around the Zoo as long as they had.

"All right." Jacobs clapped briskly to bring an end to the silence that had fallen over them. "We did a little research on the location in question, and our technical support managed to track where they've sourced their supplies from. Apparently, the idea has always been for the facility to be self-sufficient, but they still have supplies shipped to them on an almost daily basis until all that is set up properly.

"Anyway, while you were dawdling and taking your sweet time getting here, we managed to intercept their transports. Anja, our IT specialist, was able to insert a couple of new loads into the registry that will look like the crates we all have our suits in."

"Good thinking," Taylor conceded. "I'm still not sure how that will get the rest of us through their sights without raising red flags."

"Well, I have been told that you guys have managed to have someone inside one of those crates while wearing the suit." Sal looked around until Vickie nodded confirmation. "We should be able to smuggle ourselves in that way with little trouble."

"Okay." Taylor looked at the team. "Getting the pilots in should be easy, but we won't be able to convince any security at the location that they are driving the trucks and flying the helicopters. We need to have separate drivers who get into their suits while the chopper is loaded."

"Amen to that. Anyway, do we have any volunteers for the driver position? The cabins of the trucks would allow you to pretend to be inside and climb into your suits without drawing attention when we're there."

Vickie raised her hand immediately. "My suit is fairly easy to get into and I would be able to close myself inside the crate too."

Niki sighed and waved her hand as well. "My suit is similar to hers, which makes it easier to climb into. I think it's the same make and model as the one Elisa used in her transatlantic trip, so it should be fairly easy to work with. Besides, I'm fairly sure that having two women working the transit would result in less attention—or suspicion, at the very least."

Jacobs nodded. "There will be questions but answer them with aggressive retorts about how sexist they are for asking those questions and we should be fine."

She nodded. It was reassuring that they were putting a good plan in place for getting to the island, given that they didn't have much of one for when they arrived. They had mission parameters but they knew very little about what they would find.

"Well, we know what we'll do," Jansen noted and nodded at the team. "Let's get to it."

There was no disagreement from the others. Waiting was no one's favorite thing to do, and now that they had a plan to get them to the island and whatever fight they would encounter, they were anxious to be on their way.

Niki stood beside Taylor as he climbed into his suit and began to seal it from the inside.

"Be careful," he admonished simply and offered no other sign of concern for her.

She nodded and patted his helmet. "No shit, Sherlock."

He grinned, pulled the cover on, and made sure it was properly sealed from the inside before he locked it.

With a smile, she patted the crate again before she turned to where Vickie, Gregor, and the other pilot with the unpronounceable name were already climbing into the delivery vehicle.

"Do you guys really think this will work?" her cousin asked as Niki started the vehicle and pulled it out of the warehouse.

The GPS turned on automatically and displayed the road she should take. She shrugged and schooled her face into a calm expression. "It doesn't matter. Our people are prepared for a fight in there already, so if anything goes wrong, they'll tear out and secure the area. The only difference is that there will be less of a warning for the guys waiting for us if we manage to sneak through."

The hacker nodded, retrieved her laptop, and began to type furiously. Or maybe she sent messages out to make sure her friends knew she loved them before she headed into what could be her last mission. Neither would have surprised Niki.

They moved around the city, and columns of smoke rose from deeper inside the buildings. The news mentioned that the population was in revolt against an incredibly corrupt government and there was talk in congress about the possibility that the same government had been taking money and weapons from the US. Niki was nowhere near the paygrade necessary to know if that was true or not but she did wonder, especially since she'd also heard that the US officially supported the rebels. It seemed the perfect win-win scenario for duplicitous power brokers, although it might extend to people within the government itself.

All she knew was that it probably meant their American accents would be enough to draw attention, although she assumed it wasn't that uncommon given the sheer number of American military personnel in the area.

The drop-off location was surrounded by an electric fence as well as warnings in four languages—one of which was English—about how trespassers would be shot. She didn't want to think about the possibilities and grasped the wheel of the truck a little tighter as the two men in the guardhouse saw her and gestured for her to drive closer to the heavy gates. One of them moved to one of the defense locations, toting an assault rifle, while the other approached to inspect the vehicle.

The guys in the back would be able to fight their way through two guards, but that wouldn't be in time to save her, Vickie, and their two pilots.

The man returned after he ran a mirror under the truck and tapped her window, which she rolled down quickly.

"You are the replacements, yes?" the man asked and his gaze studied a tablet he held in his hands. "And the replacement pilots?"

Niki nodded slowly.

"Okay," Jacobs muttered through the earpiece connected her to the comms. "Anja said the regulars would be caught up in the protests in the city. She told me not to ask her how she knew that."

"The regulars were caught up in the protests in the city," she repeated. "I have no idea what's going on there, but we got the call at the last minute for the delivery and pickup afterward. Better them than me, right?"

"With the money these people pay, I don't blame you," the man answered, his attention still on his tablet. His English sounded like it was from southern England, which indicated that he was probably a dual citizen who had grown up there since he had almost no local accent. "These last-minute changes throw our whole system out of sync ever since they started upgrading the security systems last week. You're clear to go in. Our people will put the supplies onto the helicopter. Unfortunately, you will not be allowed to exit the vehicle for the duration of your stay."

"Hey, I got up at four in the morning to be here for this," she replied and put the truck into gear. "As long as you guys don't have a problem with us taking a nap while we wait for these assholes to get back."

The man laughed and shook his head. "No objections here." He motioned for the gate to open and it responded incredibly slowly. Niki forced herself to not show any sign that she was anything other than bored while doing a job that required little to no effort on her part. She accelerated sedately as soon as the gate was open wide enough for them to pass through.

The truck came to a halt where a handful of men waited to load everything into the helicopter while their two pilots crossed to the aircraft to start with the flight checks. Once the doors were shut and the windows rolled up, the two women scrambled through the door behind them, which gave them access to the trailer behind.

They worked frantically to suit up and hide in the crates. Niki's heart thumped uncomfortably as the door to the trailer opened and the men unloaded the crates one at a time.

After what seemed like an eternity, they reached her and she bit her lip against the instinctive protest as they hauled her crate out roughly and carried it to the helicopter. Minutes ticked past and she wondered how soundproof the suits were as more crates were added. Finally, they were cleared to leave. The rotors spun audibly above them and a sensation of nausea seeped in as the chopper began to move.

Maybe this was how Taylor felt, she thought idly. Flying was far more pleasant—or tolerable, anyway—when she had the option to see where she was going. It didn't need to be constant, but being able to look out a window and see movement was enough to settle her inner ear.

This was simply unpleasant. She didn't wait long before she shifted uncomfortably in her suit and grimaced when it pressed against the restraints inside the crate.

"Are we in the clear?" she asked over the comms once she felt enough time had passed.

"We're in the air," Gregor answered, his voice a little muffled. "That would be a qualified yes. The GPS tells me we should arrive at the location in thirty minutes, assuming the current winds hold. If we have pressure to the south, we might take as long as forty-five minutes."

That sounded unpleasant, but if Taylor could put himself through it, she could too. Niki grasped the controls of her suit to give her some kind of power over the world around her, or at least the illusion of it, which would do for now.

"I wouldn't start on that case of carpal tunnel syndrome yet," Vickie stated over the comm line.

"What?" Gregor asked.

"From patting ourselves on the back. It looks like the guy Niki spoke to inspected the cabin after we left and discovered our little deception. He's radioed the island on a private channel to alert them that there might be trouble heading their way."

"Couldn't you block it?" Niki demanded. The frustration of confinement pushed into her waspish tone.

"Desk did, but the first part of the warning got through. By private channel, I mean one that isn't connected to the facility's conventional system. It seems to be one they leave dark and only ever activate it in an emergency. Neither Desk nor Anja was able to access the on-site system at all and I haven't had any luck either. These guys have zipped it very tight and have full control at this point over what comes in or goes out."

"So it looks like we'll go in hot," Taylor noted and ended further debate by stating the obvious. "I wonder what thirty minutes of prep time will do for them."

Niki scowled. The whole idea was for them to get in without being seen so they had the element of surprise on their side. It wouldn't play out that way, which served her right for getting her hopes up like that.

"So did we have a plan B?" she asked, unhooked her suit from the crate, and climbed out gingerly. She didn't know much about flying in helicopters, but she did know that shifting a couple of tons of weight would affect the challenge of keeping it in the air.

"Well, I had a good idea of what we could do," Jacobs told them, already out of his crate and moving aside to make space for the others. "But I don't think you guys will like it."

"Is it something we might have seen before?" Francesca asked as they emerged from the crates and began to prep for a fight, moving carefully in the back of the helicopter.

"Ummm, yes. Some of you, anyway."

Taylor sighed. "You'll do that superhero landing bullshit, won't you?"

"Ugh, I'm getting predictable." The scientist shook his head dramatically. "And it's not bullshit!"

"Sure. Anyway, if I hear you right, the helicopter will do a pass over the island, and you'll drop in—"

"I'll be with him," Kennedy added.

"Right. You guys clear a landing zone for the chopper that will get the rest of us on the ground. Do I have that right?"

Jacobs nodded. "It's a nifty plan, right?"

Taylor froze for a couple of seconds and an odd, jolting movement jerked his shoulders. It took Niki a couple of seconds to realize he was laughing.

"I wish I could say we had more options, but in this case…" he said once he'd stifled his amusement. "Well, getting boots on the ground quickly to clear our landing zone is all we can hope for. If you think you can pull it off, I say do it."

Niki exchanged a glance with Vickie, immediately aware

that her cousin thought the same thing she did. That kind of trust in someone's ability was not given lightly. While she'd always known that Jacobs went into the Zoo, she had assumed that he did so as a researcher, capable of defending himself but leaving most of the heavy lifting, combat-wise, to Kennedy.

That didn't appear to be the case. Jacobs had offered to dive head-first into an unknown situation, and Taylor had not only agreed but encouraged it. She wondered if there was more to this team than what she already knew.

By the time they were prepped and ready to go, Gregor was already alerting them.

"I have eyes on the island," the Russian shouted. "And yes, it looks like we will go in hot!"

"Give us a sweep around the location," Kennedy shouted. "Open the bay doors and we'll drop in and clear an area for you to drop everyone else off."

"You know this isn't a combat helicopter, right? There's a limit to my ability to maneuver."

"Well, yeah, sure. Give us your best and we'll do what we can from there."

The helicopter banked, and as the bay doors opened, the Mediterranean receded behind them and a flicker of land appeared below when they began to turn.

Jacobs and Kennedy lined up in front of the door. They looked around for a few seconds before she held her hand up and counted down from five on her fingers.

"See you guys on the other side!" the researcher shouted as the two of them jumped clear of the helicopter.

CHAPTER TWENTY-FOUR

I t was weird to feel jealous of someone jumping out of a helicopter into the open air with a challenge much like looking to thread a needle and land on a skinny strip of land protruding from the Mediterranean.

But Taylor honestly wished that he could have plunged out with them into the middle of the fight instead of sticking around on an aircraft that would make some hellish maneuvers to avoid any attempts to bring it down. His stomach already rebelled over the fact that he was spending more time in the air than usual.

Still, he knew what his job was in this case. He would lead the rest of the team out when the time came for them to join the action. His breath dragged and his fists clenched as the chopper banked hard to the right and turned almost completely horizontal as it circled to head toward the island again.

Shooting could be heard from outside, even over the roar of the rotors above them, and he inched toward the door and waited for the helicopter to resume its approach.

Gregor wasn't kidding when he said it wasn't made for combat maneuvers, but whichever one of the two pilots was in control was seriously skilled.

The aircraft shuddered, but as they began to descend, he realized that Jacobs and Kennedy still attempted to clear the area for them. They took fire too, and there wasn't much in the way of cover around the island other than the walled-off complex where the defenders fired from.

"Let's go, go, go!" Taylor roared as the helicopter touched down. He didn't want to have it stationary for longer than was absolutely necessary and an easy target for the rockets the defenders probably had. It gave them some cover to scramble out, its nose pointed toward one of the cliffs that surrounded them. The position provided barely enough room to debark beside it.

"We're out!" He knocked on the doors as Niki, Vickie, the two members of Jacobs' team, Maxwell, and then finally Jansen climbed out and immediately began to return fire.

Vickie peeked out from behind cover and ducked her head hastily. He hadn't thought about her being present in the combat zone.

"Fuck!" He growled and stepped in front of her as the helicopter ascended sharply and moved away from where he could see them preparing rockets to target it.

The defenders looked like they were well-entrenched on the walls around the base. They wore suits too, although they were only fitted with assault rifles and not the rocket launchers or machine guns the larger suits might have provided. Giving them the armor had been an afterthought.

"They don't have any heavy suits?" Jacobs shouted over the din of the firefight as Taylor guided Vickie to a small yet dense outcropping of rock that would give her some protection.

"Sal, take your team and flank them!" Taylor called and delivered a sustained barrage of cover fire. "Break me a hole in that wall!"

"You're not my supervisor!" the researcher shouted in response.

"What?"

"Nothing. Madigan, show them the error of their ways!"

Kennedy wore a massive suit, the kind that was almost impossible to buy on the open market. He had never had much of a chance to work with those in the past since they were usually sourced from and built privately by people who knew how to maintain and repair them.

With that said, he wanted the opportunity to put his hands on it and see what it could do.

Madigan barreled forward, circled, and drew the fire from those who continued to track Sal's team. They used her heavier suit as a shield and fired consistently from behind it to force the defenders to back away from the wall and find protection against their onslaught.

The heavier suit shifted and the shoulder pivoted to bring up two shoulder-mounted weapons as the infiltrators pushed forward. A small minigun on her right shoulder was already identifying targets. The six barrels spun and once they reached the required velocity, opened fire.

What they heard wasn't so much the clatter of an automatic weapon as an uninterrupted roar as bullets pounded into the walls ahead of them. A couple of the defenders fell back with a line of holes across their suits that looked like they could have been cut with a knife.

"That's some suppressing fire," Taylor muttered and checked that he was still positioned between Vickie and the walls in front of them.

"I'm glad you approve, Leprechaun," Madigan quipped and he realized he had spoken into the comm line. "Wait until you see my finale."

"I'll let the Irish slight pass this time," he retorted and she chuckled. "That aside, I can't wait."

The mount on her left shoulder circled as the team moved closer to the walls. The rocket launchers almost didn't look fair and the weak, older structures already showed signs of crumbling under the assault from the minigun.

Flares of fire erupted from the back of the launchers and three rockets sped away from Madigan as she marched steadily forward and absorbed most of the damage that was directed at her team.

A flash of blinding light, even in the middle of the day so close to the equator, was enough to make Taylor look away. Once his vision returned, all he could see were the smoking holes left in the walls where damaged sections were still crumbling.

"Well," Niki said, "I guess we now know what we can aspire to in our training. I don't suppose we could get our hands on one of those big fuckers?"

"We could try," he conceded as the team pushed through the breach in the wall. Davis led the way which wasn't a surprise. It wasn't in his nature to hang back, but it was hard to tell that the man was missing a leg. He made a mental note to ask questions about the upgrades and adaptations they had made to his suit because they worked unbelievably well.

Martin, in a smaller suit, squeezed around him and directed a sustained volley on those who attempted to fall back to a more defensible position. Madigan continued to lay down different layers of cover fire to make sure no one could get a clean shot on her people without exposing themselves.

Sal, interestingly enough, chose to not use the holes in the walls. A pair of extra limbs uncurled from the back of his lighter, leaner suit and with their help, he managed to scale the wall where the defenders didn't expect to see him and fired at them from there. One of the extra arms drew the sidearm from its holster and added to the firepower he laid down with ruthless efficiency.

"Screw the big one," Vickie commented when she peeked out from behind the rock she used for cover. "I want that one. I want to be fucking Spider-Man, not the Hulk buster."

"Yeah, yeah, put it on your Christmas list," Taylor grumbled.

"Get down!" Niki shouted. "Do you think you can connect to their software from here?"

The hacker looked at the woman. "Hell, I would if we were in a city and I could piggy-back off its connections and this place wasn't zipped tighter than a nun's—."

"Is that a yes or a no?"

"It's a no," Taylor explained.

"Okay, we'll have to move closer," Niki muttered. "Taylor, lead the way!"

"Yes, ma'am."

He smirked as he prepared to comply. Niki taking charge was great and something he liked to see in her since she would be a founding member of his merc company. There were other reasons why he liked it, but he had no desire to mention them until they were somewhere private.

Still smiling, he took point with his rifle aimed at the top of the walls that remained, despite the fact that Sal's team held most of the attention. They approached quietly and steadily. It was difficult to not simply charge in and join the action, but he had a more important job to do while he was on the fucking island.

"Get me up," Taylor said and gestured for Niki to take the front.

She did as she was told and lowered so he could climb on her knee, then used her hands to hoist him so he could reach the top of the wall.

He kept his weapon aimed at the defenders who were still too preoccupied to notice that reinforcements had moved into the combat zone. With one hand on his weapon, he stretched the other down the wall as Niki helped Jansen up next, followed by Maxwell. Vickie vaulted up to grab Taylor's arm, and he hauled her up beside him.

It was quick, simple work, the kind he remembered them performing together on the training ground. The effort required had been particularly difficult for them at the end of the day, when they were exhausted and their coordination wasn't at its best. Watching them perform the maneuver without a hitch while bullets flew around made him feel a small hint of pride. He had a smile on his face as he dragged Niki to the other side of the wall.

There was more than enough cover for Vickie and she was already working to crack encryptions and find electronic openings in their security while Taylor guided her to where he identified the safest position for her. The hacker continued to mutter under her breath, though, so he wasn't sure they should hold out much hope while they focused on the remaining defenders.

Those topside, he reminded himself. He doubted that whoever was running the facility would have sent all their security to the surface. They would have more teams waiting in the lower levels, and these would be better equipped and prepared than those they fought now.

Taylor motioned for Maxwell and Jansen to circle from the left, while he and Niki would go right. Both men nodded and used cover where they could as they inched behind the defenders, who had holed themselves up in a section of wall. The location and their aggressive defense made it particularly tough for Sal's team to break through.

There were still about a dozen of them, but they were bunched and used the cover greedily. They took turns to step out from behind it to retaliate to the invaders but no one thought to check if anyone approached from behind them.

Their loss, he thought grimly.

Taylor retrieved a grenade from his belt and lobbed it into the middle of their huddled formation. Only a couple of them saw it in time and none were able to jump clear before it exploded.

The ordnance detonated with a vivid flash and smoke, and more masonry crumbled around the enemy. Those who were still standing were forced to stumble away from their cover, stunned and covered in dust, and they fired blindly in every direction in hopes of hitting something or someone.

Luck wasn't on their side, and with fire coming from all angles, Taylor almost felt bad for the mercs who had so clearly been underprepared for what they had to face. From what he'd read on those who had been hired for this work, though, there was very little in the world that would make him truly feel bad for them.

Sal and Madigan moved forward to confirm that none of them would be a threat any longer before they turned to look at him.

"Nice flanking maneuver," she stated and nudged one of the fallen mercs with her boot. "But you took your fucking time. I remember you being a little faster on the draw."

He wanted to say it was because he was handling a novice team, but that felt like a deflection at best.

"I guess all that time in civilized company slowed me somewhat," he admitted with a shrug. "So, I don't know about you guys, but I have a bad feeling that there'll be considerably more guns in much better positions once we get down there. Is there any chance we could simply blow this whole fucking place off the map and be done with it?"

"I'm down for that." Madigan raised her hand and was quickly followed by the other two members of her team.

Unfortunately, it didn't look like the researcher agreed.

"They have fresh life down there, directly from the Zoo. I'm worried that if we drop a ton of explosives, it will simply result in the biomass being spread into the Mediterranean biome that...well, it will result in an explosion much like the Zoo but a thousand times worse. We shouldn't take that risk."

He made a solid point and one that led to Madigan and the Heavy Metal team lowering their hands.

"Fuck me," she muttered.

"So, what do we have to do?" Taylor asked. "I assume you guys will deal with any hazardous biological materials we run into since...well, Sal's the only one with any kind of expertise in the area. I guess that leaves the job of cleaning out the rest of the trash to me and my team. Vickie is getting into their electronics now—right, Vickie?"

The last two words were shouted, although strictly speaking, he didn't need to. The comms connected them as though they were talking in the same room.

The hacker didn't answer him immediately. She was probably too engrossed in her work to pay attention to other people talking to her.

"Anja does the same thing," Sal commented while he ran a couple of checks on his suit to pass the time. "She zones the rest of the world so she can focus entirely on the work she's doing. It can be annoying, but..." He shrugged.

"The work they do requires focus and careful attention to detail." Taylor finished the researcher's thought with a nod. "There's no point in rushing these things. And if you're patient, in the end, it makes everyone's job easier."

None of them had anything to disagree with particularly, but they also didn't want to stop and wait for someone else to work while they twiddled their thumbs. Their impatience was exacerbated by the obvious fact that the folks below would use the time to solidify whatever defenses they had planned.

Finally, Vickie looked up from where she had been hiding. "Sorry, I...uh, tuned you guys out for a second. I don't know who set this system up, but I want to buy them a drink laced with fucking cyanide. There is no way to control the doors without accessing the system from the inside, which means we'll have to find another way to get into the base."

"We could blow the doors," Maxwell suggested and sounded hopeful.

"Yeah, we could." Taylor scowled. "Dammit. Although I suppose it's not too much of an issue. It's not like we're trying not to alert them to our presence."

Davis chuckled. "Yeah, that ship has sailed, I'd say." He approached the doors and studied them carefully. "Hold on."

"What?" Niki demanded and joined him quickly.

"Isn't this some kind of access thingie?"

Taylor gestured for Vickie to move closer with him and the two peered at a keypad positioned on the outside wall which included a card swipe and a slot for some kind of electronic device.

"Ohhhh..." The hacker grinned. "All that goddammed security and they hand it to us on a fucking platter."

"Okay, maybe this would be a good time to fill the rest of us non-geeks in," Madigan snapped as she strode closer, her impatience very evident.

"Yeah. Right." Vickie chuckled. "This is a...okay, I'll call it a port to make it simple. One of our very dead friends will have a keycard—or maybe all of them do?—and that there is where I can plug my tablet in."

"And?" Taylor could understand Kennedy's impatience.

"Come on, Tay-Tay. It's my access to at least some of the system. If nothing else, I can get the doors open without it being messy."

"Fuck. So why didn't you kick off with that?" Niki snapped. "Right, everyone search the bodies for a keycard. It'll likely be tucked into the suit somewhere to keep it safe."

Martin grimaced but dropped to one knee beside the closest corpse and the others moved quickly to start the search.

"That big guy over there looked like the leader—if you could call him that. They weren't particularly well led, overall." Jansen moved quickly to one of the bodies that had holed up on the section of wall. He knelt and began to dismantle the armor around the chest. A few minutes later, he whooped in triumph and brandished a small plastic card. "Well shit. This guy had no imagination. He didn't even try to hide it."

"From who?" Maxwell asked and laughed. "He needed it where he could get to it easily."

"Oh, for fuck's sake." Madigan dragged in a breath. "Give that fucking thing to Vickie and let's get this show on the road. We can share the idiot stories later."

Jansen hurried forward and put the card in the hacker's outstretched hand. She had her tablet poised and ready and pulled a nervous face as she swiped the card. The team gathered around her and someone exhaled a long breath when an indicator light turned green.

"So far...don't fuck it up, Vickie," she muttered, shrugged, and shoved the tablet connection into the slot. "Yes! Oh very fucking yes."

Her fingers moved furiously, her tense demeanor somehow exaggerated by the suit, and as if by general consensus, everyone remained silent while she worked.

"Annnnnd...done. I've managed to open the door, but it looks like it cycles so we'd best not waste time."

"Right." Taylor all but shoved the others through as the door opened slowly and gestured impatiently to the hacker, who finally unplugged her tablet and followed the team.

"I managed to download schematics that should help us navigate without getting lost," she told them as the doors closed and a muted click indicated that it had already sealed again. "It's a fucking maze down there. That's all I can do without alerting them to my presence in the system, although I'm sure they'll find out soon enough. I guess we'll have to cross that bridge when we get there. Any questions?"

Sal immediately opened the schematics and looked through them. The shared nature of the file allowed the rest of the team to see him shifting quickly through the different levels and sections of the base. He remained silent and continued until he reached one of the lower areas that had been cut deeper into the ground. This created a single large room that took up the whole of the lowest level and spread farther so it was wider than the rest of the facility with a massive arching roof.

"Okay, I'm no architect," he said thoughtfully and looked at the waiting team members, "but if I built a massive room to house my own personal bite-sized Zoo, that is where I'd put it."

"What will you do when you find it?" Niki asked and checked her weapon yet again as they started toward the doors.

"Wreck that shit," the doctor answered immediately with a small grin. "Burn every trace of it down to the last spore to make sure no part of it will ever get out."

"I like the way you think," Taylor responded grimly. "Vickie, whenever you're ready with the doors, I'm ready to run pest control."

CHAPTER TWENTY-FIVE

The facility didn't resemble anything the US-based team had encountered before.

"There's something different about this," Vickie commented as they moved deeper inside. "I'm not sure what it is, but it's not like any of the other labs where we've had to take care of cryptid fuckers. I simply can't put my finger on it, though."

"Who's we?" Taylor asked. "Isn't this the first time you've come on a mission like this?"

"Sure," she replied. "Physically, that is. But I've been involved with missions before—even if some of them were after the fact—and I've seen the pictures. There's a decided...lack of dead people around here. Well, except for those we left outside."

"Give it a couple of weeks," Niki muttered. "These places have a habit of making a mess of themselves if you give them long enough."

Jacobs chuckled softly. "You'd think they would have learned their lesson from the first time around."

"If there's anything I've learned from looking into what these assholes do behind closed doors," she commented and ran her fingers across the tiled walls, "it's that they'll always put profits above everything else. Including their employees' lives."

Taylor looked around the room. Despite the bantering, Vickie was right. There was something off about the location.

"They aren't finished building it," he muttered and tapped the walls. "Construction is still ongoing."

The others paused and looked around the room. At first glance, it looked like it had for decades. American bases were built to last, after all, but even so, exposed wiring protruded and while some sections were tiled, others were not.

"Who the hell would already start testing Zoo goop at a location that isn't even finished yet?" Madigan asked and scanned the room.

"I guess they were in a hurry," Vickie responded as she turned and hurried toward a small room where a number of servers connected to screens.

"Do you think you can work from here?" Taylor asked. It was better to not make any assumptions about things he didn't understand.

"Sure, but…yeah, I was afraid of that. They've isolated their servers into different sections. I guess they were worried about people having access to what they tested in various areas. Taylor, if you can use the fobs I gave you, I'll organize everything they have on their servers and I'll be able to pin down the fuckers who are running this facility."

"I guess that'll be my job," he muttered. "Jansen,

Maxwell, and Niki with me. Sal, you and your team will have to take care of the clean-up on your own."

"Exactly like old times." The researcher grinned, bumped his extended fist, and gestured for his team to follow him to the nearest stairwell.

"Vickie," Taylor said once they were on their way, "do you think you'll be okay up here? You have enough fire-power to defend yourself if you get into any trouble."

"I'll be fine," she insisted and waved for them to leave. "You guys have work to do. I've already highlighted the locations where you'll need to insert the little fob for me to get access. Get a fucking move on!"

"Everyone is shouting orders at me today," he mumbled under his breath and motioned for Maxwell, Jansen, and Niki to follow him as the hacker sealed herself in the room.

Their first location was still on the first level and they were able to reach it without encountering any further resistance. Taylor already had the fob out and plugged it in immediately.

"Are you getting this, Vick?"

"Yeah…and Vick?"

"I thought that was better than the other nickname I came up with for you."

"You're setting the bar very low there, Tay-Tay, and besides, Vick brings to mind a certain…quarterback who had issues with animals."

"He set it right after, didn't he?"

"Like that excuses him from doing any of it in the first place? Keep working, Tay-Tay. On the nickname and finding the rest of the server rooms."

"Work, work, work."

He stepped into the stairwell with his rifle aimed down while he checked to make sure no one was defending it before he moved fully through the door. Two stairwells led up and down from the lower levels, and with Sal taking the other one, they could at least confirm that no one would sneak in behind them.

They reached the next level with no sign of defenses being set up, and all Taylor could think about was where the rest of the security might be. He still couldn't believe they had dealt with the entire defensive team above ground. Those who had been there didn't account for the numbers they had brought in and which he had read about.

"You're worried," Niki commented as they circled into the first of the lower levels and scanned it quickly before they stepped into the hallway.

There wasn't much available in the way of cover, which meant that if a gunfight ensued, they would have to act quickly and with overwhelming force.

"I don't like this," he admitted and swept the hallway ahead of him with his rifle as they continued. "If they're not attacking us by now, it means they've found a position they can and will defend. And I'd put good money on them having teams already mobilizing from the mainland to reinforce them here, so we're on a clock. Vickie, do you have anything on cameras that can tell us what we're looking at?"

"They didn't install a camera system," Vickie grumbled over the comms.

"That's not... are you sure? That doesn't seem likely."

"Well, it's either that or they have the cameras and security running on an isolated...system..."

"You just realized that's a possibility, didn't you?"

"Cut me some slack. I'm out of my element here and their electronic security is beyond belief. Last I heard, Desk was trying to find a way around it from the outside but for now, I'm on my own. Anyway, yeah, I'll look for the security systems but there's only so much I can do from here. You need to connect me to their security servers, so... sooner would be better than later."

"Yeah, I'll get right on that shit."

Taylor paused and glanced up at what looked like a camera mount. It was in a mirrored glass seal, which prevented him from seeing what someone was watching— or if there even were people on the other side.

"Okay," he muttered. "There is a chance they are tracking our movements, so keep your heads on a swivel."

The warning proved unnecessary as a few seconds later, the doors in front of them pulled shut, quickly followed by those behind them. They were effectively sealed into the single hallway they currently traversed.

"I don't want to say this is bad," Niki noted. "But having us trapped in here probably isn't the best thing. They can't attack us, but we can't do anything either. Us hitting them is the idea, isn't it?"

Taylor didn't want to answer, given that he still wasn't sure they couldn't be attacked while in their little trap. Sure enough, as his mind considered the possibilities, something moved in the walls around them.

Niki heard it too. "Okay... I may have spoken too soon."

"You think?"

"What am I looking at?" Kennedy asked.

Sal opened his mouth but nothing came out. He wasn't sure what they were looking at either and he didn't want to make any assumptions.

Davis tapped the glass and shook his head. "Well, this shit is about four inches thick and tempered, so whatever they kept behind here, it wasn't small and they didn't want to risk giving it a way out. Could they have held live Zoo specimens there?"

"Honestly, that makes sense," she conceded. "But if so, why did they put the doors at the back? If they wanted to study the creatures they kept in here, why would they have doors open to an entirely different section of the building?"

"Maybe this is simply to display them," Martin suggested.

"That also makes sense." Sal took his turn to tap the glass. "But that also brings up the question of where the fuck these critters are in the first place."

Madigan scowled. "That is a good point. Do you think they're being used in the defenses?"

He laughed but couldn't put his heart behind it. While part of him was sure no one would be stupid enough to do that, he had been proven wrong in matters of human stupidity before.

"Get down!"

His long experience around Madigan was sufficient to know she didn't toss those orders around randomly and for no reason. He had already flung himself prone before she finished saying it, and the team followed quickly. Less than a quarter of a second later, a rocket streaked over their head and drove into one of the glass cages.

Most of the explosive force was absorbed by the thick, shatterproof glass, but it still didn't stop them from being showered by shards from the sections that did break.

Sal pushed himself to his feet using his extra limbs. A group had organized themselves at the end of the corridor and used the cages as cover, which protected them against being gunned down by the return fire the Heavy Metal team now leveled at them.

"Push them back!" he shouted.

Madigan realized that the order was meant for her and she marched toward them, using both her shoulder-mounted weapons. It didn't stop their retaliatory fire, but there was no way they could have stopped the team from closing the distance.

He focused on the three who stood on the left side. They wore heavy suits, and while they were more than effective, they were also a little hampered in the close quarters.

Madigan and their teammates would have to deal with the other seven on their own.

Sal powered himself forward and fired around the corner a couple of times with the extra limbs on his suit before he took control of his weapon back. He let the suit move him as the enemy aimed for where they assumed his center of mass would be as he advanced on them.

Matt Davis had a good idea of how the suits were built —or, rather, he knew more than most about how to disable them—and Sal had paid attention to what he had to say. Most needed vents to operate, which were the most vulnerable places in the armor if you could get in close enough and behind them.

In his case, moving around them was made a little easier as the suit assisted his vault over the other mercs where they were crammed too closely together. This allowed him to open fire on two at the same time. He targeted the cooling vents immediately and used his knife to disable the third.

It wasn't a clean strike but it did the trick, and smoke began to issue from inside the suits almost immediately. The damage wasn't severe enough that they were unable to move—the suits had a handful of different vents that could keep the machinery cool—but it ended up being a problem for whoever was inside as the noxious and toxic gasses could kill them in minutes.

Ten seconds passed before the pilots evacuated, coughing and hacking while tears streamed from their eyes.

Someone would correct the vulnerability soon and he didn't want to be caught in it himself, but while it was there, he would use and abuse it.

"If I let you fuckers go," he asked with his weapons aimed at the three men, "will you go topside and stay out of this whole debacle, or will you cause trouble and end up like...those guys?"

He nodded his head toward the group who were in the process of being eliminated by Madigan, Davis, and Martin.

The three mercs exchanged a glance and raised their hands in surrender.

"We don't want any trouble," one of them said with a French accent.

"Any more trouble, anyway," an American amended.

Sal smiled but kept his weapons trained on them. "Awesome. Get the fuck out of here and don't stop running until you see blue skies. Go!"

They didn't need to be told twice, turned immediately on their heels, and sprinted in the direction from which Sal and the others had come.

"Do you think that was a good idea?" Madigan asked while her weapons reloaded and cooled for a few seconds.

"I don't know why but killing humans still feels wrong for me," he admitted and walked away from the still-smoking suits. "I can do that shit if I need to and there was a time when it didn't worry me so much. But given the option, I'd prefer to let the humans get away—at least in this kind of situation, where they probably don't know what the fuck is going on. They weren't actively trying to kill me so it seemed like a good idea."

Madigan smirked and patted him lightly on the head. "I keep forgetting how naïve you can be. It's adorable."

"Shut up."

"It's true!"

"I said shut up!"

Taylor narrowed his eyes as sections of the wall began to slide apart and open what looked like a series of tunnels into the structure itself. It revealed how much work had been put into the facility.

"What the hell am I looking at?" he asked.

"Remember how this was supposed to be a nuclear base?" Vickie replied over the comms. "Those were designed as vents for the rockets in the event that something needed to be launched. When that was scrapped, they started…building around that, I guess. I told you guys. This place is a fucking…maze…"

"What?"

"I've managed to get eyes in the area. I'm working on opening the doors again, but…it looks like you're about to have company."

"What kind of company?" Niki asked.

A low, rumbling, rolling hiss issued from inside the tunnel.

"Never mind." Taylor growled belligerently. "Get away from the hole and give me a shooting pattern. I want to put as many holes in whatever comes out as possible, got it?"

There weren't many opportunities for a choke like this in the Zoo or even hunting cryptids. Hell, humans usually had enough sense to avoid these kinds of situations, but from what he could hear barreling down the tunnel, whatever approached was more than willing to risk it.

The hissing grew louder. He could see the shadows of something moving toward them. It was big and moved fast —a little too fast, he realized suddenly.

"Oh, you have to be kidding me," he whispered. "Change of plans—we'll need explosives instead!"

CHAPTER TWENTY-SIX

He wasn't sure why he hadn't recognized the sound. It had been a frequent flier in his nightmares, one of the few monsters he genuinely dreaded facing in the Zoo.

It wasn't the creature that made the hissing noise but the carapaces gliding and scraping over the walls. With its tremendous size moving through the narrow tunnels, it would grind against the wall no matter how well it could move.

Niki looked at him instead of the hole in the wall. He didn't know what went through her mind, but he wanted her focused.

"Eyes off me!' he roared and yanked a grenade from his belt. He still couldn't see the mutant and could only focus on the twitching shadows within the tunnel.

Waiting for it to circle was killing him. It wasn't fear, he tried to tell himself. He didn't fear these things. But his inner voice contradicted him and left him with only the determination that he would fight it anyway. The self-preservation instinct that nagged and told him that running away was the right option only meant that he was still alive and more or less functioning between the ears. It didn't mean he had to listen.

"I fucking hate killerpillars," he whispered and froze when he caught a flicker of movement down the passage. He narrowed his eyes to focus as its antennae peeked around to 'see' what was happening at the entry.

The grenade bounced on the wall and circled the corner while the fuse wound down. The flash and explosive were enough to drive the fucker out of hiding and forced it into the fight maybe a few seconds before it would have preferred.

"Come on, you big fat bastard!" Taylor roared and fired at the creature with his assault rifle in one hand while the other pulled another grenade from his belt. He flicked the pin out with his suit's thumb and lobbed it without so much as a pause.

He wouldn't be able to kill the bastard on his own. The concussive blasts of the grenades kept it slightly disoriented and unbalanced, but it was still about half a ton of monster that should be about the size of his boot, at the most.

At over five meters long, it slithered across the floor toward him at an impossible speed. The carapaces shielded it like armor and prevented his bullets from punching through.

Any weaknesses were in the rear, and as it surged toward him, those vulnerabilities would be exposed to the other three members of his team.

He had to trust them to take the fucker down before it eviscerated him.

Entirely focused on his attacker, he backed down the hallway and away from his team and drew the mutant along with him, firing with every step. Jansen was beside him and while he tried to fight, he didn't move fast enough. The creature realized this almost immediately and shifted its efforts to tackle him as the weaker adversary.

"Stay on me, dumbass," Taylor snapped at the killerpillar. He fired into its eyes and dragged its attention away from the other man. Damage had been done to Jansen's suit, but he had more than enough to worry about without adding his teammate's armor issues to it.

The mandibles cut in first and grabbed and squeezed his legs. He tried to draw back and pull himself free from the mutant as it attempted to run him over.

He dragged his leg out of the monster's jaws and they snapped shut a fraction of a second after he pulled free. The assault rifle clicked empty and there was no time for him to reload it. The dozen or so black beads that passed for eyes were locked on him and the mandibles reached for him again. He was less afraid of those since all they could do was crush him like a hydraulic press. Hopefully, he could recover from that.

His real fear came from the first five rows of legs. The points were stingers and as sharp as razors, thin enough to punch through weak areas in his armor to deliver a fatal dose of venom.

"Fuck no," he whispered when the wall pressed against his back and left him no space to retreat farther. He was out of space and out of time.

"Fucking...get the fuck off me," he demanded, pushed back, and tried to use some of the suit's power to stop the creature from crushing him against the wall. He moved one hand to the mandibles and tried to hold them despite the fact that they were covered in slime. As he was pushed up on the wall by the sheer weight of the creature attacking him, his feet lashed out to shove the poison-tipped legs away from him.

When only one limb was left, Taylor stretched desperately but couldn't reach his sidearm. His fingers closed around the handle of his knife and he drew it and tried to run the blade up the carapace. If he had to, he would climb inside the fucker and cut his way out.

Too late, he realized he hadn't mentioned the killerpillar's vulnerabilities to his team. In the moment of impending combat, he had made a rookie mistake and simply assumed they knew. Little wonder that they hadn't been able to deliver much assistance, and he cursed when he realized he was probably well and truly on his own—unless he could manage to explain what was needed and keep himself alive at the same time.

Explosives detonated somewhere ahead of him, but the noise was lost in the sound of the clacking mandibles of the monster that tried to tear through him and savage what defense he had managed to put up. He was close enough to see that the eyes had been damaged by the first grenade. They were bleeding, and the creature was mostly blind and enraged.

"Fuck!" He hissed and felt like the breath was being squeezed from him. The mandibles clamped around his arm and dragged it aside. He twisted his body and pain arced up his spine at the unnatural position as he rammed the knife between the jaws. The beast shrieked with pain as he twisted the blade in place.

Another explosion made his ears ring, and this one reverberated through the creature's body and his. He was shoved harder against the wall until he saw spots all around him.

Suddenly, the weight disappeared. He moved, rolled across the floor, and sucked in deep breaths he had been unable to take while pressed up against the wall by the creature.

"Holy...shit," he whispered, pushed slowly to his feet, and looked to see what had happened to the killerpillar.

The part he had been violently up close and personal with lay bleeding and twitching. It made sense since that was more or less all that was left as the bottom half of the mutant was all but gone.

Well, not gone so much as redistributed through the generous use of explosives.

"I managed to get the doors open," Vickie announced over the comms. "Are you...are you guys all right?"

"A-Okay," he announced but teetered a little on his feet. His suit had taken damage but it was still mostly functional at this point. He flicked his knife until it was no longer covered in cryptid blood and shoved it into its sheath. "How's the rest of the team?"

"Still here," Niki announced and negotiated over the dead creature to pump a couple more rounds into the creature's mouth to be sure. "We thought you were fucking dead, Taylor. Don't you fucking do that again."

"Well, you should know by now that I'm tough to kill,"

Taylor replied and straightened with a grimace. "But I admit, I dropped the ball on this. I forgot that you aren't Zoo-experienced and that you've never fought one of these. My bad. And believe me, if you have to deal with one end of those bastards, you'll want to target the back end. The tactic usually dictates that a heavy draws the front while everyone else takes the back. In this case, it was me."

"That means one of us needs to get a heavy suit next," Maxwell muttered and patted him on the shoulder. Jansen did the same.

"Well, I've dived through the software I have access to," Vickie announced on the comms. "Sal's team has been able to put in some of the fobs I gave him, and I have access to the security system. I...think you guys need to get to the bottom levels. They're about to get themselves into serious shit."

Taylor nodded and focused down the hallway. "Okay, we'll beeline it there right now. Grab your collective shit and let's get going. Jansen, are you good?"

The DOD agent nodded. "You took more damage than I did. I'll be fine."

The defenders almost seemed like they were giving up. A handful of them continued to fight, but the others hung back and rushed out of the way as soon as bullets were exchanged. It was logical that someone had told them to get the hell out of Dodge, and Sal could only imagine it was because they were prioritizing other locations.

Hell, with their kind of luck, the place they intended to

protect so vehemently would be Heavy Metal's ultimate target area.

"I don't like this, Sal." Madigan trotted ahead of the group and acted as a shield for them. "More and more, I'm starting to feel like we're heading into a trap."

"Yeah," he answered quietly. "I have the same feeling."

"What do you think we should do?"

"Do we have a choice? We spring the trap and get them to come to us."

"How creative of you. Charging head-first into something you know will be a trap."

He grinned. "They'll never expect that."

They reached the lowest level, but it didn't look as he imagined it would. He had expected vaulted ceilings and a wide room, but they stood in a section that appeared to have been merely carved into the rock of the tiny island.

Vickie worked efficiently and the door opened for them as soon as they pushed toward it. Groups of over a dozen security men in suits of varying sizes waiting for them. They used massive crates as cover but didn't look entirely ready for a fight.

Unfortunately, it seemed they wouldn't have more time. As Sal stepped through the door, what he had assumed was a wall slid slowly upward with a low mechanical grinding sound that echoed through the massive chamber behind it.

He couldn't help a small seed of dread that planted itself in the pit of his stomach as he looked into the chamber beyond. Massive UV bulbs hung from the ceiling, illuminating the whole room so it looked like they stood in the great outdoors.

His brain recognized the weird relevance of that, given

that they stood on the edge of a jungle that grew underground. Trees that would have taken years—decades, even —to grow anywhere else in the world had sprung up in a matter of weeks since the facility had been established. He could think of nothing else other than that it was way too familiar.

"What the fuck?" Davis hissed through clenched teeth and shook his head.

"Yeah, it's a Zoo," Sal responded. "Bite-sized, but yeah, there's no doubt."

"But how?" Madigan asked, an edge of horror in her tone. "Everyone knows the Zoo needs biomass…" The words trailed off and silence settled around them.

"I…I think I have some of those answers," Vickie said tentatively. "And yeah, when I get out of here, I'll most likely be sick."

"Why?" Sal asked, his scientist mind already clicking into high gear.

"Well…first, they brought in loads and loads of soil from the Zoo—"

"Which contains a huge supply of what a jungle like that would need," he interrupted. "Sorry. I think aloud. Don't let me put you off."

"Okay, this is where the sick comes in, so be warned. That soil was sourced through contacts in the Sahara Coalition and was removed from the Zoo by locals. Some of them, according to this, were criminals and lowlifes. But some…"

"Some were poor people willing to do anything to earn something to take home to their families." Martin sounded disgusted.

"Yes," the hacker said, her voice much quieter. "But it gets worse. The biomass you mentioned?"

"Oh, fuck no." Madigan had stiffened and her voice reflected something close to rage.

"I'm afraid so. Those workers were shipped in with the last load and...well, they never left. From what I see from some of the notes here, the researchers had stores of goop sacs they bought, whatever those are, and when everything was ready, the workers...uh, they fed them to the Zoo, which is what kick-started the process."

Sal cursed and shook his head. He dragged his gaze from the spectacle that had them mesmerized and his brain engaged the reality that they were in a combat situation. Already, they'd spent too much time gaping at what none of them wanted to admit was real. He vaguely registered that the defenders seemed as surprised as his team was. It appeared that they had been out of the loop in the decision to expose them to the mini-Zoo that some dickhead had grown in the area.

After a moment, he recognized the fear they manifested when they backed away from the jungle. The reaction told him that something in there terrified them enough that they didn't want to fight, which explained why his team had been able to stand and gawk like tourists on a Sunday stroll.

They seemed oblivious to anything but the scene directly ahead as if they waited for the something to appear. He had a few theories as to what could generate that kind of reaction, and the trees themselves only factored into a couple of them.

"You don't think they would have been stupid enough

to put the creatures inside there, do you?" Madigan asked although he had a feeling she already knew the answer to that. He wouldn't tell her what to think about what was being done on this island, but the testing he had seen so far made it clear why it had been done on an abandoned island in so much secrecy that intelligence operatives were killed to keep it hidden.

"We'll have to burn this whole facility to the ground," Sal whispered, and almost as if the jungle heard him, a rustle of movement followed that could only have been from the animals inside.

He grasped his weapon a little tighter and gestured for Madigan to move toward the defenders who were still in place. Their team had a job to do, and it wouldn't be accomplished if these guys were still in position to shoot them in the back.

A couple of rockets streaked into their cover, knocked the defenders back, and reminded them that they had a job to do as well.

"Clear this place out!" Madigan roared and motioned to her teammates to join the action. This meant it was on him to ensure they weren't attacked on the flank by whatever emerged from the jungle to their right. One of the extra arms drew his sidearm and he focused it in on the men pushed back by his team.

His assault rifle remained at the ready and he began to sweep it across the tree line less than ten meters away from where he stood. The movement was already visible and his heart rate accelerated. His mouth was dry and his whole body tingled with adrenaline as the disturbance registered on his suit's motion sensors and coalesced into a wave that surged forward.

There were too many of them—dozens, he realized—that now closed in on the sound of gunfire. Sal noticed that a small light flicked on above them. He used his HUD to zoom in on what was happening and his gaze identified a group of men in lab coats who took notes on tablets and talked among themselves. Scientists, he thought sourly, who watched, recorded what they saw, and discussed it like it was merely another research project.

Sal's blood began to boil with the need to kill or destroy something. He wanted to make those guys take notes about what he would do to them when he reached their little observation room.

The creatures moved toward him, focused on the closest origin of the fighting noise.

"Come on, guys," he shouted. "You lived long enough in the Zoo. You come out to die here!"

And with that, he pulled the trigger.

CHAPTER TWENTY-SEVEN

"Three companies."

"What?"

Vickie sighed. "They routed a considerable number of transactions through dummy corporations, but I'm tracking it to three different companies in Serbia, Sweden, and Venezuela. All have pushed their investments through the same bank in the Caymans. I can see that they put a ton of money into this and they won't be happy to see all that investment disappear."

Taylor sighed and pressed against the wall. "What do they know about what we're doing here?"

"I thought they would get live updates. Well, I hoped since that would let me track them. Unfortunately, the last outward transmission happened around five minutes after they were alerted about us, and I'm still working through that."

"So what you're saying is…"

"These people covered their tracks. As much as they were invested in this, they like their privacy better. Also, if

I were a betting gal—which I guess I am now—I'd say they probably spread their investment so not all their eggs are in one basket."

"We'll leave that to the DOD," he muttered. "Are you sure these people are in here? Why would they be this close to the...what do they call it—the eatery?"

"Yeah, and...well, I guess they want to see what their work has wrought so far. Which is why they set up a fail-safe on the whole facility to burn it down lest someone discover their secrets. I've used Desk to keep the system from going down now that I could give her access from inside, but it won't last. They intend to incinerate every-thing but leave the structure intact. Just in case."

Taylor shook his head. "Well, let's take the trash out quickly, then."

"The door should open in three, two one..."

It clicked on cue, and Taylor pushed it open immedi-ately and stepped through. Going in, he already knew it wouldn't be a fair fight. Neither was it a fair fight between an executioner and some guy on death row, but it still needed to happen.

The view below almost distracted him from his purpose. He looked out into an area that seemed to have been sliced from the Zoo and transplanted under artificial lights. It was weird to look at it from above like this—empowering seemed like a good word. He could almost see how these people could develop a god complex over it.

"Knock, knock, assholes," he announced and they turned in shock. Even with his delay, the twenty men and women who stood near the window looking down hadn't realized they had company. "It's time to die."

The numbers made no sense. A handful of mutants could be shipped out of the Zoo by the people who knew how to do it—those who had been around almost as long as he had —but there were too many here to be explained by that. The researchers had either been breeding the creatures or allowed them to breed.

These idiots simply never fucking learned.

The monsters drew back when he opened fire. Most of them like the hyenas and the giant locusts looked like those he had fought before. Something larger held back and remained in the cover of the trees. It resembled a lion with a massive mane, and it uttered an ear-splitting roar that drove the beasts out of the jungle again, this time to attack in earnest.

The merc defenders were in disarray. They were either dead or turned to face the monsters that surged forward, no longer in the mood to fight humans. Sal couldn't say he blamed them.

His teammates wasted no time, held their weapons ready, and gave them the same offer he had given to those they had run into on the second level. They could climb out of their suits and run or stay and die.

To a man, the survivors chose the first option. There wasn't any amount of money that would convince them to stay when they could take the reprieve offered and get the hell away from the monsters. They left quickly, and Sal turned his full attention to the oncoming creatures. He noticed that they seemed to run almost in fear of the larger beast that remained the trees and refused to come out.

They wouldn't be routed easily, but Madigan had already turned her full attention to them. Her rockets launched, the minigun fired, and tracer rounds were the only sign visible to the human eye of what decimated the creatures that surged in what seemed like a mindless assault.

"There's something wrong with these!" she shouted. "They have the same instinct but nothing is guiding them. There's none of the tactical bullshit we see in the ones from the Zoo!"

"They're disconnected," Sal whispered almost under his breath.

"What?"

"Something bigger is driving them from beyond the tree line," he shouted to cover his whisper. "Keep an eye out for that one with your next rockets."

"My next will be my last," she told him. "We're not flush on ammo at this point. How exactly will we incinerate this whole fucking jungle?"

"I'm…uh, still thinking about that."

"Think about it a little quicker, dammit!"

Before Sal could think of an appropriate or even witty response, his attention was caught by the sound of gunfire from above. He turned as the window the researchers had been watching through was suddenly shattered. A handful of bodies fell, their white lab coats spattered with blood. Suits were suddenly visible in the aperture—familiar suits, even if a little damaged.

"It looks like you guys have been busy," he called to where Taylor stood above them. "Is there any chance I can get you guys to come and help us, or will you simply stand there and watch?"

"It is a great view but I have always been more of a participant than a spectator," the man replied. It wasn't a huge drop, but he still needed the help of grappling lines to get to the bottom. They ended about ten feet from the ground and Taylor let go and executed a smooth three-point landing.

"I told you the superhero landing would be a thing!" Sal shouted.

"Get back to fighting the fuckers!" Madigan retorted. "We're not here for your goddammed amusement."

"And yet I can be amused, that's how easy I am," he replied and resisted the urge to wink as she wouldn't see it. At least with the two teams together again, he could feel a little more hopeful about their chances of getting out alive.

"We need to get out of here," Taylor shouted. "They plan to burn it to the ground. They've lined the whole place with incendiary bombs that will obliterate the facility from existence and leave only the structure."

"We can't let any of these creatures escape with us," Madigan shouted.

"They won't," Sal decided. "Not if they don't have that big fucker in there to egg them on. We need to get him out of the tree line and kill him."

Taylor nodded and took a grenade from his belt. It was the last one he had, although it looked like the others in his team had some that could be fired from the launchers under their assault rifles.

It wouldn't be the best way for it all to start, but Sal

didn't want to wait around to find out if it would burn with them still inside.

The grenade was thrown, along with a handful of others from Taylor's team. All fell behind the tree line and forced the massive creature out from where it had remained hidden.

The rest of the animals fell away as if to avoid being too close to it.

Sal stared in amazement, not sure if his eyes interpreted it correctly. The mutant was about twice the size of a lion, but the skeletal and muscle structure was the same. Instead of fur, however, its body was covered with scales of pure black. In place of a mane, what looked like a stiff but flexible membrane expanded and retracted into its neck.

"Ain't he gorgeous," Taylor said and sounded almost in awe.

The creature didn't care for their surprise and attacked immediately. The size belied how quickly it could move, and as they opened fire, the membranes around its neck extended and stopped the rounds to leave the animal intact.

"Trond!" Maxwell shouted, but it was too late. His teammate's shoulder was snatched by the monster and Sal winced as he was hurled almost casually into the wall. He made impact with an ominous crunch before the lion-like mutant turned its attention to the others. Taylor and Niki dove out of the path as it attacked again and rushed toward them. It struggled to skid to a halt as they evaded the charge.

Maxwell swung immediately into an assault and he bellowed his fury as he opened fire. The scales on its side provided less protection than whatever was on its neck, and the creature winced, twisted, and uttered another bone-shivering roar before it snapped its jaw at the agent and extended the shield membrane to block the fire.

Taylor and Niki added a combined volley that struck it on its side. Sal wasn't about to stand by and let them have all the fun and delivered a burst of fire as well.

The monster, now attacked from all angles, roared even louder than before. It sounded like it was calling for help, but the other animals balked and tried to stay as far away from it as possible.

Madigan chose not to wait for something to happen and launched her last salvo of rockets. The ordnance streaked into it and it fell as three smoking holes appeared along its body.

It was still alive and roared its fury and frustration when it couldn't stand. Sal realized that its hind legs weren't moving, which indicated something wrong with the spine.

"I'm so fucking glad that we didn't run into that bastard in the Zoo," he noted. "I can only imagine how well it would be able to fight when it has the rest of the jungle supporting it."

Taylor nodded, but he looked around quickly and noticed that the rest of the creatures, with their oppressor disabled, began to look less fearful and more curious. "Come on, we have to get out of here now!"

Maxwell helped Jansen to his feet. The man was still alive but the damage to his suit and deeper injuries made it difficult for him to walk without help. Once they reached the atrium where they'd started, Taylor paused.

"Vickie, do it now."

The wall that had lifted began to descend again and closed with a thud that created a vibration they all felt.

It wasn't long before the floor shuddered with consecutive blasts. Explosives were detonated inside the miniature jungle and they shook the foundations of the old base.

Even with one of their team wounded, they reached the top level in time, where Vickie waited for them.

"I have everything I need," she announced and gestured impatiently toward the door. "We need to get clear. Desk can only hold off the incineration for so long."

They hurried out and felt the heat on their backs as the facility sealed again. The foundations still seemed intact and there was no evidence to the contrary outside, but Sal doubted they would risk it for too long. The helicopter's rotors were already spinning where Gregor and his co-pilot waited for them.

Those mercs who had surrendered stood in silence. They looked afraid and unsure of what to do next.

"If you guys want to live out the rest of the day, I suggest you get in. Quickly!" Sal motioned them on and they scrambled in eagerly, not waiting for a second invitation.

The helicopter was practically already off the ground by the time they were all inside and none too soon. Those parts of the structure that protruded above ground suddenly sank as a column of flames roared up from the inside.

"I hope that burned everything in there to a crisp," Madigan stated and moved beside him at the window to watch with him.

Sal narrowed his eyes and could only nod as the chopper banked sharply and accelerated away.

"So," Gregor called from the cockpit. "Does anyone know where we'll land?"

The teams exchanged a look of surprise, and Sal realized that none of them had thought about that. They obviously couldn't go back the way they'd come.

"Are there any landing zones nearby that we can use?" Taylor asked. "Within fuel range?"

"Sure," Gregor answered. "But we need to be cleared for landing first. I'll make some calls."

"Relax," Desk interjected in a voice that sounded inordinately cheerful and highly amused—probably at their oversight. "Now that I no longer have to hold the flames of hell at bay single-handedly—"

"Hey," Vickie protested. "Single-handed my ass."

The AI chuckled. "We can debate that later and I'll show you the errors in your logic. In the meantime, I'll devote a teeny portion of my Earth-saving skills to land your asses in a safe location. No thanks necessary."

CHAPTER TWENTY-EIGHT

S al leaned forward in his seat. "I don't understand. I didn't think any of the governments wanted to be involved in this mess. You guys made that very clear."

Jansen smirked, nodded, and adjusted the sling his arm was in before he took a swig from his pint glass. "Sure, we did and they did. If things went badly, they wanted nothing to do with it. But since it was a success, everyone wants to get in there to find out exactly what happened. They need to dot the I's and cross the T's, you could say."

The young researcher had no response to that and simply grimaced and shook his head.

Taylor grinned at the reaction and even Niki couldn't help a smile as she recalled the days when her response would have been similar. Life had taught her instead to expect people in high places to be as greedy as they were eager to cover their asses.

"Well, since it's a win, everyone wants to get involved with medals all around and a flurry of pats on the back,"

Taylor explained. "I'll bet you Jansen's taskforce and our involvement will barely warrant a footnote that will probably be redacted and covered in black ink to make sure none of the people signing the checks know about it."

"That's what we all signed up for," Maxwell agreed and took a generous sip of his beer.

The bar wasn't quite as full as Niki had imagined it would be, but a handful of booths were filled and the people inside were deep in their cups. She imagined she would do the same if she had to spend too long this close to the Zoo. American base or no, she would never feel safe with that fucking nightmare in spitting distance.

Kennedy pushed from her seat. "Well, I'll pick up the next round. Niki, do you mind helping me to carry all the glasses?"

"Sure." She wasn't sure what to make of the invitation but she didn't mind spending time with the woman. Most of her work had been with Jacobs, and while she was aware of the former sergeant's involvement in Heavy Metal, very little of it made it into the research Sal sent to her.

"So," the ex-sergeant started once the order for the next round of drinks was placed, "you and Taylor, huh? I never thought I'd see the day when the guy settled in for anything…uh, long-term."

She narrowed her eyes. "You and he never…right?"

Kennedy shook her head. "Don't get me wrong, I like them crazy but I draw a line at suicidal. Which was what Taylor was like when he was here. He was a great fighter, but I wanted to get the people in and out as fast as possible. I always got the feeling from him that he…well, he liked being in there, even if he didn't care to admit it. It's a matter of taste, of course, but it killed my lady boner but good."

"I feel like that was a dig at me."

The woman smirked. "Well, you chose him. I can only guess you're a similar kind of nuts and that makes you both feel comfortable around each other. Like I said, it's a matter of taste. There's no accounting for that."

Niki turned to where Sal and Taylor were in conversation. There was something casual and calm about them, but the researcher was excited as he talked about something that was drowned by the din of the bar around them.

"What do you think they're talking about?"

"If I know Sal, I'd say he's commenting on Taylor's three-point landing technique." Kennedy sounded like she was only partially kidding. "Or maybe they're going over ideas on how to make better suits and stuff. Sal always has crazy ideas that sometimes pan out and sometimes don't. The fact that he listens to Taylor when the guy says something is a little too out there simply encourages him to talk about that shit when the two get together."

She turned her head to the woman and smiled. "You like them crazy, huh?"

"You know it."

"So you're saying you and Madigan never—"

Taylor shook his head firmly. "I don't think there was any interest from her side. I always thought she didn't like me—which, you know, fair enough—and when it's not there, it's simply not there. And, well...I was never her type, I guess."

Sal nodded and took another sip of his beer. "It's not that she doesn't like you. In fact, she asked me a couple of times about bringing you into Heavy Metal while we were setting up. Before you left, of course, but it never worked out. That's why I assumed...but yeah, I guess not."

The larger man shrugged. "I could never get a read on her. I'm very sure that fighting through a crazed swarm of Zoo critters with a plucked Pita plant in one hand and a machete in the other would be easier than understanding what goes on in her head. Niki, I kind of get, and I can more or less anticipate what she'll do next. Right up until she goes and does something crazy like not betting on me in a fight because she wants to make a point or something."

"She...wait, what? What fight is this?"

"Oh." Taylor drained his mug and set it down with a thud. "There was a situation with two mobsters in Vegas. They were assholes, and I wanted to knock a couple of their teeth out for it. Anyway, their boss agreed but realized he could make money off of it and turned it into this whole event, with a cage match and betting. Long story short, people didn't think I could beat two guys and lost a ton of money because of it. I, on the other hand, made out like a fucking bandit."

"So you won, then? Fighting these two guys?"

"Sure." He nodded. "And the whole team had the opportunity to make bets, but when it came to her turn, Niki turned it down and said that...she didn't want our relationship to seem transactional or some shit like that."

Sal was about to respond but his expression turned into one of instant panic and he nudged his companion in the ribs before he changed the subject. "So anyway, you need to make it look natural. Your landing looked like it was improvised at the last minute, right, but you should make it seem like that was what you planned all along."

Taylor looked around to see why the man had panicked and realized that Niki and Madigan were returning with their next round of drinks.

"Okay, fair enough." He went with the subject change. "But my suit was all kinds of damaged anyway after a killerpillar tried to French me. I'll try to make my next three-point landing look a little more natural."

The researcher nodded. "Sure, and if you want to film it and send it to me for pointers, I'd be happy to help you."

Madigan laughed and placed the glasses down on the table. "Do me a favor and don't encourage him with that. I'm still trying to break the news to him of how he might want to focus on other areas of his combat ability rather than how to land after a short drop."

"Killjoy," Sal muttered under his breath, took his glass, and winked at him.

Niki stretched gracefully on the bed, groaned softly, and turned to face Taylor who lay next to her.

"You can't deny the benefits of having a bed to do this in," she murmured and ran her fingers through his reddish beard. "We couldn't do what we did in that cot you call a bed."

He nodded slowly, took her hand from his beard, and laced his fingers with hers. "I guess you're right. We do need the space."

She propped herself on her elbow and narrowed her eyes. "I—wait, did you agree with me on that?"

"I never intended to live at the strip mall forever. It was practical and served a purpose while I looked around for the right property where I could put roots down."

Niki dropped onto the bed and stared at the ceiling of the small apartment they had rented for the night on the American base. "Huh. So that's what it feels like to be right about something. It's strangely addicting. But moving on. Have you started to look for something already or will that process only begin when we get back?"

"I'm a little past that process." Taylor smirked and studied her face. "Weirdly, it was Rod who dropped me a line on the opportunity. A so-called friend of his had to liquidate his assets rather hastily and that included a nice home at Sunset Mountain. It's about forty acres and was built like a fortress by the owner who was...shall we say paranoid about personal security, which suits me fine. I can use the eighteen-car garage for mech work, and it also has a pool and other nice amenities along with the three bedrooms. On top of that, a few smaller living areas aren't connected to the main house but would be useful if we need them."

She raised an eyebrow. "You do have a tendency to pick up strays."

"Said the kettle."

With a grin, she nudged him in the ribs. "Okay, so Rod

simply apprised you of this opportunity for cheap real estate? Just like that? Out of the kindness of his heart?"

"That and the hundred thousand dollars he'll take as a finder's fee off of the top, I assume. Be that as it may, it's still cheaper than almost anything else in the area, so I took it."

Niki turned on her side and slid her fingers down his chest to trace idle patterns across his skin. "I guess it would be nice to have a location like that to work from. Plus, if Vickie ever needs somewhere to stay, it's probably best that we have a situation set up for her if she has to hide from people."

"You never did tell me exactly who has it out for her."

"That's her secret to tell."

"Huh. Yeah, I guess. Also, we?"

She smiled and leaned closer to place a light kiss to his cheek. "Sure. I'll need a place to stay if I move to Vegas. I have a property of my own, but I've been renting it out forever and I guess it's time to let go—to liquidate my assets, I guess."

"Well then, I guess I'll expect you to front half the cash I'll pay for the house since it'll be the headquarters of our new business. What did you call it again? Since everyone hates McFadden's Mercs."

"You hate it too," she reminded him. "And it's a shitty name. No, the one I had in mind was McFadden and Banks Consultancy—no, McFadden and Banks, Consultants for Hire, Incorporated, has a better ring to it, I think."

"And I'm the one who comes up with the terrible names?"

"Alliteration is lazy. When you have two surnames at

the beginning, people think you're a firm that's all professional and shit."

"Aren't we?'

"Well yes, but we need to give them that impression. McFadden's Mercs makes it sound like you're running it out of your dad's garage since you're not allowed to bring guns to your place after the neighborhood started a Homeowner's Association because of you."

"That's an oddly specific mental image."

Niki nodded. "And one that comes to mind every time you say that name, so I suggest you drop it if you want any business to come in. Good business, that is."

He drew in a deep breath. "McFadden and Banks, Consultants for Hire. I like that. You're right, it has a ring to it."

"I know." She rested her head on his chest and paused for a moment, enjoying the closeness, the sound of him breathing, and his heartbeat against her ear. "I guess I should be in charge of all the naming situations while you can be in charge of setting up a training course at our new base of operations. It does have space for that, doesn't it? Forty acres is a large area."

"I suppose I could do away with all those lawns and shit. I'd have to do proper planning when I go out there again. We'll also have to think about the details like caretakers and gardeners and shit. I won't spend my days taking care of that whole fucking property on my own."

"Holy shit, I already came up with the name and everything. You need to pull your weight a little, McFadden!"

She squealed and giggled good-naturedly when he

grasped her by the hips and dragged her on top of him before he placed a long, tender kiss on her lips.

"How about I pull your weight instead?" he whispered.

"You know, I could live with that, yes. We can decide on the details later."

He grinned. "Sounds like a plan."

THE END

THE BOHICA CHRONICLES BOXED SET

Have you read *The BOHICA Chronicles* from C.J. Fawcett and Jonathan Brazee? A complete series box set is available now from Amazon and through Kindle Unlimited.

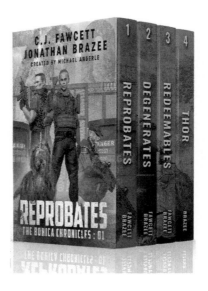

Kicked out of the military for brawling, what can three friends from different countries do to make some needed money?

Grab your copy of the entire BOHICA Chronicles at a discount today!

Reprobates:

With nothing in their future, Former US Marine Charles, ex-SAS Booker, and ex-Australian Army Roo decide to give the Zoo a shot.

Without the contacts, without backing, without knowing what they are getting into, they scramble to get their foot in the door to even make rent in one of the most dangerous areas in the world.

With high rewards comes high risk. Can they learn on the job, where failure means death?

Relying on their training, they will scratch, claw, and take the most dangerous jobs to prove themselves, but will it be enough? Can they fight the establishment and the Zoo at the same time?

And what the heck's up with that puppy they found?

Degenerates:

What happens when you come back from vacation to find out your dog ate the dog-sitter?

And your dog isn't a dog?

The BOHICA Warriors have had some success in the Zoo, but they need to expand and become more professional to make it into the big time.

Each member goes home to recruit more members to join the team.

Definitely bigger, hopefully badder, they return ready to kick some ZOO ass.

With a dead dog-sitter on their hands and more dangerous missions inside the Zoo, the six team members have to bond and learn to work together, even if they are sometimes at odds with each other.

Succeed, and riches will follow.

Fail, and the Zoo will extract its revenge in its own permanent fashion.

Redeemables:

NOTHING KEEPS A MAN AND HIS 'DOG' APART...

But what if the dog is a man-killing beast made up of alien genetics?

Thor is with his own kind as they range the Zoo, but something is missing for him. Charles is with his own kind as they work both inside and outside the walls of the ZOO.

Once connected, the two of them are now split apart by events that overcame each.

Or are they?

Follow the BOHICA Warriors as they continue to make a name for themselves as the most professional of the MERC Zoo teams. So much so that people on the outside have heard of them.

Follow Thor as he asserts himself in his pack.

Around the Zoo, nothing remains static, and some things *might converge yet again if death doesn't get in the way.*

Thor:

The ZOO wants to kill THOR. Humans would want that as well, but they don't know what he is.

What is Charles going to do?

Charles brings Thor to Benin, where he can safely hide out until things calm down. Unfortunately for both of them, that takes them out of the frying pan and into the fire.

The Pendjari National Park isn't the Zoo, but lions, elephants, and rhinos are not pushovers.

When human militias invade the park, Thor and park ranger Achille Amadou are trapped between the proverbial rock and a hard place. How do you protect the park and THOR Achille has to hide just*what* Thor is...

Can he hide what Thor is when Thor makes that hard to accomplish?

Will the militias figure out what that creature is that attacks them?

Available now from Amazon and through Kindle Unlimited.

AUTHOR NOTES

JULY 29, 2020

THANK YOU so much for supporting this series about Taylor McFadden and the family which is pulled into his gravity.

Let's talk a little about 'why' I did a series with Taylor. As you know, a lot is going on in society, and much of it shows up on the Internet. Some of these things are a little upsetting to me. (Remember that this started last year (2019) – the COVID wasn't even on the radar at that time.)

Why do the series, Mike?

(I'm glad you asked! Or rather, I'm glad my mind assumed you asked.)

Because life isn't nice and all packaged up. People don't *HAVE* to act a certain way all of the time and THAT IS OK.

People are messy, problematic, strangely honorable in their odd behavior's and there are reasons adults can consent and consent ethically (even if one questions the morals of the lifestyle if you are morals focused.)

Like Taylor McFadden.

When we meet Taylor in Book 01... He is messed up.

Like most, he seeks and wants a relationship, but realizes he is damaged goods. Not physically (ok, mostly not physically) but mentally he questions his own reality.

And why shouldn't he? He has lasted 83 trips into that damned ZOO full of alien monsters which want to eat him and everyone around him.

The arms of a willing woman for a night of passion is what the Dr. ordered. I should know, I made his first liaison with a doctor. Funny how that worked out, isn't it?

Happenstance, I swear.

Really though, what I wanted to point out is that society creates what is permissible and not permissible all of the time. And just because the largest (or loudest) group screams what they want to set into law doesn't make it right.

At least not right for everyone. Humanity has too many outliers to even consider one rule to rule us all. Right now, everyone who has time, a keyboard, an internet connection and fancies they know the truth has a podium.

But where would they have thrown Taylor if they had done that? Had they known a woman, arguably as damaged in her own way as Taylor, needing someone who understood what made her tick would they have realized they needed each other?

I doubt it.

I have a pretty good imagination and I can't remotely touch the number and variety of people who are broken, and just want the ability to get through life and heal.

Not everyone is a monster to others, even if they have a monster inside of them.

Taylor McFadden, when unleashed, *is a monster.* But for

those of us who are human, we can thank God he is our monster fighting those who would try to consume us.

Now, Taylor and Niki have found each other and are setting off on another set of adventures. New jobs, new responsibilities.

Monsters out there in society who believe they are the wolves among sheep.

Be careful wolves... There are monsters who will consume you like the tasty little snacks you are.

McFadden and Banks, Mercenaries for Hire.

Book 01, coming to you... Soon.

Ad Aeternitatem,

Michael Anderle

P.S. – McFadden and Banks is for people who realize that life is full of gray and we won't all agree on how dark or light that gray happens to be. But in the end, those that do unto others will absolutely have horrible endings done unto them.

Like I said... *They are snacks...*

CONNECT WITH THE AUTHORS

Michael Anderle Social
Website:
http://lmbpn.com

Email List:
http://lmbpn.com/email/

Facebook Here:
https://www.facebook.com/groups/lmbpn.thezoo/

https://www.facebook.com/LMBPNPublishing/

One Crazy Set Of Stories (12)

SOLDIERS OF FAME AND FORTUNE
Nobody's Fool (1)
Nobody Lives Forever (2)
Nobody Drinks That Much (3)
Nobody Remembers But Us (4)
Ghost Walking (5)
Ghost Talking (6)
Ghost Brawling (7)
Ghost Stalking (8)
Ghost Resurrection (9)
Ghost Adaptation (10)
Ghost Redemption (11)
Ghost Revolution (12)

THE BOHICA CHRONICLES
Reprobates (1)
Degenerates (2)
Redeemables (3)
Thor (4)

BOOKS BY MICHAEL ANDERLE

For a complete list of books by Michael Anderle, please visit:

www.lmbpn.com/ma-books/

Printed in Great Britain
by Amazon